PREFACE

Dear Reader,

When I was still teaching, I would say to every class, "If I had magical powers and could grant each of you one gift, it would be the gift of curiosity. If you would be curious, you would be an avid reader and researcher, so that you might quench your thirst for knowledge, fulfill your desire to know and understand. This would make you a lifelong learner. I can think of no greater gift than that to make your life's journey fascinating and worthwhile by constantly learning something new."

I mention this to you because I have always been curious, wanting to know and understand. It made me an avid reader of books, newspapers, and magazines. This all comes in to play with this book because I read two articles in the paper, one years ago, and one more recently.

A very short article in the Sunday paper caught my eye. It was maybe four paragraphs about finding a young woman on the steps of a Catholic church in South Philly nude, save for a pair of socks, shot in the back of the head, with the gun lying on the sidewalk at her feet. My curiosity got the best of me as to why she was murdered. Who was she? She was somebody's daughter, perhaps a wife, maybe a mother. What happened and why was she shot? The idea that she was naked made me wonder if it was a sex crime, but the fact she was shot in the back of the head made me think it might have been an organized crime hit. I also wondered if there was some other explanation, something I was not considering or overlooking.

The other article, also in the Sunday paper, regarded a fourteen-year old boy being shot and killed in Florida under very weird, almost inexplicable, circumstances. Again, my mind went to work contemplating how something like this could happen.

I had aspirations of writing after retiring from education after forty-eight years, but kept putting it off, probably for fear of failing. One night my wife and I were out for dinner with friends and I happened to be seated next to Wendy. She politely asked me what I was up to during my retirement and I mentioned my desire to write a book. I went on to relate the two articles, which I thought would be a great stimulus for an interesting story. She too was intrigued and shared some ideas and possibilities. We then made a commitment to one another to pursue this to the end.

The book you are about to read is our attempt to explain how tragedies of this magnitude that cut short lives as full of potential as anyone else's – if only the circumstances differed, may have occurred and developed to their tragic conclusion.

We sincerely hope your curiosity is piqued by these stories and that you enjoy reading how we constructed and arrived at our own conclusions as to what happened and why.

We live in a difficult age and we recognize, a valid argument could be made that every age has had its challenges, but to us, the time period we write about appears to be so much more daunting than ever before; particularly for young people. Hopefully, our society can right itself and pursue solutions to overcome the roadblocks to family unity and love, and also to civility with our neighbors and fellow Americans.

Sincerely,

John Toppin and Wendy Frantz

The Girl in the Argyle Socks

It had rained earlier in the evening. It had been one of those steady, gentle rains that farmers and gardeners claim to be so beneficial and young lovers approve of as perfectly romantic. I didn't find it to be so. Oh sure, we hadn't had rain in over a week, and the plants were drying out and the grass looked as if it should be cut and baled like a field of hay, so we really did need it. And I suppose a case could be made there was a picture-pretty quality to it. The street lights sparkled in the puddles like so many diamonds, swaying more than a Cuban rumba dancer. And while it might be a great night for new lovers to take that romantic stroll, I wasn't a new or an old lover. Well, at least for the moment I wasn't, and probably the foreseeable future too.

No, to me, the night was just plain tiring. It was the kind of evening that pulls you down and once you're there, won't let you up, a real heavyweight wrestler making the move and slipping a hold that makes you pant fitfully fighting for each breath and you don't even know if that next one's even coming. And at that point, self-doubt, the other member of this tag team, jumps on you from the top of the ropes and the count begins. Then, while you're being counted out, the night takes a sharp downward spiral turning into a turbulent river of remembrances, a contemplation of what you did

4

and didn't do, of what you should and shouldn't have done. And the night's got you in a chokehold, and your oxygen starved brain begins to see images and corresponding memories of things best forgotten. Of course, that's when old man melancholy jams his size thirteen shoe in between the jam and the door you're trying desperately to close, forcing it to open wider so it can grab you, which it does. You can feel its power. Yeah, you begin to feel its strength as it throws a headlock of sorrow controlling all your thoughts. On a night like this, you'd better be damn wary of feeling too sorry for yourself or you'll be climbing to the top of a bottle of Jameson, jumping in feet first and sinking to the bottom like a big heavy stone. But I've always been a fighter. I wasn't about to let this night use me and abuse me, and then lay me out in the corner of the ring like some limp wet rag. If I was going down, I was going down fighting. I was raised to persevere and never give up. I wasn't about to pack it in now.

Of course, the flip side of a night like this was business. In my line of work, a night like this could keep me busy, real busy. A night like this could bring out the beast in anyone. It could strip away all semblance of civility and human kindness and leave you with a heartless, vicious killer. It was, after all, a Saturday night in July. It was a steamy, rainy, weekend night in July to boot, and the greeneyed monster was loose and on the prowl. I could feel him, like underwear creeping up, sneaking up on me, to the point where I just wanted to grab and yank him from his hiding place. But, it's not something done easily. On a night like this, the beast would definitely be loose, and jealousy and vengeance would be in his heart and murder would be on his mind. Yeah, it was definitely the kind of night that could easily bring me a new client and keep the monster in a neutral corner. Not that I was desperate for a job, but the insurance work was three weeks west of now and my bank account was slipping lower than a pair of pants on a fifteen- year old skater with a ring in his nose. So, you could say I wasn't at all surprised when she sashayed into my office.

She was dressed in a two-piece, blue, serge suit with shiny silver buttons. Her hair was cut short and swept to the side like a breaking wave, but instead of white caps, it was as dark as a chunk of bituminous, and shined as much as her buttons. I took a deep breath and was enveloped in a bath of rose water. She was one tall lady, and carried herself in a regal, self-assured manner. In fact, I felt she was used to giving orders that others heeded, me included. I sensed she believed and operated as if her ends justify any means. She was polished granite, slick, shiny, hard, and very cold. Her eyes were all over me like grease on a grille. They slipped up and down, and hummingbird hovered on mine. She stood mute, I guess expecting me to initiate the interlocution. So, I reached out to her. I needed a break-through line.

Quick witted, I pounded her with this chisel, "I've been expecting you."

"You have? How did you know I was coming?"

"I'm a detective. I detect. People pay me large sums to learn things and tell them all about it, to expose secrets, to reveal the unknown. I gather facts, and then I sift through those facts. I separate the chaff from the wheat. And then I make an educated guess, a deduction. We detectives do a lot of deducing. Besides, I watched you from my window. I followed you as you strode across the street and entered my building. With your looks and fashionable attire, it was a pretty safe bet you weren't part of the cleaning crew and since I'm the only one here this time of night, I deduced you were coming to see me."

Perhaps the ice age was ending. She smiled and deigned to speak to me again. I was in suspense as her lips, full and oh so kissable, pushed out, pulled back slightly, and began to form the word in a bright red lipstick probably called something like "Enchanting Red." Well Mr. Bridge, are you always as sharp as a straight razor or did you just run up and down a leather strap a few times too often?"

Her banter was snappy. I wasn't surprised nor was I disappointed. She could make a phrase sit up and bark. I'd met many a verbal gymnast in my line of work. Certainly, two can play that game, which often makes mischievous repartee exciting and stimulating. But for the time being, I opted to remain on the sidelines. I wasn't sure I knew the rules of this game, or any game the ice-maiden would opt to play. I answered her question with a question of my own. "What can I do for you?"

I was stunned by what happened next. I was stunned because this lady had not given me the impression, she had a vulnerable bone in her body. To show any kind of weakness did not seem to be an option for my rainy night visitor. Her cold and polished veneer melted, and she began to sob uncontrollably. Striving to be a gentleman, I offered her a handkerchief from my back pocket. Thank goodness it was clean. Through tears and muffled sniffles, I barely managed to hear her weep, "My sister's been murdered over six months ago and the police still have no leads and I want to hire you to find her killer."

I could've said no, been done with it, but at that moment I felt sorry for her and hated to be so abrupt. I don't usually handle this kind of case as murder is best left to the police, who aren't great dance partners. When you step on their toes, as you're bound to do in my line of work, they don't forget and hold it against you forever like the proverbial woman scorned. No, I mostly do research for divorce lawyers, and insurance companies. Those pursuits are a lot safer than murder. I figured, smart guy that I am, a large fee and retainer would dim her enthusiasm for tilting at windmills. "Five hundred a day, plus expenses, and I want a week's worth up front."

Well, just call her Don Quixote. I had been wrong on both counts. There were unusual circumstances, and I noticed both of them as she uncrossed her legs, shifted in the chair ever so slightly, then deliberately and seductively, crossed them as before. And my exorbitant rate didn't faze her in the least.

"I expected this kind of investigation would cost a great deal. Do you prefer cash or a check Mr. Bridge?"

I had been right straight out of the gate. She was polished stone, and cold, very cold. I'd never seen anyone turn it on and off as quickly as M. J. McKay. She certainly regained her original composure post haste. All too quickly for my liking. And I'm usually not that particular. And never more so than when someone leads me like they're Igor Stravinsky or I'm Rex, the family dog, on a leash with a choke collar. But there was something about her, and I couldn't quite put my finger on it. "I'll take the cash," I said.

She handed me twenty-five crisp Franklins without so much as batting an eye.

Maybe that was chump change for a woman like her, but I must admit surprise, I sure wasn't expecting she'd have it on her.

After we completed the exchange of money and a receipt, I asked her to provide me with as much information as she could about her sister. Thus, she began the introduction of Jack Bridge, me, to her sister, Margo McKay. If you hadn't already guessed, I'm a private dick. I'm a retired Philadelphia detective. Like any job, being a dick has its ups and downs. I'm my own boss, which is good. I get to make all the decisions and call all the shots, which is good, too. But I'm not going to win any contest either for popularity or having the biggest income. It's an iffy profession in an iffy world, which makes for a very iffy life style. But then again, I'm a pretty iffy guy, at least according to my ex-wife. Detecting and Bridge were the marriage now. A fairly successful marriage, kind of like mustard and the famous Philly soft pretzel. I had a consistently successful success rate. I got the goods for my clients. But murder, I didn't know.

"My sister was a good kid. She was always a little head strong, but she was really good at heart. She was sensible all through school and at first when she went out on her own. After graduating college, Villanova, she landed a job with a law firm in center city, Barrow, Nickerson, Smythe, and Fuller. I'm sure you've heard of them. They're one of the top firms in the city. This was her ticket to law school.

She was getting her feet wet and earning some money at the same time. Then, about a year ago she began to change, subtle at first, but more rapid right before her death."

"What kind of change?"

"She went out almost every night and appeared to me to be leading a very risky lifestyle. It seemed as if there were more men in her life than normal. This was contrary to high school and college, where she dated, but nothing too serious. Her studies were most important then. She was conscientious and had established some pretty lofty goals."

She went on about Margo like she was the world to her. She made it sound like her kid sister meant everything. Margo was this, and Margo did that. Everyone at the law firm thought highly of Margo. She was a conscientious and loyal employee. "All I ever heard from partners in the firm was what a great gal Margo was. They were proud to have her as part of the team, and after law school there would be bigger and better things in store for her. I was really proud of my little sister."

Only time would tell if any of it was true or would help in any way to solve her murder.

At that point she gave me the newspaper clipping:

Woman found fatally shot in head and naked

By Joseph Bellows

Staff Writer

Police are investigating the death of a woman who was found naked and shot in the head outside a Catholic church in South Philadelphia early Wednesday.

Investigators are combing the area for any forensic evidence and have put on a full court press to find anyone who may have seen something at or near St. Paul's Church on Christian near the Italian Market.

The woman, said to be in her mid to late-twenties, was wearing only a pair of argyle socks when police found her, Chief Inspector Wesley Plank told reporters at the scene. A pistol was found five feet away from the body. The serial numbers had been filed off.

Medics pronounced her dead at the scene about 3:15 a.m. Wednesday. Her name has not been released.

"I assume that's your sister?"

"Yes. She was found less than ten blocks from her apartment. The autopsy indicated she had some alcohol in her system, but not over the legal limit. Whoever did this to her, needs to pay. You must get to the bottom of Margo's murder for me."

That sounded to me more like a command than a plea.

"Had she been seeing anyone on a regular basis?"

"She dated Tommy Harris for a while. He's with Scanlon Financial out on the Main Line. And I know she would still see Jimmy Malkovich who was more of good high school friend. She'd known him since middle school. And she had also been seeing a Bobby Knickerly lately, but I only met him once and don't know much about him."

It would seem Margo only dated men who had a "y" at the end of their given name. That would've left me out of the parade, because no one calls me anything but Jack. Well, that's not entirely true, but none of those ugly handles ends in "y."

I was interested in Margo's last known movements and whereabouts. According to M. J., Margo had indicated she was dining on Tuesday night with Tommy Harris at Spots on Bank Street. The plan was to go clubbing afterwards. The next day, Wednesday, she had planned to meet M. J. down the shore at Stone Harbor for a long weekend. A get together that never came to fruition. M. J. indicated it took a while to I.D. Margo because no one at work was expecting her since she put in for vacation days.

"When she didn't come down on Wednesday, I called around, but no one knew anything. I contacted the police, but it took a couple more days to connect the Jane Doe they had in the morgue with Margo. The police contacted me, and I went to the morgue and made the identification."

"I'm really worried. Since it's been more than six months, the likelihood of solving this case is greatly diminished. I'm a realist. I don't kid myself, Mr. Bridge. I've prepared myself that too much time has passed, but I'm also a woman of conviction and perseverance. The police don't seem to be moving on this. Jack, can I call you Jack?" I nodded affirmatively. "Jack, I need you to find my sister's killer. I want justice for Margo. It's the least I can do on her behalf. I expect you to get to the bottom of her murder and bring it to a closure that satisfies me. That's why I am willing to pay you whatever you ask, Mr. Bridge. That's why I came to you."

It was quite a speech. It almost made me want to applaud and then hurry to find out more about this hero, Mr. Jack Bridge. What a guy he must be. Able to leap tall buildings in a single bound. Of course, some would probably say, "Hey, he's a man. Able to leap on tall women is probably a more accurate description of this guy." I couldn't help wondering what led her to the Bridge Detective Agency, 'an agency that spans all mysteries and problems to connect you with the truth.' I was puzzled. With her kind of money and influence, why had she come to me? I didn't want to be too committal, so I replied, "I'll do my best. You'll hear from me at least once a week, usually at the beginning of the week. I'll relay what happened the prior week and what my next steps will be. Do you have a number where I can reach you?"

After we squared away the rest of the arrangements and contact information, she took my hand and held it. Her hand was cool and soft as the cotton swab from the top of a bottle of Aspirin. I began to feel dizzy. And as I looked into her limpid blue eyes, I couldn't help but think, they're just like that bottle of Jameson, inviting, but deep and dangerous. If a man isn't careful, he could definitely be sucked into an eddy of emotion and never come up again. And, if by chance he did come up, he'd need every damned drop of that Jameson to sooth his tortured soul.

"Mr. Bridge, Jack, I mean. I'm counting on you. I hope you won't disappoint me." Was that a plea or a threat? Before I could fully contemplate this or why so much fuzz seems to collect in my navel, she was up and moving quickly. She had turned on her heel and was on her way through the door to my office before I could respond with a lame "Good evening, Miss McKay," which chased after her through the outer office but may not have caught up to her speedy departure. Or had it been an escape?

With questions like that, it was time to call it a day and close up for the night. I hit the lights and glanced out the window prior to leaving. I watched her, mesmerized by the manner in which she carried herself. If dictionaries had pictures, her picture would be right beside the word self-assured. She was hurrying across the street, but it couldn't be described as disheveled flight or slipshod scurrying. I'd say, and you would too if you had watched, it was purposeful. It had begun raining lightly again and she seemed to move between the droplets. The sky looked to be on the verge of unleashing a virtual downpour. It was and it did release a deluge just after she made it across the street and into the parking garage. I stayed by the window and watched as a white Corvette slid down the exit ramp and slithered down the rainsoaked street also seemingly between droplets. I assumed M. J. McKay was behind the wheel. I could see it was a woman, but it was too dark to determine any more specifics. She took a left and sped off on Walnut. After she had made the turn and right as I was about to leave my window, I noticed a dark, perhaps black, navy, or maroon, Ford or Mercury four-door sedan parked just past the garage turn on its lights and glide to Walnut making the same turn as the Corvette, which had already disappeared from my view. I wondered, was it merely a coincidence? Or, was it simply my overly active imagination? The rain was easing. I decided to go home and sleep on it. And sleep on it I did, but it was not a deep sleep. It was a sleep encumbered with dreams of the McKay sisters. The question, had I made a mistake taking this case, tossed me around the bed like so much Caesar salad. It was not a peaceful night for this aging detective.

Chapter 2

After a strong cup of coffee and a couple of pieces of buttered rye toast, I was ready to hit the ground running. My first inclination was to back track Margo's last movements, but following a bit more contemplation, I thought it would be more advantageous to find out more about Margo's background. I decided to start with her neighbors and then a thorough search of her second-floor apartment on Pine. M. J. had given me a key to Margo's apartment and permission to go through it with a fine-tooth comb, if I deemed it necessary.

I drove through relatively moderate traffic despite the fact it was late rush hour. When I came to Pine Street, I had to circle the block a few times until I found a spot I could squeeze into. The homes were old, fashionable and mostly brick, while the neighborhood appeared to be relatively quiet. It was probably a nice place to live, particularly if you were young and single. A number of restaurants and bars were nearby, and transportation, bus or taxi, was readily available to get to center city or work. The subway was a brisk walk away. But without off street parking, in my mind, it would be a nightmare to live here. It would be a nightmare unless of course one didn't own a car. With a car, I could imagine circling the block many times, in all kinds of weather, trying to find legal parking.

After I found a parking spot, I peeled my 6'2" frame from my beige Mazda Protégé and stretched as I studied both sides of the block. Now you might think my choice of wheels to be odd, but I lived with my transportation decision every day, so I better like it. In my line of work the proper vehicle is critical. I didn't need speed in the city. So, what does a Protégé have to offer? It's small and I can park easily; particularly in tight spots. Plus, it's good on gas, and that makes it cheap to operate. It's not a glamorous car, who'd want to steal it? And perhaps most importantly, it's pretty innocuous and great for tailing someone without being conspicuous. Besides, it was all I could afford.

I moved on down the street past Margo's place and I noticed an old man through a window in the brownstone next door. He was sitting in a high back chair and appeared to be engrossed in a television show as there was a glow emanating from the far side of the room. I knocked on his door and after a short time I could hear him shuffling toward me and grousing about it under his breath. I stood there focused on how substantial the door was, obviously amply constructed to keep out intruders.

He growled at me twice. "Who is it?" "What do you want?" They almost ran together so that I could not answer the first before the second charged from his lips. Was he cranky or just bothered by a visitor interrupting his schedule?

I introduced myself and held up my PI license to his peep hole and announced in a baritone voice I was looking into the murder of his neighbor Margo McKay and that I hoped he would be willing to answer a few questions. After a laborious undoing of several locks, the door swung open and in a less nasty tone, he invited me into a charming hallway, a trip into the past. The hardwood floor was covered by a beautiful oriental rug and there was an antique cherry sideboard and matching chair along the wall. Fresh flowers adorned the top of the sideboard in an old pitcher sitting in a bowl with the same print. I followed him to a sitting room where he resumed his seat in the high back chair in which I first saw him. It was the kind of room you might picture when someone mentions a parlor. The furniture was well polished and formal with little lace doilies that came up short if they were to protect the floral upholstery. Maybe I was being unfair. Maybe the furnishings reflected him and his life. Maybe the furnishings were older than the old man sitting in front of me. He appeared to have good manners though, as he turned off the game show while offering me a seat across from him on the couch. As the screen flickered and faded to nothing, I took a seat on his surprisingly comfy couch. He had a serious look on a face lined by the wear of living so long.

He stared at me with dark penetrating eyes that twinkled like Santa Claus after filling all the stockings hung with care. In some ways he reminded me of a little bird as he cocked his head side to side, inspecting me from different angles. And then he ruined the mental image my observations had just created.

"Well, what the fuck do you want to know? I ain't got all day."

I had been a bit hasty with my assessment of his manners. It was now pretty obvious he didn't know Amy Van Buren from Martin Van Buren or the fork on the far left of the place setting from the left fork in the road. He was not the man I thought he was.

"I'm Jack Bridge, and I've been retained by M. J. McKay, your neighbor's sister, to look into her homicide. But I didn't catch your name Mr. ..."

He interrupted, "That's because I didn't throw it. You know, you're rather obtuse for a detective. How do you detect anything? I'll bet she's not going to get her money's worth out of your efforts. How does a guy like you make a living for Pete's sake?"

I didn't make much of a living and I didn't humor him with a response that, no matter how clever, this selective son-of-a-bitch would have found wanting. No, when they go low, it's good to go high. I took the high road and demonstrated that I, at least, had manners. Instead of any glib quip, I asked another question. "Do you remember when you last saw Margo?"

"My name's Ralph Pitcairn, Sport. And I saw her four days before she was killed. It was a Friday."

"How is it you're so sure, Mr. Pitcairn?"

"I may look old, Sport, but I've still got a mind like a steel trap."

I wondered if that meant nothing got out once it was in, or nothing gets in because the trap sprang a long time ago. If I said what I really wanted to, sure as there's no Easter bunny, he'd have clamped shut and closed on me quicker than a greyhound on "here's bunny." I decided to play it controlled and easy. I merely fed him another question. "I'm sure of that Mr. Pitcairn, but could you fill me in just a bit, expand on how you're positive?"

He couldn't help himself. It was a combination of being old and living alone. He wanted to talk and have somebody listen. In this case, I was the somebody. He knew he had me strung like a marionette and could pull the strings to make me dance his tune. I quickly recognized the stage was his and knew enough to shuffle my feet to whatever he choreographed. And that's what I did. I smiled, asked some innocuous questions, and nodded my head at all the right times and in all the right places.

"It was Friday afternoon garbage pick-up. That's how I know. I was taking my garbage out, as the truck would be along pretty soon, and I saw her. She was walking up the street, I suppose coming home from work. She said, "Hello." And I commented that I hadn't seen much of her lately. Margo had always been nice to me and friendly enough. That's when she told me how it was Friday and she was looking ahead to a weekend of fun. I asked her if she had any particular plans, and that's when my neighbor said, "I'm going out clubbing tonight and Tuesday I'm having dinner with my boyfriend and then I'm making a mid-week trip to the shore to spend some quality time with my sister."

I tipped my head up and down ever so slightly. "Did she offer anything else?"

"I didn't understand it, but she said something about patching things up. I don't know, maybe they weren't getting along so good."

"Keep him talking" was my mantra. "And?"

"Yeah, there was something else. She did comment that it would be the last date with that slime ball. And no, she didn't mention his name."

I asked if he had noticed men friends visiting her apartment and he answered me, "Not the first year she was here, but about six months before she was murdered, there was a procession of men, different men, usually late at night." He added, "Some were repeaters, but many were one night only. I never saw any of them again. I just know it was a hell-of-a lot of men."

He did admit, "One night, maybe it was June, I was sitting on the stoop when she and this fellow she introduced as Ronny or Tommy Harris. The traffic was heavy, and I couldn't hear clearly so I'm not sure what his first name was. But I can tell you he was a smug bastard. He treated me like I was something he wanted to scrape off the bottom of his shoe. He couldn't wait to leave. He kept tugging at her, while she was still speaking with me. That son-of-bitch I knew was just plain self-centered and downright mean."

The old man made me think of the black kettle. Was he too smug, as smug as the "cat that swallowed the canary," or was I being unjust? This time I lifted an eyebrow to keep him talking.

"I don't know what a nice girl like Margo was doing with a bum like that. You can't make a silk purse out of a sow's ear, and I was only hoping for her sake that she didn't feel a need to try and fix him. That never works out. Heartaches and tears are the only things a woman ever gets from a reclamation project. But they think they can do it, so they keep on trying. It sure puzzles the shit out of me."

But the real question is can you make shit out of shine-ola? I nodded again and it made me feel like one of those little toy baseball players that some folks have on the ledge in the rear window of their cars. The little head bobs up and down with each braking and starting of the car, or when bounced by hitting a pothole and God knows Philadelphia's got a lot of them.

At this point, I strove for a higher plane, ditching that train of thought, replying, "Sometimes the moth is drawn to the flame. Sometimes good girls like the excitement of bad boys. Sometimes, they think bad to the bone is better."

"Gees, a dim-witted philosopher too. Your limited talents are endless, Sport."

I couldn't help myself and snapped, "You haven't seen my good stuff yet. Wait 'til I whiz a fastball under your chin." But as soon as it escaped my lips, I knew it had been a mistake to say anything in rebuttal as he got a glint in his eye.

"If your fastball compares to the other fluff you've been pitching, I'll lean into it, and take my base." Why is it that the older old folks get, and I'm talking late seventies and eighties, the feistier they become? Maybe they begin to believe, since they've lived so long, the simple rules of human interaction don't apply to them anymore. They form an attitude that observing some social etiquette is no longer required. It passes and is gone like so much broken wind. Of course, there's always a chance I'm whistling in the wind. Maybe I see my own fate all too soon. On the other hand, maybe their brains are just oxygen starved and they operate in a vacuum stupor. I realized I didn't know. But I did know if I contemplated this line of thinking much longer, I'd be stupefied. I decided to move on with a snappy comment and question. "While you're on first, Ralph, can you think of anything else about Margo that might be helpful?"

"Not really, Sport. I don't know what I know that could help a dumb flatfoot like you."

I thanked him for his time and left him with my card and instructions to call me if he thought of anything else that might shed more light on her murder.

I wasn't expecting to hear from Mr. Ralph Pitcairn. If he had any more pertinent information, I'm sure he would've been happy to divulge it right then and there.

My next move was to check out Margo's apartment. M. J. McKay had given me permission and a key to look around her sister's digs. I walked the few steps to the building next door and enter the small vestibule which had two mail boxes on the left, a door facing the entryway, which I assumed to be the ground floor apartment based upon the letter A on the door, and a door to the right with a B showing me the way to the second floor. I unlocked the door and took the narrow flight of stairs to the second level.

I entered the large front living room somewhat winded, reminding myself to use the gym membership more than once a month. I noticed the rug was somewhat thread bare and the furniture, including a long couch and end chairs, appeared to be well used. I surmised that on her salary at the law firm the contents had come from Good Will or a secondhand shop. Across the room stood a self-made bookshelf utilizing cement blocks and long wooden boards probably purchased at a

Home Depot. It was filled with mostly paperbacks. There were a few hardbound books dealing with tax law and such. Next to her library was a small television, with a screen that looked to be no more than nineteen inches. Beside the couch was an end table supporting a large brass lamp. I continued to peruse the area and walked into a small kitchen with a tiny space for eating, basically a table for two. Peeking into the refrigerator I discovered a few essentials, milk, eggs, soda, a few apples that had become soft and mealy, and not much else.

I'm an okay cook, my pantry was better equipped to prepare a pleasing meal than Margo's. Off the kitchen/dining area was a short hallway. On the right was a bathroom which I decided to check out more thoroughly later. Straight ahead was a closet and when I opened the door, it revealed clothing hung neatly with a shoe rack underneath and a fulllength mirror attached to the door. It was a sparse but satisfactorily trendy wardrobe. She showed a clear preference for black and seemed to have a penchant for expensive looking pumps. There seemed to be no fewer than a dozen handbags ranging in styles and shades of red and pink. On the left of the hallway was a door leading into the bedroom. The bed had a checkerboard pink and white quilt with a pink stuffed elephant guarding pink pillows. It would seem to be a sure bet that Margo liked pink. There was a standing lamp in the corner beside a little table which went on when

I hit the wall switch. There was a clock-radio on the table. Opposite the bed was an old, antique looking, bureau covered with three jewelry boxes which, when opened one at a time, revealed mostly costume necklaces and bracelets. One box did contain a string of pearls and a gold bracelet that reminded me of braided rope. I looked up at my reflection in the mirror hanging on the wall behind the chest. A thoughtful looking middle-aged man with graying hair and a neatly trimmed beard peered back. I rifled through everything and found nothing of note. It struck me as weird that one drawer contained nothing but argyle socks. My heart was palpitating because that was the only item she was wearing when she was discovered. Time to check out the bathroom.

I returned through the hallway to the small bathroom which held a toilet at the far end, a very small shower, and a sink with a medicine cabinet hidden by a mirror showing its age the many cracks running across and in the corners. I opened the cabinet door and found what was to be expected, such as deodorant, toothpaste and brush, cologne, combs and brushes. However, I also discovered a number of prescription bottles and looking them over realized that Dr. Elena Chow, M.D. had freely prescribed a number of pain medications, namely oxycodone and tramadol. From what I knew, these were pretty potent pills, which led me to wonder, if Margo was suffering from some ailment, and what was wrong that she needed such dangerous drugs? This seemed significant to me and I took several pictures with my camera. I went back to the living room feeling as if I missed something. I stood there in deep thought, considering a series of questions regarding mail, bills, a checkbook, or savings account. Where was everything? She had to keep those things somewhere. Had they been in her purse? I asked myself, "Where was her purse?" It wasn't at the scene of the crime. "Had it been stolen? Had she been murdered for the drugs? But then, who would've known she had them, if that's why she was killed?"

In short order, I answered my own questions since the walls and drapes were of no help. I noticed a bit of room behind the side table and couch and it was just wide enough to carefully slip through, if you were small. I wondered why. I wasn't small, I turned sideways and moved around the couch to answer the question, "Why the space?" "Why not establish the furniture flush with the wall?" As it turned out, when I got to the back of the table, I discovered it had been facing backward toward the center of the room. Perhaps this was intentional to somewhat disguise a hiding place for her personal papers. I pulled open the drawer with much anticipation, as if it was a wrapped package for me to open at Christmas, and inside were all of the items in question. I glanced through the bills and there was nothing unusual. Typical rent, heat, and charge card statements. The same could be said for the checking and savings accounts. They revealed nothing unusual. There were no telltale letters, but the drawer seemed deeper to me. I emptied everything onto the couch. The drawer was definitely empty. I dropped to a knee and sure enough gauging the drawer from the outside and the depth from the inside, it didn't jive. I reached to the very back and exactly as I suspected there was a gap between the bottom of the drawer and the rear. I could inch my fingers in and to my surprise lifted a fake bottom. There was a notebook hidden at the bottom of the pile. I opened it to the first page which was dated about six or seven months before her murder. It clearly was a diary and rifling through it revealed many entries of varying lengths, but each one I saw was no more than four or five pages. I turned to the last entry, which had been made the day prior to her murder. I paged back to the front. There was listing of names with phone numbers and addresses. I sat down on the couch to study my discovery in greater detail, then thought better of it. I'd go through some entries later. In the meantime, I took out my camera once more and took copious pictures of the entire apartment: the living room, the closet, the kitchen, and the bedroom.

After returning to the street, I took note that Margo's apartment had no neighbor on the other side of her building. There was a small walkway and an apartment house, but the entrance was all the way at the other end. It was a pretty good distance from Margo's entrance. I contemplated if it was too far to really get to know anyone living there.

I scanned the other side of Pine, and there were several brick houses, not row houses, single homes, but all the same design and construction. I crossed over to them and knocked at each one, but no one responded to my inquiry. I did notice a small garden with a swing beside the house with the blue door. The flowers were gorgeous, and I'd bet it was very relaxing to sit on that swing with a cup of coffee in the early morning hours. Whoever lived in the house took good care of the flower beds because I didn't see any weeds. I have to come back again, hopefully when the occupants of these two houses would be home.

I turned, looked back at Margo's place, and again wondered what had happened to this young woman. Then I turned and walked back to where I'd parked my car, deciding I would have to return another time to follow up on the other neighbors. I drove to my apartment through stop and go traffic, cursing under my breath all the way at the traffic and the possible mess I got myself into this time.

Chapter 3

I didn't want to spend all day going through a dead woman's diary, but I felt obligated to scan an entry or two believing it might shed some light on Margo and her life. I read the first one knowing I would have to go through all pages at a later time.

Diary Entry – June

I feel sentimental today. Don't know why, but I can't stop thinking about Rich and wondering where he is right now and what he's doing. The last time we were together, everything went horribly wrong. I didn't want to break up with him – not that night, anyway. If he had just listened to me and stayed home instead of showing up at my dorm, none of this would have happened. And who knows? Without that fight, maybe we'd still be together today and instead of sitting here alone on my second-floor walkup, Rich and I would be out for a drive enjoying the sunshine and planning our wedding. I can so easily picture myself being married now and perhaps raising children with him. I picture three kids – two boys with curly blonde hair and deep blue eyes like Rich, gangly and thin, glasses starting in elementary school, smart, funny, cool. A daughter who looks like me – auburn hair, green eyes, a teacher's pet, a homebody – her mother's little mini-me. We would garden together and bake cherry pies, and we'd argue about when she could get her ears pierced and start wearing makeup. But none of that will ever be. It's all over now and I've lost touch with him or what's become of him. I don't know where he lives or even if he ended up going to graduate school or if he met someone else – or if his drinking got worse, or if he ever hurt anyone again after that night.

I thought to myself, this Rich character sounds like a winner. Is it possible he held a grudge and over time stoked it building higher and hotter flames until he cracked and followed Margo with rage in his heart and murder on his mind? Maybe. I'll have to add Rich's name to my list of interviews. I resumed my reading.

It all started with one of my headaches. I had one of my awful migraines, when the phone rang. Tammy was waiting for a call from her mother and I thought this call might be her. In my hurry to get to the phone, I tripped on the cord and stubbed my toe on the leg of the table. And then I just lost it. Picking up the headset I screamed, "Damn it all to hell, that really hurts." I rarely cursed. I was raised by a loving mother and an adoring father to act like a lady, but the pain in my toe was so intense and sudden combined with the migraine the words just slipped out in fury. Rich launched right into me for taking the Lord's name in vain. He could be a sanctimonious prick at times. I could predict at this juncture the conversation wasn't going to go well. He didn't accept my excuse about my migraine and the toe. It hadn't been my intention to swear. To change the subject, when I told him my sister was coming for a visit that weekend, he was really pissed off. He claimed he had been planning to come and had some surprise plans, but MJ and I had set everything up weeks ago. After more back and forth, we agreed Rich would come the following weekend.

I felt uneasy even though we worked it out. It makes me so tense whenever things get complicated like this. I crawled into bed and tried to take a nap. My head was still pounding along with my toe which was starting to look a dark black and blue. I hope I didn't break it. I wondered, will I ever stop getting these headaches? It seems like I've had them for such a long time. It really is maddening. Maybe it's time to go see Dr. Chow again.

The two bottles of heavy-duty pain pills, oxycodone and tramadol, had been prescribed by Dr. Chow. Apparently, she had made an appointment and tried to get help for the headaches.

That weekend, Rich showed up and refused to leave even when I reminded him, we'd agreed he would come the following weekend, and that got everything off to a rocky start. But MJ was okay with it, and I had renewed hope we could make everything workout.

We decided to throw a floor party and MJ bought the booze. Everyone on our hallway pitched in and we had enough drinks to float a small raft. I was mixing drinks and not keeping count, and the next thing I knew, I was plastered and slurring my words. Rich and I snuck away to my room and I heard the click of the lock when he shut the door behind us. I don't know why we lay on the floor instead of my bed, but we did. He was kissing me passionately and I responded. We couldn't undress quickly enough. We had talked of waiting until marriage, but sometimes the heat of the moment overwhelms good intentions. The sex was gentle at first, but it became rough and I didn't like it. That's when we fought and both of us said some pretty nasty things. We dressed, but instead of returning to the party, Rich pulled me into the stairwell and told me that my hurtful comments cut him to the core. He grabbed me by the hair and pushed my head back and I hit the wall so hard my mind fogged over. I called him an asshole and he slapped me hard across my mouth. He said I was a spoiled bitch. I don't know where all the blame lay, but I knew this much. I had to break it off.

I wonder, will he ever let me go?

That was all for that entry, but the last line made me think he could have been stalking her. I definitely had to look into Rich, but first I'd have to talk to MJ and find out his last name and where he lived or worked. I proceeded to my office and sat at my desk contemplating what steps I should take next. To date, I had a previous boyfriend named Rich who apparently had a track record of booze and abuse. I had a wealthy Main Line financial guru named Tommy Harris, who was apparently a smug bastard. And didn't have much else. Obviously, I wasn't doing much better than the police. This was turning into the kind of case where luck might come into play. Sometimes, good fortune helps to open things up, making all the facts and key details visible like a cheap can of sardines opened wide and all laid out in neat rows. Sometimes with a bit of luck, everything falls into place with one fact or piece of evidence leading to the next, and so on and so forth. Would I have some of that good fortune with this case? Only time would tell. But for Margo and M.J., I hoped I would. I really wanted to solve this one, but was it really for the McKay sisters, or was it for my own ego. I didn't have an answer to that question. Well, at least not yet I didn't.

Chapter 4

Margo had worked as a secretary in a prestigious center city law firm and M. J. had indicated that this was how her sister was saving to finance her law degree.

She went on to add that Margo would've matriculated in the law program in Rutgers University School of Law, Camden, New Jersey campus the coming September. M. J. told me that Margo received a monthly stipend from the family business, which covered her living expenses. I decided this was a day I needed to pay a visit to Margo's workplace and see what the scuttlebutt was around the water cooler.

It took about twenty minutes to drive there and another ten minutes to find a parking spot. I managed to ride the elevator to the 38th floor without getting a nosebleed. Exiting into a spacious outer office, I was greeted by either a friendly, or overly efficient, receptionist. She assumed I had an appointment and had more questions for me than Alex Trebek for his Jeopardy contestants. Miss Friendly Efficiency inquired as to the time of my nonexistent appointment and with whom, as well as the nature of my business. Knowing these questions could trip me up and nix any further efforts to do some serious detecting, I tried a little of my famous charm. I gave her my best Little Boy Lost facial expression and indicated that I hadn't scheduled an appointment, mainly because I wasn't sure who I should see regarding the murdered Margo McKay. This gregarious gal Friday informed me that it would be Tyler Quentin, and she also offered to check and see if Mr. Quentin could squeeze me into a very busy schedule for a few minutes. I was officiously appreciative to the point of nausea – mine, not hers. She got up from behind her desk and as she strolled down a long corridor, she told me to take a seat in the waiting area across from her desk. I did as I was told. What a good lad. Although I worried my stay would be a lengthy one, I could only hope it wouldn't be. Why? Other than the old saw, "Time is money," the chair swallowed my body and threatened to cause such a feeling of relaxation that I would be unable to win the battle with sleep-induced gravity and keep my eyelids up. I prefer a chair be solidly under me rather than envelope me in a bear hug. The arrangement of these luxurious arm chairs with overly plump cushions was, as expected, around a coffee table, the size of a small pool, covered with a host of fashionable and highbrow magazines. Certainly, no one could validly claim boredom in this waiting area. I contemplated my choices, but I really wasn't in a mood to scan the pictures of modern art I would never understand or appreciate, nor was I in a mood to attempt reading any article way over my head or way under my interest level. I left the impressive assemblage of journals to collect dust and continued to scan the room.

A number of expensive-looking prints adorned the walls. Not being an art museum junkie, I could only surmise why anyone in their right mind would spend the kind of money these prints surely cost. They looked to me to be a step up from finger painting, and not much of a step. As my gaze rounded the room my eyes focused on the long hallway down which my helpful receptionist had disappeared. I could see a number of closed doors on either side and at the end a double door which had just opened. Miss Effervescent was on her way back with a huge smile upon her countenance. She called me over to her desk with the good news that the busy Tyler Quentin had a few minutes to see me regarding Miss McKay. I thanked her profusely and, as directed, I walked "this way," right through the double doors, ushering me into a huge office with a stunning view of the city, Delaware River, and New

Jersey. I was duly impressed. Not about the view of New Jersey with its dismal skyline, but the size of the room, Quentin's desk, and the beautiful walnut conference table for twelve with matching credenza, a sideboard and bookshelves. In addition, my eyes came to rest upon a stunning redhead seated at a smaller desk to the right of her boss's massive desk. She was smiling broadly and nodding her head at apparently something Quentin had said prior to our arrival. He was standing behind her and to the side. This well-known counselor, a tall handsome man with a touch of gray at his temples, eyed me up and down. He smiled broadly, too. Maybe these two thought I was an ad man for Colgate toothpaste, and this was their big chance to be discovered. Maybe they thought if they gave me their best toothy smile, I'd hire them for a new campaign of toothpaste commercials. Then again, maybe they were just friendly and polite. I expected the fees charged in this office would buy a lot of friendly and polite. He invited me into his office and to have a seat across from the big desk in one of two chairs. I sat down and he sat in the other. Obviously, he was arranging for a friendly chat. Any minute I was expecting coffee and scones would be served.

And I wasn't disappointed as Red turned back from a sideboard across the room with a tray of cups, a pot, cream and sugar, and sure enough scones.

"I understand you have some questions regarding Miss McKay. What can I say, but all of us were terribly upset and saddened by the news of her untimely departure from us?"

I wondered if that meant there were timely departures, but I couldn't really think of one. After introducing myself and the nature of my business, I jumped right in, beginning with low level groveling and then in short order arriving at my question.

"Mr. Quentin, I really do appreciate you seeing me on such short notice. You knew Margo McKay quite well?"

"As well as one might or could know an employee, I suppose."

"Did she have any difficulties here at work or with any of her colleagues?"

"Not that I'm aware."

"I realize you must maintain a certain level of confidentiality, but was Margo working on anything that may have led to her demise?"

"I'm not at liberty to go into any particulars, but I wouldn't expect that her murder was work related."

"Might it have been related to her social life?"

"Perhaps. I overheard a conversation with another secretary, Miss Levine, that she was unhappy in her relationship with Tommy Harris."

"How so?"

"You'd have to ask Miss Levine for more details."

"Would that be possible at this time?"

Quentin turned to Red and said, "Please show Mr. Bridge to Miss Levine's office and explain his mission to her."

I thanked him for his time and offered one of my cards in case he thought of anything else that might be helpful.

As directed again, I walked "this way" out of the office and down the hall to a door which Red knocked and entered, all the while thinking it sounds like I'm one of the Round Table Knights on a mission, a quest. Call me Lancelot. She introduced me to Miss Carol Levine, a young lady in her midtwenties, who was a bit chubby, or as Jerry Blavat might say, "More woman to love." After explaining the nature of my business, Red turned as quick as a top and was gone.

I opened, "I understand you were friends with Margo."

"Yes, we were close."

"What can you tell me about Margo's relationship with Tommy Harris?"

"Well, at first she was flattered that this goodlooking successful broker took an interest and pursued her, but she found out he was very possessive, and one didn't say 'no' to Mr. Thomas Harris."

I called upon one of my clever interrogation tools, "Go on."

"Margo viewed him not only as a lover at first, but as a mentor as well. As time passed it revealed how self-centered he was. All his relationships were a power play. She had definitely outgrown him and had begun to despise time spent with him. That's why she was ready to call it quits. Even her sister advised her to break up with him. I'm not sure that would be easy to do. Tommy Harris just isn't rejected. He comes from a well-connected Main Line family. There always in the society pages of the Sunday "Inquirer." Members of the family are on a variety of charitable boards and organizations. They're a big deal. The more I think about it, the more I think it's unlikely someone from such a highprofile family would get involved in criminal activity at all, much less murder someone. I can't imagine he would actually hurt Margo, but he did have a terrible temper, so it's not impossible, I guess."

I stifled a snort and couldn't help but think many wealthy individuals have low morals and aren't the big deal the general public thinks they are. Sometimes, all the charity work masks their true nature. It isn't only poor people who commit ghastly crimes. Wealthy individuals' shit stinks too.

As always, after thanking Carol for her time and help, I left her my card with the expectation, if she remembered or thought of anything else that might help, she'd give me a call.

As I stepped out of the building into a very hot, muggy summer Philadelphia day, I thought about all I learned at Barrow, Nickerson, Smythe, and Fuller. It would seem that the logical next step was to go see Tommy Harris. At the very least he'd been dating the victim and he may have been the last person to see her alive. I unlocked my car and decided lunch was in order prior to my visit with Mr. Harris. I drove to Pat's Steaks for one whiz wit.

I shouldn't have, but I'm a real Philly man, and real Philadelphians can't resist an occasional cheesesteak at Pat's or Gino's. Personally, I like both sandwiches, so I alternate each time I go. I am never disappointed, and wasn't this time either, although my tie was. I'm sure if my tie had anything to say about it, it would whine emphatically, "Wear a bib, bub."

After lunch, I drove the notoriously treacherous Schuylkill Expressway to the Main Line office of my next interview. You'd swear many drivers on that highway got their license at Sears and Roebuck. Slow drivers and speed demons on twisting lanes make the highway into a demolition derby. There are always accidents followed by rubbernecking and road rage. Generally, one needs to add thirty or forty minutes to an estimated travel time. After arriving at one's destination, an airplane bottle of Jameson is required to calm one's frayed nerves.

Investigative procedures involve a lot of interviews and research that requires much leg work and can be relatively tedious and boring at times. It certainly isn't glamorous, but it is a critical component of the job.

I believe it was George Santayana who said, "Those who forget the past are doomed to repeat it" or something to that effect. I do try to learn from my mistakes. Not wishing to be held captive in another waiting room, before eating lunch I called for an appointment with Tommy Harris. When he learned the nature of my visit, he was able to "squeeze" me into a very tight schedule for Miss McKay's sake. Was his very tight schedule real or just the pretense of a self-important man? I was going to have a few minutes of his time-is-money time to inquire about Margo and their relationship.

I parked my car in a crowded lot and walked what seemed like a mile to the office building of Scanlon Financial. Again, a very cheery and loquacious receptionist welcomed me. When she was satisfied as to my identity and the nature of my business, she picked up her phone and spoke to someone in another office. I barely had time to glance at my surroundings, which were certainly not as ostentatious as those of Barrow, Nickerson, Smythe, and Fuller, probably due to a different culture, a different client expectation, when a door at the end of the room opened and a stunning brunette invited me once again to "walk this way." I had some trouble getting my hips to sway in such an inviting manner, but I did manage to follow her down a long hallway to another small reception area where I was handed off to a matron lady with her hair in a large gray bun, and cold, calculating eyes piercing me from behind a pair of spectacles. She had been introduced to me by the brunette as Miss Grim, and she certainly was. Her nose, a hawkish beak, and countenance would have scared the shit out of me had I been a little bird. That, of course, was not a very nice first thought. I had never met the lady and certainly didn't qualify as a judge of personality on such scanty evidence. She escorted me into an expansive office and straight ahead was an array of windows with a nice view of the trees and beyond them even more trees, apple trees to be exact. Johnny Appleseed would've been pleased. Seated behind the desk lodged in front of that window on the world was a man with light brown hair slicked back in a pretty fair impersonation of Jack Nicholson. Even his eyes had that dangerous look which Jack managed to convey in "The Shining." He stood up and greeted me, extended his hand and shook mine when I offered it. The grip and shake were firm and brief. And then he motioned me to a chair on my side of his platform called a desk.

With what came across as a sneer, he asked, "So, M. J. hired you to look into the murder of Margo?"

Brilliant. So much so, maybe he should be the detective and I should be the one uncomfortably squirming with each and every precise and probing question. "Yes, I've been retained to look into the homicide. I understand you had a dinner date with Margo shortly before her murder."

He studied me carefully as if he were looking at a microorganism under a microscope, and he slightly arched his right eyebrow. It made me feel as if I should be slithering around on a petri dish. I wondered if the eyebrow effect helped to improve his focus, or if it was meant as a not-so-subtle message that he had doubts about me. Hell, he wasn't alone, I had doubts about myself.

"We did have dinner, but Margo indicated she didn't want to make a night of it. She had some things to do, who knows what, and then she said she had to pack for her shore excursion. I dropped her at her apartment about 11:00 p.m. and continued home."

"Do you know what things she may have been referring to?"

"Not in any detail. I do know however, she had been going over some client's tax forms for one of the lawyers and was having some reservations. This client, I believe she called him Baxter, had received an extension, and was filing late. I also recall she had mentioned some kind of irregularity, but never expanded on that. She always observed attorney client privilege and wouldn't confide such with me. And I respected her privacy and didn't push it. Actually, I really wasn't interested, and it wasn't any of my business. I don't pry into other people's affairs."

The last line was delivered with all the holiness of a television evangelist, and it was obvious he was taking a slap at my profession. This was the kind of guy you might have eaten lunch with in high school.

And all you wanted to do was to grab the back of his head and push his face in the chocolate pudding. Mr. Pitcairn hadn't gone far enough when he called Harris a smug bastard.

I inquired whether he was aware of any problems Margo was having or if anyone might have had a grudge against her.

He couldn't think of any obvious problems and certainly, as popular as Margo was no one could possibly have had an issue with her.

I asked if she had broken up with him on that last evening together.

"It was more a mutual agreement to part ways. I believed we'd still be friends as there was no animus when we split up. She had her interests and I had mine. Plus, I wasn't happy with Margo at the end. She was changing and it wasn't for the better, at least from my standpoint."

My mind was growing into a kind of post-lunch metamorphosis state and I couldn't come up with any other lines of inquiry to pursue. I thanked Mr. Harris, handed him my card, and suggested the possibility of meeting again at a later point in my investigation. I'm sure he was thrilled with that possibility. In fact, he was so enamored with it he stifled a yawn with the back of his hand. His expression revealed what I perceived to be a false disinterest. I filed this thought away and left his office. By the time I reached my car at the end of another grueling walk, I concluded it was time to head back to the office.

At this time of day, traffic was heavy but not so heavy for me to miss the dark Ford sedan following at some steady distance. I decided to take my normal route through the city, which had a few turns. And everyone I made was also made by the mysterious dark Ford. There was no doubt in my mind I was being followed, but why? This was probably a question which had an answer that would only be revealed by time.

When I pulled into the garage across from my office, I noticed the license plate of the now obvious navy-colored Ford. I wrote the tag down on the back of an old envelope which had slipped to the floor next to the console. As a lovely lady I once knew was wont to say, "It pays to let the trash pile up in your car, because you never know when some of it might come in handy." How right she was. For once I was glad that my anal-retentive personality had not kicked into gear the last day or two removing any receptacle for my questionable memory. I crossed the street and entered my building. I should've been paying closer attention, but my mind was elsewhere. I was mulling over too many unrelated facts and trying to determine relationships and if they, or how they, fit together. When I entered the elevator, I was unprepared for Mutt and Jeff, totally caught off guard. Mutt was by the panel controlling the elevator and Jeff was standing opposite in the back corner. Once in, the doors closed quickly. Mutt pushed and spun me around before I could react, and Jeff threw an incredibly strong arm around my neck and grabbed my right arm with his. I tried to pull his arm from around my neck with a free left hand but couldn't budge his bear trap grip. I finally got a hold of his thumb trying to bend it where it shouldn't go. All the while, we danced to our right and hit the elevator wall. My shoulder felt needles of pain emanating into my arm and elsewhere. Next, we shuffled toward the front and bounced into Mutt, who promptly punched me in the stomach and then hit me with an uppercut. Jeff wanted to lead, but he was no Fred Astaire. And had I known, I wouldn't have accepted his invitation to do the two-step rumble. We continued to dance around for what seemed an eternity, but I had made some progress escaping his grasp, freeing me to better defend myself.

While Jeff and I were jitterbugging our way around the elevator, I sensed the pre-stop bounce elevators make right before reaching a floor. Mutt had apparently stopped it, I assumed, between floors as the doors never opened, and now he was looking for a way to join in and change the number we were doing to the Bristol Stomp. I, of course, was Bristol and Mutt and Jeff, after dropping me to the floor like a sack of potatoes, were doing their very best to win the stomp contest. In my mind, and the way my body felt, they were doing onehell-of a job. By the time I hit the floor and the elevator was moving again, all I saw were a couple of shiny black shoes finishing the job. I had two or three bruised ribs, maybe even broken, a black eye, various sore spots all over my body, and guessing a slight concussion as my head swayed in a dense fog of nothingness but pain. Finally, the elevator stopped, presumably at the ground floor, and as the doors opened, they immediately departed the scene of the crime. I, on the other hand, wasn't going anywhere, at least not quickly. I was thankful the beat down was over. I just lay there attempting to mentally check my body. It was hard to do, so much of it hurt. I didn't move. Even the trickle of blood sliding down the side of my face tickling me could not be wiped away. I lay still for a few more minutes, any effort to move an exercise in futility.

I was hoping someone from one of the offices would be entering or departing and come to my aid. But no one came to my rescue and, after a while, I gave up hope. It was either do it myself and get to ice or suffer some more on the floor of that elevator listening to "It's a Small World" over and over. Just put me out of my misery, please. I finally found the fortitude to get to my knees. It was a prolonged struggle. With the help of the metal handrail running around the three walls of the elevator, I stiffly got to my feet. I was wobbly. Probably more so than one of those dancing hula girls on the ledge above the backseat of granny's car. Could I make it to my office?

I pushed the appropriate button and the door closed. I could feel the elevator gliding up and up. It stopped and the doors opened. It was my floor, and the office was probably only a hundred or so steps down the hall, but it seemed like it might be a difficult, if not impossible, haul. I dragged one foot after another leaning on the wall for support. What a pal, and he didn't leave me down. He was a loyal and sturdy friend. Even though I tried to slide to the floor several times during the trek to the office, my buddy kept me upright time after time. With his unswaying strength I slid along, held up precariously by him until I reached an oh so welcoming door. I opened it and went in where I slumped on the couch. In a while, I stirred and made it to a small fridge I kept mostly for ice. The ice came in handy as I dumped the entire tray in a towel and placed it on various spots that cried out in pain. The incredible cold did make my head feel better, and the little black dots stopped circling in front of me. I had to do some serious thinking, but before I could, I needed to close my eyes and just rest, which I did for several more hours. It was dark by the time I awoke and although I knew I should get moving, I just couldn't. I didn't have the fortitude, the strength, or the desire to begin moving. I just slipped off into a shadow filled sleep. It was not restful as I kept seeing Mutt and Jeff and the elevator scene and then I was falling, falling into a deep dark chasm. Then black and nothing. I was lost in the darkness.

Chapter 5

Although it was one of the roughest nights I could ever remember, I awoke determined to get up to continue my investigation. I decided to go back to my place, take a long hot shower, and change clothes, but I couldn't help wondering who paid those thugs to give me a solid beat down and why.

Steam covered the bathroom mirror as I contemplated my next move under a prickly spray of running water. It felt so warm, I almost forgot my discomfort. And all the while the water ran down my aching body, I mulled over the who and why. All I came up with were blanks. Enough already. I turned off the healing spray and toweled down, then put on fresh clothes, and quickly devoured some leftover pasta and clams. I realized the police department needed to be an early stop. But before that I need to see Dr. Preston. I drove to his office and since it was early, just as they opened, he squeezed me in to what must have been a busy morning considering the number of people in the waiting room. He checked me out and gave me a prescription for Percocet, along with a warning to be careful. He emphasized the pills were highly addictive and dangerous with the consumption of alcohol. He strongly suggested I stop taking them as soon as I could handle the pain from my ribs. I thanked him, paid the receptionist, and on the way to the police department, stopped at a pharmacy and filled the prescription. Right away I popped a pill and hoped it would kick in quickly.

An old pal, Lenny Andrews, still worked homicide and he happened to be at his desk when I arrived at the precinct. He looked up from a file and after perusing my appearance, asked "Did you get any licks in, or was it a one-sided beat down?"

I had to admit it was pretty one-sided. I relayed what happened and shared the license plate number I had copied down. While he checked on it, I volunteered that I had been hired by Margo McKay's sister, M. J., to look into her murder. "The plate was stolen from a Chevy in the Mayfair section of the city."

I   wasn't surprised. I didn't think Mutt and Jeff would have been as obvious in their tail otherwise. In fact, the Ford was probably stolen too. I asked Lenny, "What can you tell me about the McKay case?"

"Well, there were no witnesses when the body was dumped and no camera footage. She had been shot in the back of the head with a 22 slug about one to two hours prior to the body's discovery. There was no bruising on the body, and no signs of rape, although semen was present. Obviously, there was no purse or

I.D. Basically, at this point we've got zip."

"Were you able to trace her movement prior to death?"

"Yeah, she had dinner with a financial wiz named Tommy Harris, but he dropped her off at her apartment about 11:00 p.m. We know she went out again. A neighborhood canvas turned up a visit to the local gin mill. She was seen about midnight at Grumpy's Bar and Grille which is just a few blocks from her place. The bartender, Sally Turner, recalled she had one drink and left. She couldn't have been there for more than a half hour. That's where her trail ends until she was shot sometime between one and two."

"What about the gun?"

"The revolver found near the body was the murder weapon. Ballistics show it was used about a year ago in a murder in South Philly. The serial numbers were filed off and what was left was treated with acid – kind of a double whammy."

"Where does the case stand at this point?"
"Nowhere really. It's still an open case, but probably for not much longer. It'll end up in the hands of detectives from the unsolved crew, as if their plate isn't already too full. The sister, a Mary Jane McKay, has applied a lot of pressure. She must have friends in high places because the push is top down. She's been a real pain in the ass. We're doing all we can, but we haven't had a break that would open the case up for us. I doubt once it lands on the desk of unsolved cases, not much will happen. Those detectives are really swamped."

"Thanks for your time and the information, Lenny. I owe you one."

"No buddy, you owe me at least three, but if you discover anything that helps, maybe I'll call it even."

I spent the rest of the morning looking at mug books, but Mutt and Jeff continued to lurk in shadowy corners, just like the shadowy corners of my office elevator. It seemed to be an exercise in futility. Finally, I had seen one too many ugly mugs and called it quits. It was time to move on to other avenues of inquiry. An effort that might kick start the case and help me establish some solid leads.

I drove home, to my apartment, to plan my next move. Traffic was exceedingly light and I made it there in almost record time. It was a good thing too, because the pain was growing intolerable at that point, all I could do was take a pill and try to fall asleep for a while. After about a half an hour of news, the Percocet kicked in big time and I thankfully dozed off, minus the pain. I slept hard until the morning sun was shining through my window disturbing my slumbers.

Chapter 6

The sleep helped, as did the pill. When I woke up, I felt much better, which was good as I planned to spend the later hours of the evening at Grumpy's Bar and Grille watching the clientele and interviewing Sally Turner, according to Andrews, the bartender on duty the night Margo was killed.

About eight o'clock I awoke and was terribly hungry. I opened the fridge and took out a small filet, some spinach, and then got a yam and shallot out of my counter basket. I proceeded to anoint the steak with olive oil and Montreal Seasoning, then I cut up a shallot and along with the spinach put them in a pot with a little bit of water and some butter. Finally, I washed the yam and poked holes in it with a large fork. The yam went into the microwave, and then the oven. When it was almost finished, I started the steak. After several minutes on high heat, I flipped it and put the pot of spinach on the burner. In short order, I had a pretty tasty meal, if I do say so myself. I was fortified and ready for the evening.

It was 9:25 p.m. when I cruised into Grumpy's. I took a seat at the end of the bar. The barkeep wearing a tag which read Sleepy, came over to me, and since it was probably going to be a long night, I ordered a Yuengling rather than a Jameson over two cubes. The two cubes, it's an idiosyncratic thing with me. My ex-wife accused me of being a bit OCD, but I'm not sure one can be a bit of something like that. You either are, or you're not. It's like weight – you're either overweight or you're not, there's no hazy in between. After taking a healthy swallow of my beer, I put the mug down on a little cardboard mat that said, "High Ho. Off from work I go!" and scanned the room. The bar itself was long, maybe thirty-five or forty feet. There were two rows of tables for four in the center of the room that could seat maybe thirty patrons. And on the far wall, were five booths each seating six people. The walls were covered with a wall paper portraying a mine and, of course, there were dwarfs working away. The air was stale, and the heat was oppressive, probably the kind of conditions in the mine on the wall. Away from the mine scene on a back wall was a cute little cottage with Snow White sitting on a stump. I suppose she was waiting for the Sleepy, Dopey, Doc, Sneezy, Happy, Bashful, and Grumpy to come high-hoing home. It seemed to me that if I was picking and digging in a mine all day, which would be really hard, really demanding physical labor, grumpy is what I'd be, and I'm not bashful to admit it (ha, ha – I chuckled to myself). I probably wouldn't have any energy or inclination to be singing all the way home. But hey, it's a fairytale and anything's possible in one of those, I suppose.

By 10:00 p.m., I was ready for another beer, as the room started to fill up. The bar had about twenty customers and the tables and booths held another twenty-five to thirty. The noise level had drastically increased and would best be described as boisterous.

Sleepy, I actually discovered, was named Phil. At the other end of the bar was a woman bartender, who I assumed was Sally. I checked with my man Phil and learned his bar mate was indeed Ms. Turner, but tagged Snow White.

I decided to move to her end and took an open seat near the entrance. She quickly arrived on the scene with a "What'll you have?" In short order, I had another Yuengling in front of me on one of the High Ho coasters.

When it eased up a bit and she came to my end of the bar to survey the crowd, I took the opportunity, introduced myself, and asked her what she remembered about Margo's last night at the bar.

"Margo was a regular and many nights she would stay until she was picked up, or maybe more aptly, when she picked some guy up. That night it was pretty busy, but I remember she was sitting where you are now. I served her one drink and moved down the bar to take care of other customers. By the time I returned, she was gone. She couldn't have been here for more than ten or twelve minutes."

"Did she leave with anyone?"

"I really didn't see. But now that I think about, Buck was sitting next to her.
Maybe he saw something."

"Is Buck here now?"

She scanned the room. "No, but he usually comes in Wednesdays and Fridays about 9:00 or 9:30 and stays until closing."

I thanked her and indicated I'd be back. At this point, I decided to head back to the office and take a look at more diary entries. I read through the remaining pages of June and started into July. I came upon an entry that gave me pause. I read it and then I reread it.

Diary Entry – July

Today was a good day. Taking a job as a secretary was hard at first, but it's a pathway to law school. It seems like everyone at Barrow, Nickerson, Smythe, and Fuller think of me as inferior because I'm just a secretary, like I can't follow the thread of a case being discussed or reviewed. The men look at me as a pretty young thing, a distraction from the daily grind. I think they see me as someone with whom they can exchange pleasantries, and for some, a bit more than that. Carol, another secretary, has befriended me and she agrees there's a lot of sexism in the office. A few of the lawyers like to take secretaries for drinks after work, and according to Carol, whose been here longer, sometimes more than just drinks.

Last night, we went to Oscar's Tavern to get the weekend started. I was feeling extra happy because I had received some positive feedback from one of the partners regarding my recent research work on taxes and editing his briefs. To my surprise, Tyler Quentin, whose wife rarely gives him permission, so I'm told, to go out without her, was there for a while. Carol said, "He's on a very short leash." He was so much lighter and engaging without his wife around, and of course, away from work. J.D., Anthony, Rachel, Carol and I did vodka shots and played darts in the back of the bar where we met some people our age from another firm.

They were fun, rowdy, fraternity types. One, a guy named Pete, asked for my number. I thought he was a stud, so I was flattered, I gave it to him. Maybe he will call.

People were leaving due to the late hour. By this time, I was feeling a little woozy from one too many drinks. My head was spinning a little which made walking a bit of a chore. I was talking with Carol and was embarrassed as I recognized how slurred my speech was. Thankfully, all the top brass had departed long ago and no one else was there from the firm except friends. My reputation would remain intact, which is a good thing because I really need this job.

Anthony was still there as we approached the front of the bar. I asked him if he would hail me a cab, but he drove to the bar and offered to give me a ride home. I vaguely remember giving him directions to the apartment, and how lucky we were to find a parking spot right in front. He insisted on helping me to my apartment and after opening the door urged me to let him help me maneuver the stairs. I don't remember much after that.

This morning I woke up in bed, naked, and with a splitting headache again, but I can't, for the life of me, remember how I got there. Did Anthony carry me into the bedroom, take off my clothes, and tuck me in under the spread? Did I do it all by myself? As I took my morning shower to help wash away the fog, I couldn't help but notice the bruising on my thighs. Maybe he did more than put me to bed. I have no idea and obviously, I'm not going to ask him.

Miss Margo got around. She had an awful lot of men in her life and maybe one of them killed her. I added some more names to my list and decided to call M. J. and find out more about two of those names, Rich – the drunken abuser and Jimmy Malkovich – the high school buddy and family friend. If Margo had a one-night stand with the guy who shot her, my chances of success were zip and nil, but if it was one of these schmoes she was seeing and screwing, well, that might just be in my wheelhouse. Yeah, maybe under those circumstances I would find out who. After all, I was used to trailing cheating husbands and scammers trying to pull a fast one on the insurance company and getting the goods. Most criminals aren't mental giants, they make glaring mistakes, and I had a pretty good track record of finding those errors and getting justice for either the wife or the company. But then again, this was a murder case and the perp could be a smidge more careful and dangerous; particularly, if I got too close.

Chapter 7

M. J. was quite helpful. The Rich from the diary was Rich McConnell who had indeed gone on to grad school at the Wharton School of Business. He was working on a master's degree in Business Administration. He lived in Ardmore. She gave me his address.

As for Jimmy Malkovich, M. J. had lost touch with him. The last she heard he was still living and working in Kennett Square. She reminisced about growing up together, although she was a couple of classes ahead of Jimmy and Margo. Jimmy's dad was an executive at DuPont and the sisters' dad was a big-wig at Sunoco Oil, she told me. When pushed, she remembered Jimmy being on the math team and Margo sharing he had gone to college for accounting. She thought Jimmy had his CPA and was working for a firm but couldn't remember which one.

I thanked her for the info and gave her a quick but detailed update, including the good old-fashioned beat-down in the elevator. She was horrified, I knew, because her facial expression was a revelation. Her look reminded me of a jack o'lantern with a gaping mouth frozen in terror. After a few more shared thoughts and plans, she thanked me and we agreed I'd touch base again in about a week, unless I needed her help sooner with any other background facts.

I rode out to Ardmore, but it was a dud as no one answered the doorbell. Maybe I'd have better luck searching for him at Penn. From Ardmore I proceeded to Kennett Square, the mushroom capital of the world. As you approach the area, you can't help but notice the distinctive odor. Many tourists and some locals find it offensive, but it never struck me as unpleasant, just unusual. It's possible my sense of smell is not very discriminatory, like my old pet dog's. She smelled everything and never seemed to wrinkle her nose. All these long windowless cement block buildings contain mushroom beds which require fertilizer for the mushrooms to grow. And that fertilizer gives off a very pungent odor. I used to stop at the Mushroom Museum on the way to my folks in Lancaster. The museum was very informative, and I learned a lot. I like to learn something new and expand my knowledge base. One of my best teachers impressed upon me that learning is a lifelong activity. He told me to stay curious. But usually I only stopped to pick up a crate of fresh mushrooms for my mom and some mushroom pâté for my dad, rather than visit the museum again. Tasty stuff on a cracker, that pâté was. My dad loved it with his scotch on the rocks, usually Dewar's. I stopped at a gas station and borrowed their phone book. There couldn't be that many accounting firms in the area. I made a list of seven from the yellow pages, along with phone numbers and addresses and thanked the manager who was not only friendly, but helpful as well. I felt obligated to fill up my tank as an appreciative gesture. He smiled a toothy grin and I was reassured he took it that way. My next task was to narrow down Jimmy's place of employment, by calling each of the seven firms. Either Jimmy worked for one of them or he didn't and then the difficulty of my task would rise exponentially. It took about an hour of calling and transfers to a variety of efficient and somewhat inefficient secretaries, receptionists, or personnel individuals, but I finally narrowed the firm down to Pierce and Sons. After making sure that Jimmy was in and could take a few minutes to meet with me, I got the address, directions, and drove there.

I parked in a lot next door to the Pierce and Sons office, approached the building, and took notice of how busy everyone was through expansive picture windows on the ground floor running the length of the office. The stairs to the side of the building and curtains in the windows suggested apartments on that second story. I entered an office that was very well lit with many cubicles in the center of the room, and approached the receptionist, a Mrs. Palmer, who sat at a desk in front of it all. After viewing my identification, she directed me to a small office toward the back of a row of a series of little work boxes or stations. His was not one of the little cubicles. It was a real office. I don't know why, but I pictured pigs, each in their own little pen, as I walked by them.

The door to the office to which I was directed was open, and I knocked on the jam. Jimmy Malkovich was sitting behind his desk, directed me to come in, then stood when I entered, and offered his hand. It was limp and clammy like a dick after unprotected sex. It made me want to wash my hand with Lava soap before he even let go. After all the formal graces, we sat down and then it struck like a bolt out of the blue; he reminded me of a turtle with glasses, like a turtle in cartoons I watched when I was a kid, but I couldn't come up with his name. I remembered that the cartoon turtle's speech was slow and deep, and he guffawed yuck, yuck a lot. Jimmy talked that way, too. He even threw in an occasional "yuck." At least that's what I thought I heard. I inquired about any information he might have regarding the McKay sisters and Margo's death.

"Tell me what you know about the McKay family."

"We moved to the area when I was in the middle school. This was a really difficult time for me socially. You probably remember what middle school was like. Yuck, yuck." Oh, then it dawned on me, it was Cecil Turtle, who always got the last laugh, yuck, yuck. "I was new, and it was hard to break into the circles of friends. I can remember eating lunch alone a lot for the first few months. But Margo and I were in a number of classes together and we became friends. The next year we entered the high school and remained friends. I got to know MJ then, although she was a two-years ahead of us. Mr. and Mrs. McKay were really good people and sometimes Margo would include me at dinner, and I was always made to feel welcome."

"Had you seen Margo recently?"

"We got together for dinner, usually in the city, about once every two or three months. The last time was about three weeks prior to her murder. Yuck, yuck."

"Did she mention any problems she might be having, or anyone that might have been giving her a hard time?"

"Not really. We talked mostly about old times. She did complain of having terrible headaches. She had just gotten another appointment with a doctor to do something about them."

While he was talking about the headaches, I couldn't help but wonder what could be causing them.

I asked what else he could tell me about Margo, and he said she was very popular in high school with both girls and boys. He added that she hadn't dated anyone seriously then, but since college her whole approach to dating and men seemed to loosen up.

Again, I couldn't help but wonder, why the huge change in dating habits? Some young ladies like the party scene, and others like to date around, but Margo seemed hell-bent for leather on both. Over the past few months her personality changed so drastically from what I gathered as an outgoing, popular young lady to more or less a tramp. Why? What happened that transformed her so? I didn't learn anything else for the moment. I left him my card in case he thought of anything he hadn't shared and suggested I might be back to speak with him another time, and that was fine by him.

I decided to head back to the office and on the way grab some lunch. I was hungry for a hoagie, one of those Joe Gentile Italians with extra onions and hot pepper spread. That might have been the best idea I had for the day. After picking up my sandwich, the smell that permeated throughout my car told me I was definitely right about that. It was such an inviting odor, I had a hard time getting it back to my place still in the wrapper and whole. That was particularly true when I stopped off at a Quick Stop 'n' Shop to buy a bag of chips. I had to fight off giving into the temptation to open it and take a huge bite, both before I got out of the car to enter the store, and again when I got in behind the wheel. But somehow, I managed to control myself. Of course, the heavy traffic and erratic drivers helped me to focus on something other than food, and that guaranteed the sandwich arrived intact, still wrapped.

Chapter 8

Parking my wingtips on the corner of my desk, I leaned back, and took a huge bite of my lunch. The salami, capicola, onions, and other condiments blended perfectly into a nirvana of deliciousness. While I ate, I scanned the "Inquirer" sports pages. The god-awful Phillies had lost again to the lowly Marlins. Like any true Philadelphian, I had a lovehate relationship with a franchise that has lost the most games in major league history. I needed to lick my sports wounds by remembering there's always another game, another season. Or even another sport, but the 76er's and Eagles were no great shakes either. What the teams needed were scouts who recognized sincere talent that could and would blossom over time and with good coaching. Oh shit, forget it, it was time to get back to the girl in the argyle socks.

If she left Grumpy's about 12:30 a.m. or so, and she was shot between 1:00 and 2:00 a.m., it didn't leave much time to dump the body in front of St. Paul's where it was discovered by a waitress on her way home from work at 2:45 a.m.

And why was she nude, except for the argyle socks. Her body had traces of semen, but no signs of rape. Had she had sex with her killer, who then shot her, drove the body to Christian Street and dumped it along with the weapon?

It seemed important to know if she left Grumpy's that Tuesday evening, or technically, Wednesday morning with someone. I needed to return to the bar and interview the elusive Buck who, sitting beside her at the bar, was probably my only witness to when she left, and if it was alone.

But first, I needed a nap. Again, I slept on the couch. Only this time it wasn't so fitful. I woke up and went to the can. What relief! It was Wednesday and Snow White said Buck was fairly regular at about 9:30 p.m. I got some Chinese takeout and while I ate, I pondered the evolution of my interviews and evidence.

At 9:00 p.m. I was once again ensconced on stool with a little Hi Ho disc blotting the extra head gliding down the side of my mug. While enjoying my second Yuengling, a crusty old man, who looked like he hadn't shaved in a couple of days, came in and sat down next to me. When he grinned, I could see he was missing a few teeth. I considered whether that forced him to eat mostly soft foods. Snow White came over to us interrupting my thoughts about teeth by flashing me a mouthful of dazzling white enamel. She introduced me to this fellow sitting next to me as Buck.

I bought him a drink, or should I say drinks? Four Roses and a beer were Buck's beverages of choice. He downed both rather quickly before I could even begin my line of questioning. Then he smiled, displaying a huge gap where his two upper center teeth should have been. I contemplated asking what had happened, but I didn't want to offend him, and the answer to that question could've had all kinds of offensive stuff attached.

"You were sitting next to Margo McKay that Tuesday in January when she was murdered?"

"Yup. Say, how about another round?"

"OK." I signaled Snow and in short order we were both refilled. "I understand she was only here about thirty minutes and left around 12:30 a.m. Did you see her leave with anyone?"

"Nope."

"Did you notice anything, perhaps which direction she took when she left the bar?"

"Well, now that you put it to me that way, I was looking out the window to check if it had started to rain. Channel 6 weather report called for rain on Wednesday beginning early morning."

I was feeling impatient but didn't let on for fear he'd clam up, so I resorted to another one of my patented questioning strategies. I nodded like I understood, empathized and said, "Yes."

It seemed to satisfy him as he came back to topic. "Margo had left the bar and had taken no more than three or four steps headed east when a car pulled up and stopped right by her. The window slid down; it seemed she talked for a minute or two, and then got in and off they went."

"Did you see who was driving or did you recognize the make or color of the car?"

"Nope, it was too dark. I did see it was a four-door and dark. That's all I know."

I thanked him for his help and left money for him to have another round on me. Buck had been a help, but not a great one. At least, I now knew she did depart the bar with someone, and probably someone she knew.

I thought best to call it a night and get an early start. Maybe it was time to try and contact Rich McConnell either in Ardmore at his home or at the Wharton School. I drove back to my place, had one more beer while I thought things over, and then called it a night. Sliding into the cool sheets was a comfort. Funny how small things become significant as one ages.

Chapter 9

I rose early, like the early bird I've always been, although I wasn't looking for a worm simply a breakfast bar which is preferable. I took a quick shower, dressed, grabbed a couple of those bars and was on my way to Ardmore. This time my trip wasn't a dud as I caught Mr. McConnell at home. An older woman, well maintained I might add, answered the door. I identified myself and explained my need to speak with Rich regarding an old flame named Margo. She said she was Rich's mother and he had just gotten out of the shower.

She'd let him know I was here and why.

"Before I go upstairs, would you like a cup of coffee and a muffin?" She was certainly very accommodating. How could I resist?

"That would be very nice."

She sat me in the living room, like I might have been a newly arranged vase of flowers and brought me coffee and the muffin on a beautiful crystal plate. Then she excused herself and went up to notify Rich I was here and waiting. I couldn't help but notice all the religious paraphernalia on tables and shelves around the room, and pictures of Jesus and Mary on either side of the fireplace mantel. The muffin was a pleasant surprise and reminded me of my mother's cooking.

It was a short wait before Rich came downstairs dressed in khaki slacks, a maroon pullover cashmere sweater, and a pair of Docksiders sans socks. Without a doubt he was a handsome man, a real chic magnet.

I introduced myself and explained a little of my investigation. Then I launched into my inquiry. "When was the last time you saw Margo?"

"It was probably about six months or so prior to her death. We broke up."

"Any particular reason why?"

"I felt she was changing, and not for the better. Those changes didn't fit with my beliefs or lifestyle. It was as simple as that. In case you hadn't noticed, I come from a very religious upbringing."

"What kind of changes did you notice that didn't fit well with you?"

"She stopped going to mass, for starters, and used way too much foul language, which I found unbecoming. She was pushing the boundaries of decency, and I was raised to expect more from a woman I would marry."

"Did you part on friendly terms?"

"I would say so."

"Could you tell me where you were and what you were doing the night she was murdered?" "Why?" he demanded.

"It would be exceedingly helpful to rule you out as a suspect. I really don't want to waste my time looking down or traversing rabbit holes." He became sullen and then haughty.

"Am I a suspect?" he growled. And then, without so much as a breath, "Sure, I've got nothing to hide." We had a big test coming up in one of our

classes and my study group and I were cramming that
Tuesday evening.'

"Do you recall what time you completed your," I paused for effect, "cramming?"

"It was about twelve-thirty or twelve-thirty-five."

"Where were you studying?"

"We were at Kitty's apartment on Locust."

He proceeded to give me the names and contact numbers for the other three members of the fourperson study group. I decided I needed to track them down on the way back to the office and verify Rich McConnell's alibi.

I spoke with the two men in the study group and learned zilch. Both remembered the night but neither one could remember how long they studied. All they were good for was verifying there was a study group, McConnell was part of it, and they had studied the night Margo was murdered.

Kitty on the other hand, was able to enrich my knowledge of the evening in question. She was a veritable fountain of knowledge.

"We got together at my apartment, ordered pizzas and soda, and began studying around 7:00 p.m. We worked pretty hard and only took two breaks. Rich was really up on some of the material, and Dan slammed the rest. So, our review went pretty smooth. I think we finished about 11:30 p.m., but no later than midnight. I'm positive about all this because we all aced the test. I couldn't forget

that." That meant he lied to me about the time. I wondered why.

"No, I guess not. By the way, do you know if Rich drives, and if so, does he own a car?"

"Yes, and yes again."

"Do you know what model?"

"I know it has four-doors and is black, but I don't really know cars. I'm sorry."

I said it was okay and thanked her and slipped one of my cards to her as I departed. It was time to return to my office and determine what to do next.

I got back to the office and sat at my desk pondering the possibilities. The dark four-door car matched what Buck saw sitting on the stool, when he was looking out the window, checking the weather. But was it possible for McConnell to get from Kitty's apartment to Grumpy's in time to pick up Margo, as she departed for wherever she was going at that time of night? Presumably, she went from there to her apartment? It was, if Kitty's timing was correct. If they finished anywhere from II:30 to 11:45 p.m., he had time to make the drive and pickup. If the session ended later, say closer to midnight, it would be a close call, and after midnight would be impossible. But how would he know Margo was in Grumpy's? I couldn't answer that question. The gun had a body on it. Where would he have gotten the weapon? I'm not naïve. I recognize if a guy wants a gun, he sure can buy one in the right neighborhood. Hell, for the right amount of money, anything can be obtained.

My mind started to wander, and I had to refocus on the problem. I had nothing, even with greater concentration.

That led me back to the diary, which I picked up off my desk and thumbed through to where I had left off last time. I read through a number of entries, but nothing jumped out at me as significant. It did reveal that Margo was becoming more promiscuous as she had started having sex with a number of pickups and one-night stands, all dutifully recounted in her diary with apparent pride.

I paged back to the front of the diary. On the back of the cover page, Margo had listed a number of her contacts with phone numbers and addresses. I slid my finger down the list and paused on Bobby Knickerly. It was time to make his acquaintance and see what light he might shine on this perplexing case.

I drove into South Philly near the stadiums and parked in front of one of the many brick row houses. Bounding from my car and up the steps to a bright red front door, I rang the bell, and after a short spell it opened. I was facing a young man with curly brown hair and a scraggly beard. I said hello and introduced myself, indicating why I had come to see him. I asked if he could spare a few minutes.

Bobby invited me into a small, but nicely and fully furnished living room.

"When was the last time you saw Margo?" I began.

"I had dated Margo maybe three or four times before she was killed, and the last time was maybe a week or two prior to reading the story in the paper."

"Is there anything you can tell me that would help get to the bottom of this? How did you meet? Did she have any problems? Did she have any enemies?"

"We met at a club on Bank Street called Mansfield's. We went back to her place and, I don't mean to brag, had really great sex. She was an insatiable broad."

Sure, he meant to brag. He wanted me to know he was a killer stud. I just wanted to know, was he a killer?

"How about problems and enemies? Were you aware of any?"

"I guess it was a problem and he was an enemy, but an old boyfriend, I think his name was McDonnell or McConnell, something like that, called her a couple of times over the three or four weeks we were seeing each other. Each time she seemed pretty upset afterwards. I really wasn't interested. We weren't really dating. We were just seeing each other for the sex. She was an animal in bed. You know what I mean, buddy. You look like you've been around the block a few times."

Yeah, I'd been around the block a few times. In fact, I'd like to drag this bastard around the block once or twice and see what would happen to that pretty boy smile and thin-lipped sneer he gave me when describing her as an animal in bed.

He said he had to get going. We got up and I'm not sure why, but I gave him one of my cards. I wasn't expecting a call from him, but I might be calling him or calling on him again. Time would tell, along with the direction the evidence I was gathering would lead.

I got in my car and drove back to the office. I wondered where he had to go.

Did he have a date set up, or was he going to pick up some unsuspecting young lady? He was a problem for those dabbling in the night life, but he was not my problem, yet.

As I drove toward Center City, I noticed a red panel truck some distance behind me but making all the same turns. I wondered whether Mutt and Jeff were back, and how they were involved in this case. Or was it just a coincidence? I reached parking for my office and didn't see the red truck anywhere.

I wasn't going to barge into the elevator as I did before. Today, I stood back and watched as the doors slid open. I was ready if Mutt and Jeff were once again lurking in the shadows to give me another beat down or worse. The elevator was empty and the ride to my floor was uneventful. Well, uneventful except for the monotonous song emanating from the speaker in the ceiling. I must hear the same song two or three times out of four when I ride, either up or down. It's nauseating. A Muzak version of the theme song from "Phantom of the Opera."

I sat at my desk and looked out the window. Dr. Elena Chow would be no help due to doctor patient-privilege. Even though Margo was dead, Dr, Chow wouldn't be at liberty to divulge any medical information. Where did that leave me? It left me with zip.

Time to go home. My body was still a bit sore and I confess I was beat. I don't bounce back any more, like I used to when I was younger. A little sack time, I hoped, would help me rejuvenate and invigorate the old body for another day of sleuthing.

I was out seconds after my head hit the pillow.

Early the next morning, while drinking a cup of coffee, I perused more entries to the diary. Most were of little value as they didn't shed light on what could possibly have happened to Margo. No mention of enemies and no apparent motives. But an entry in August caught my attention.

Diary Entry – August

MJ moved in with me – it's been a long couple of weeks, so far. I never thought she would get divorced. She was always going on and on about Lorenzo and what a super fabulous husband she had, always bragging about the great love they had for each other and how she just couldn't wait until I fell in love, too. We all liked Lorenzo. He was quite a bit older – in his thirties, and ready to settle down. His parents had a place on Shunk with lace curtains in the windows that his mother had made herself to remind them of the home they left behind in Naples, and, of course, his family had figurines of the saints in every room. Lorenzo's parents didn't have much, but they had deep pockets when it came to giving to the church, and always managed to give, even when they were just scraping by. Lorenzo started working by the time he was ten, helping neighbors by running errands, sweeping their pavements, shoveling snow from their walks, and washing their cars. In high school, he began working at the diner. He started out as a busboy, worked his way up to waiter, and by the time he graduated college, general manager of one of the most popular diners in South Philly. This was an accomplishment we all respected. On top of that, he looked like a movie star with his slicked back black hair, big brown eyes, olive skin, and muscular physique, and he always dressed to the nines.

On his first date with MJ (a blind date arranged by a mutual acquaintance who worked with her at Cavatello's Pastries), he arrived in a large black Cadillac Escalade. We were all there when he arrived, and though I didn't say anything to MJ until much later I was so jealous at the time, it was hard to ignore that he looked like a million bucks in his French cuff shirt, Italian silk tie, tailored slacks, and Ferragamo loafers. MJ was beside herself. She liked the fact he was older; he was stable, he had money, he had style. I thought she was lucky. Within six months they were engaged, and by the end of the year they were married and looking to buy a house.

How could such a perfect marriage come to an end?!? Mom thought maybe he was having an affair. That's what dad had done early in our parents' marriage. He would tell her he got caught in traffic after working late at the office. Eventually they resolved their problems, but MJ and Lorenzo couldn't. It turns out he hadn't been cheating but had gotten involved in some high stakes poker games and owed some very scary men, the kind with bent noses who didn't say much. I guess they didn't need to. I wonder how this could've happened. Lorenzo seemed so grounded and focused. I wonder what else I didn't know about my brother-in-law. MJ has been super depressed. She's really angry and feels betrayed. We're crammed into my one bedroom like sardines in a can, sharing my double bed and closet space. There's no privacy whatsoever, so she goes into the shower to cry. Yesterday, I heard a very faint noise emanating from behind the closed bathroom door. I'm not sure, but I think she was sobbing. This has happened several times. I've tried to get her to go out with me, but to no avail. I can't convince her there's a whole world of interesting people out there, including men, who would like to meet and maybe date her. She won't have anything to do with the idea. It's just pathetic and I don't know what else I can do.

It would appear that M. J. McKay had not been totally forthcoming with me either the first time we met, or the times since then. I was now curious if she was withholding anything else from me.

I called M. J. and set up time to meet with her for lunch at Bene's off Head House Square. Driving there I tried to plan a line of questioning that would reveal whether any of the last entry had any impact on Margo's promiscuous behavior or created a motive for murder.

I wanted to know whether Margo's jealousy had led to any involvement with Lorenzo. I wanted to know how long M. J. stayed with her sister after the divorce and when she left and why. I wanted to know whether Bene's still had the grilled octopus salad.

It didn't take me long to find the answers to all my questions. The "Ice Queen" was already seated at a window table when I arrived. She was drinking a glass of white wine and nodded to me. Was the nod a hello, or a direction to take the seat opposite her?

I sat down opposite her and said, "Good afternoon." She smiled and resumed her study of the menu. I picked mine up and was gratified to see grilled-octopus salad prominently placed in the salad section of the menu.

In short order, a waitress arrived to take our order. M. J. ordered a shrimp scampi and another chardonnay. I ordered my heart's desire and a Jameson on two rocks.

I opened with all guns blazing, "Did Margo sleep with your husband?"

She hemmed and hawed and stammered a bit, "Well, I didn't think, I wasn't sure, no, of course not!"

"When and why did you leave Margo's apartment?"

"I finally had enough feeling sorry for myself, moping around, sobbing in the bathroom, and decided I needed to move on and move on I did. I put all my energy into working for our father and moved up from one position to another. I didn't need a man to give me an identity. I could create one on my own."

"Then what?"

"Our mother died in a car crash a few years ago, and last year dad died of a sudden heart attack. I took over running the company."

"What is the business?"

"It's a real-estate investment firm called Downtown McKay. My dad built it up to a high level, but I took it to the top! I've really given it my all."

She certainly didn't pull any punches regarding the firm's success. I wondered how Margo factored into that equation. Did Dad treat both daughters equally, or did he favor M. J.?

Nothing more of any merit transpired during the remainder of lunch and I left thinking, somehow, I wasn't privy to the big picture. Was M. J. holding something back?

I wanted to check out Pete and then Anthony, two of the men mentioned in a July entry.

I called Carol Levine who helped me locate Pete's firm and called him to see could he meet with me for a few minutes. He agreed to see me later in the afternoon. In the meantime, I drove to Barrow, Nickerson, Smythe, and Fuller to have a chat with Anthony. He was in and readily ushered me into his office upon learning my interview concerned Margo.

I explained the entry in the diary referring to him.

"Yeah, I took her home that night and I got her upstairs into her apartment. She was cogent, just a little wobbly. She offered me a drink and one thing led to another, and before I knew it, she had me in a lip lock and was asking me to carry her into the bedroom. I picked her up and in we went. After I laid her down, she sat up and started to undress. She looked at me and asked, "What're you waiting for?"

"That was all the incentive I needed. Margo was a real looker with a great bod. I wasn't going to say no. So yeah, we had sex, but it was consensual. That was it. It was a one-night stand."

"You didn't see her again?"

"Only at work. She didn't even say anything to me about the evening. I just let it go. We had a good time, nothing serious, that was it."

"Thanks for your time."

As always, I left my card in case.

I spun over to Pete's law firm an after a short wait in an outer office was ushered in to see him. After introductions and handshakes, he motioned me to a chair, and I sat down.

"Margo kept a diary and mentioned your name in a July entry saying you asked for her number. Did you ever call her?

"Yes, in fact, we went out clubbing a couples of times and had a great time. At least, at first we did."

"What's that mean?"

"We partied hard and had great sex. But then the third time we went clubbing I lost her."

"How so?"

"We'd been dancing, and she said she was hot. It was pretty hot. The 222 Club was mobbed, and it was hard to move around. I was sweating, but I wanted to hear the next number. Margo declined my request to dance. Said she was going outside for some fresh air. When she didn't return a few numbers later, I went looking for her, but she was gone."

"Do you know what happened to her?"

"I asked the bouncer if he had seen her. He said she was talking to this guy and then they got into his car and drove off. I called her the next day, and the day after that, but she didn't answer my calls or return any of my messages. I couldn't believe how rude she was. Cutting out like that, and not saying anything. So, I said the hell with her. It was fun while it lasted, but what are you going to do, lose sleep over it? I just moved on to another pretty lady. They're all over the city."

I didn't think he lost any sleep over Margo. In fact, I didn't think he'd lose any sleep if he drank too much strong coffee. I thanked Pete and left a card, more a habit because I really wasn't expecting any additional information from him.

I was famished and stopped at Pietro's for some linguini and clams. The breadsticks were outstanding and by the time clams in white sauce came, I had devoured the whole jar of them, along with two glasses of the house chianti. I ordered another wine and enjoyed a most delicious repast.

After dinner, I called it quits for the day and drove back to my place. I was tired and needed a night cap and a good night's sleep.

I read through a few diary entries while I sipped my Jameson. Margo was seeing a lot of different men, but nobody for very long. It seemed as if sex was her main objective and a relationship was not sought or expected. What was driving her? This compulsive behavior was all rather new, but she never wrote in her diary about its motivation. At least not the parts of it I had read.

I finished my night cap and called it quits. Sleep caught up with me as I chased Margo's sexual escapades. It was not a good night's sleep. I dreamed of scenes of Margo and a variety of men. The scenes were unpleasant. They portrayed a misplaced desperation for some kind of what, sexual validation, or proof that she was in control? And I was powerless to help this vulnerable girl, guiding her away from her descent into hell and eventually death. All I could do was get her some kind of justice, if I was good enough. I hoped I would be.

Chapter 10

I started the new day off with some baked Spam on a bagel (if you fry it, it smells like Taylor Pork Roll and tastes like shit). When I was about four my mother served Spam for dinner, way too often for my liking, and she fried it. It stunk and I couldn't dump enough ketchup on it to hide the awful flavor. But I had to sit there until my plate was clean. The first week I was married, I came home from doing a stakeout, and asked what we were having for dinner. My new bride said, "Spam." I panicked. How was I going to possibly eat her cooking? I didn't want to hurt her feelings. But when she served it, low and behold it tasted good, a little salty, and smelled like ham. She had baked it, not fried it. I enjoyed my Spam with coffee, and Margo's diary. An entry in September caught my interest.

Diary Entry – September

My headaches are back with a vengeance and I've been feeling dizzy and a bit nauseous again. On Monday, my head hurt so badly, I thought it was going to explode. I dry heaved in the bathroom, and I'm not sure, but Anthony may have overheard me. When I left the ladies' room, he was standing outside the door. It was if he was lurking, and he had this strange look in his eyes. That look frightened me. I've been trying to avoid him ever since that night back in

July when he drove me home from Oscar's. It's not easy to avoid him. Even though the office is large, we work in relatively close proximity. He spoke as I passed him, asking if I was okay. I told him I was and cracked, "Why wouldn't I be?" I wasn't expecting an answer and moved on to my desk and a pile of work I'd been avoiding.

On Tuesday, I woke up with another horrific headache. It felt as if there were a couple of railroad linemen replacing the spikes holding the rails down by pounding in new ones with huge pile-driving hammers. I couldn't remember driving to work, and when I got to my desk wondered if I could concentrate enough to complete some vitals tasks I'd been assigned. I poured myself a mug of coffee, hoping the caffeine would suspend the pounding, but as I walked back to my desk I collapsed. I don't know what happened. I just fell and there were shards of glass and pools of coffee everywhere. I was totally embarrassed. I had to go home to clean up and change clothes. By the time I got home, I felt really sick again and climbed in bed under the covers. The cool sheets helped to ease some of the tension. I called the office and then tried to sleep. MJ's call woke me sometime after lunch. When I told her what happened, she wanted to know if I was pregnant. I told her she was ridiculous. Maybe it was anger, maybe it was the nagging pain, but I laid her out. I told her to mind her own business and slammed down the phone has hard as I could.   This morning my head feels a little better, not the pounding from before, just a residue of pain. It was manageable and I decided to get ready and go to work. On the way, I called

Dr. Chow's office, but I couldn't get an appointment to see her until December. I made the date, but I wasn't happy with the asshole secretary who gave me a hard time.

After work I felt much better and knew clubbing would lift my spirits. I decided to head over to Oliver's. I had a good time there before. It was really crowded, and I had a hard time getting near the bar to get the bartender's attention, so I unbuttoned my blouse a couple of buttons until my pink lace push-up bra and the top of my breasts were clearly visible. That grabbed his eyeballs and he responded to my order with a Scotch on the rocks. I downed it quickly. Perhaps too quickly, but I didn't care. I was feeling strangely free and horny. When the tall dark and handsome man next to me asked if I wanted to go to one of the private rooms in the back of the bar to have a more intimate party, I said sure, if the drinks are free, and you know how to handle a real woman.

I wasn't surprised by Margo's direct approach. Each entry reflected a more sensual woman who for some reason had abandoned a quiet desperation found in a younger, perhaps more naïve, Margo. I had to stew on this for a time. I parked those thoughts in the back of my mind – there was plenty of empty space and moved on to more investigative pursuits.

I spent a good part of the day at the Philadelphia Public Library researching a cast of characters. It was a day well spent as I taken copious notes and learned a few things about the players in this unfolding mystery.

I drove back to my place and took a piece of striper out of the freezer, that I caught on a recent fishing trip to Kent Island, Maryland. Both days we caught our limit, and all came home with numerous plastic bags of fillets. I cut up a lemon into thin slices and arranged them in a row on some Reynolds Wrap, placed the fish on top of the lemons and with a squirt or two of extra virgin olive oil covered the fillet before wrapping the foil and sealing my dinner. Then, I popped the package in the oven and commenced to cut up some asparagus which I dumped in a pot with some water and chunk of butter. In about fifteen minutes, I had a decent dinner. I ate every morsel of food and was ready for the evening.

It was my plan to visit the bouncer of the 222 Club and see if he recalled the night Margo fled the scene with someone other than Pete. M.J. had given me a picture of Margo when we met for lunch at Stella's.

I was in luck on two counts. I found parking close by and didn't have to walk far, and the bouncer, a gentleman named Brutus, was standing at his assigned post. I wouldn't want to try to sneak past this behemoth for love nor money.

After introducing myself and my mission, I showed him Margo's photo. He recognized her right away, but he didn't see the person driving the car, other than it appeared to be a man. He claimed, however, remembering the car to be dark, maybe black, with four doors.

I thanked him, but this time didn't leave my card.

It would appear possible that Rich McConnell may have picked Margo up at the 222 Club and then again at Grumpy's. As I drove home, I wondered why she would have anything to do with him after breaking off because of his abusive ways. She had to realize he would never change. Chances were, if anything, he'd only get worse.

I made it back to my place, and luckily found a spot to park. I had one Jameson and watched the news. When I hit the hay, I tossed and turned and had a tortuous night's sleep. I awoke several times thinking about what Margo's life had been like at the end. It made me shudder. This case certainly had been having too much of an impact on my sleeping habits. If I didn't solve it soon, I probably be so tired, I'd fall asleep after lunch.

Chapter 11

The next morning, I made scrambled eggs and buttered rye toast. While I ate, I contemplated a course of action. Elimination of some of the people on the list of suspects had to be a priority. I probably needed to retrace my steps and recheck alibis.

Arriving at Barrow, Nickerson, Smythe, and Fuller I asked to speak with Carol Levine again. She wasn't there and my ever-efficient receptionist friend informed me she called in sick. I was able to wheedle an address from her and drove to Carol's apartment.

My knocking on her door delivered the sound of approaching footsteps. I suppose she was checking me out through the peephole as there was some hesitation prior to the door opening. Ms. Levine invited me in and offered me a seat on the couch. As she did so I apologized, "I'm really sorry to bother you at home when you're not feeling well, but I had a few more questions."

"Oh, that's alright. I think I've got one of those summer colds. I'm really stuffy and just don't have any energy."

And with that she pulled a tissue from a box on the coffee table and promptly blew her nose. It sounded like a fog horn. I knew then and there I was not going to touch anything, and I would try to wash my hands as soon as possible after leaving her place.

"I'm sorry to hear that. Did you know Margo and Pete from the Snyder and Sons firm were dating?"

"Yes, Margo told me, but she also told me after several dates she dumped him at the 222 Club."
"Do you know why?"

"She said he was nice enough, but she was angling to possibly renew an old relationship."

I was tempted, but didn't ask if she was contemplating reeling him in.

"Do you know with whom?"

"She didn't say, but I gathered from the way she talked it had been pretty important to her at one time."

"Is there anything else you can tell me regarding Pete?"

"Margo said he tried contacting her a number of times and she didn't answer or return his calls. I did see him at Oscar's again weeks after that and we chatted, but he didn't even mention, or ask about her. In fact, he asked me if I wanted to go clubbing with him the following night."

"Might I inquire, if you did go clubbing with him?"

"Sure, I don't mind telling you. I told him no. I knew what he was after. He wasn't interested in a relationship, just sex."

"Good insight. You'll know when Mr. Right comes along."

She extended a hand, and I couldn't be impolite, so I took it and gave a cursory shake as I thanked her for her time and passed along a wish for a speedy recovery. I took the elevator down to the lobby. I remembered seeing doors marked Gals and Gents off the lobby and I made for the Gents door and after approaching the bowl lathered my hands with soap and washed them in very warm water.

While I attacked germs, real or imaginary, I picked up from Ms. Levine or from her apartment, with the weapons at my disposal from the sink, I ruled Pete out as a suspect. It didn't appear that he cared a great deal that it was a short-lived relationship. He got what he wanted, free sex, and didn't hold any grudges.

What next? Good question – I didn't have an answer for it though.

If Margo was trying to instigate a renewed relationship with Rich McConnell, that could put him high on the list of suspects. He was abusive, an opinionated prude, and probably a very jealous individual. Maybe I needed to take a closer look at his movements the last month or two before her body showed up nude, save for the argyle socks, on the steps of St. Paul's. I drove to the precinct and spent the afternoon reviewing too many mug books. It's amazing how after staring at one bad man after another, they begin to look the same. It's in the eyes. They're cold, calculating, with no empathy or semblance of regard for someone else. To me, they look like they have no soul. Page after page I turned, but all to no avail. Mutt and Jeff continued to remain elusive, hiding in the recesses of my memory.

It was soon time to meet with M. J. and give her an update as well as get paid.
She was in New Jersey for the day, apparently wheeling and dealing real estate. If I wanted to meet with her it would have to be in Jersey. We established a noon lunch meeting at the Italian Connection Restaurant in Collingswood. I had read many articles in both the "Inquirer" and "Philadelphia Magazine" what a great restaurant town it was, and that our meeting place was one of the best. Fortunately, I did recall Collingswood, an old Quaker community, was a dry town, and I stopped at a liquor store off of Route 130 to pick up a BYOB on my way into Collingswood.

I got to the restaurant before M. J. and was seated in a window table. I scanned the menu while I awaited her arrival. It didn't take long. I stood as she approached the table and before I could maneuver to pull out her chair, an ever so courteous waiter had already moved into position to do so. His mother must have been just like mine, a stickler for manners. M. J. and I exchanged pleasantries and then spent a few moments scanning the various selections. Our waiter arrived to inform us of the day's specials, which were tempting, but I opted to stick with the insalata salad with lump crab meat and the grilled salmon. M. J. selected asparagus soup with lump crab meat, and the filet mignon rare.

After our garçon departed, I gave a brief update. There wasn't a lot new, as I hadn't made much headway. As I relayed these disappointing details, I thought I detected a Cheshire smile briefly flicker across her lips. Maybe it was my imagination.

At this point, the waiter showed up with our salads and we continued our conversation with small talk. Both of us were quite pleased with our choices. M. J. claimed it was the best asparagus soup she ever ate. We didn't have long to wait when our entrees arrived. Again, we resorted to minor chit chat, with a little more chat than chit.

We declined dessert and M. J. paid the bill. As we prepared to leave, she handed me an envelope with another week's salary, plus expenses for the previous week.

I indicated I would stay in touch, and we parted ways.

Next, I drove to Ardmore hoping to have another go at Rich McConnell. I was in luck. A black four-door Chevy Malibu was in the driveway. I knocked on the door and McConnell answered. I asked if he had a few minutes to clear up a few questions that were nagging me. He opened the door wider and backed into the living room. I entered and we sat down.

"I just want you to know, I have to get moving in about a half an hour. So, make it quick."

Short and sweet, that's what I was angling for.

"I have two witnesses that saw you with Margo the last few weeks before she was murdered. You want to explain that?"

His jaw dropped slightly, and one eyebrow shot up in consternation. He appeared to be contemplating whether or not he wanted to evade answering my question, lie to me, or give up the truth. Finally, after what seemed an endless time, he went with the truth.

"I was trying to get back together with Margo. We had spoken over the phone a few times. She called me from Oscar's, and I went to get her. We went to the Gold Card Diner and talked over coffee. It seemed to me she wanted to get together again, but something was holding her back. I took her home and before she got out of the car and went in, I pleaded with her to reconsider. She said she'd think about it."

"Why'd you want to get back together?"

"I missed her and thought maybe I'd been too judgmental. And I was optimistic I could get her to change, if she hadn't done so already."

"What happened the night she was killed?"

"I finished with our study group and called her. She was walking to Grumpy's for a nightcap. She said she was still thinking things over."

"You were outside waiting for her when she came out of the bar?"

"Yes, I had to see her. I thought maybe seeing me in person might help sway her thinking."

"She got in the car with you. Then what?"

"She said she was tired and had a bad headache and asked me if I would just take her home, which is what I did. We sat in the car a few minutes talking, and then she got out and went into her apartment."

"You didn't go in with her, and coerce her into going to bed with you?"

"No, I didn't. I'm a gentleman and that would never be my motive."

He was pretty emphatic and seemed desperate for me to believe him.

"Oh really, what about the incident in the dorm stairwell when you got rough with her, and banged her head on the wall like you were cracking walnuts?"

"I don't know what you're talking about. How do you come up with that cockamamie story?"

"I have my sources and I don't reveal them unless subpoenaed."

"Well, your sources don't know the real facts. They're merely blowing smoke up your ass."

Maybe that was better than the proctologist's thumb? I wasn't sure, but I knew I didn't want to experience either one.

"Ok, let's move on, what time was it when you drove off?"

"It was maybe twelve-forty-five, twelve-fifty."

"What then?"

"I left and drove home to Ardmore."

"And I'm supposed to believe that, when you've already lied to me before?"

"Yes. Wait, I do remember stopping for gas on the way home, and I've got the charge receipt somewhere."

He went to the desk, an innately carved Italian antique, and rummaged through the top center drawer for a minute or so and then I heard an ever so slight squeal like a baby pig. He found the receipt and proudly handed it to me.

It had the date and time, as well as a purchase of thirty-two dollars of gas. Being at Ardmore buying gas at one-forty-eight in the morning eliminated him from murdering Margo and dumping her body and the gun in front of the church. There just wouldn't have been time.

I thanked him for his time and cooperation, but as I walked back to my car, I was more puzzled than ever. He was a self-centered, pious, abusive prick and a liar. He clearly could have had the motive and the ability to do such a dastardly and horrific thing to Margo. I also was puzzling what my next move would be.

I drove back to my office. I poured a Jameson over two cubes and sat at my desk looking out at a bustling Philadelphia. Eventually, I turned around, and spent the next thirty or so minutes updating my files. When I was finished, I decided to go home, cook dinner, and spend some quiet time watching television. I didn't realize how tired I was. I woke up at three or so in the morning, still in the chair. Disgusted, I dragged myself off to bed, hopeful I would find the ability to fall asleep again and get some much-needed shut eye. After some brief wrestling with a stubborn pillow, the softie won, and I fell asleep. And for some reason unknown to me, the dreams never slipped in disturbing my nothingness.

Chapter 12

The next morning, after a hearty breakfast of bacon and eggs, I drove into the office. I sat at my desk and reviewed my notes. The big question on my mind was who did Margo sleep with on the night she was killed? If McConnell was telling the truth, and the gas station receipt seemed to point to that, either Margo had unprotected sex with the killer, or with someone else before she went to Grumpy's. Which was it? I needed to backtrack all that Tommy Harris told me. Maybe Mr. Smug hadn't been honest about the dinner date. I decided to recanvas Margo's neighborhood to see if I could locate any witness to Margo's coming and going that last evening of her life.

I drove to her apartment, but parking was really tight. I ended up parking a little over a block away. I briskly walked the block and a half back to Pine and stood in front of her apartment, scanned the street, crossed it, knocked on the fire engine red door of a three-story brick home. A young woman came to the door carrying a baby. Her hair was askew and looked a bit like Medusa's dreadlocks of venomous snakes. I introduced myself, by showing my identification, and the nature of my inquiry, which was Margo's murder. I told her I was looking for help from neighbors who might have noticed some behavior or someone creating a problem for her neighbor across the street. But she informed me that normally she and her husband are in for the night by the six o'clock evening news. She added they didn't really know Margo and wouldn't have been aware of her late-night activities. She apologized as if she felt guilty not helping me solve the crime. I assured her it was okay. She closed the door with a comment regarding the sad state of the world.

I thanked her and moved down the street to the next house. It too was brick but had a blue door the color of a Maryland crab before it's cooked in boiling water. Again, I knocked. It took a little time, but this time the door was opened by an elderly woman, the keeper of the little garden. The only way I can describe her is regal. She was probably a real looker in her time and had all the men chasing her. She eyed me up and down while the little dog she was holding hurled a ferocious growl my way.

"I hope you're not selling anything. I don't buy anything from anyone at my door. There are just too many scammers in this world today."

"No ma'am, I'm not selling anything. I'm seeking information."

I introduced myself, flashed my I.D., and told her of my search for a witness to Margo's whereabouts prior to her death.

"Come in and we'll talk."

 I shuffled along after her down a narrow hallway and into a sitting room. It surprised me, as I was expecting a décor similar to Mr. Pitcairn's living room. Instead, it was very chic and modern. She motioned me to a chair and then asked if I would like a spot of tea.

I thought the libation might lubricate our conversation – give it an air of sharing gossip over a cup of tea – so I said, "Yes, please."

She departed the room through a door in the far corner and I could hear sounds of preparation. I took in the room and decided it definitely wasn't my style. The chair she assigned to me was exceedingly uncomfortable. I did take note that Ms. Weaver was an arduous reader as two large floor-to-ceiling bookshelves were jammed full of books. On the coffee table lay four more all with bookmarks and on each end table at either side of the sofa were two more books with visible markers protruding from the top. I tipped my hat to her. How did she keep all the plot lines and characters straight? Hell, I have trouble reading a book and a newspaper in the same day and keeping track of what's what and who's who.

She brought a tray with ornate tea cups, a matching sugar and creamer, and little silver spoons, and placed it delicately on the coffee table. She then poured tea in both cups and handed me one sitting in a saucer with the little spoon on the side, and said, "Help yourself to sugar and cream if you like." I thanked her and waited for her to sit, which she did.

"Mr. Bridge, how do you think I can help you?"

"Did you know Margo, your neighbor across the street?"

"Why, yes. What a lovely young lady. She was always friendly and helpful. I can tell you, she was quick to come across the street and shovel the snow from my walk and make sure my steps weren't icy. If she was outside and saw me coming with grocery bags, she'd run across the street and insist on carrying them for me."

"That's really great. I understand from a number of sources Margo was a thoughtful young woman. My investigation has led me to some inconsistencies the night she was murdered, and I'm trying to piece together her movements. Knowing more about them might help me explain incompatible facts. I reminded her of the date and asked if, by chance, she had seen Margo at all."

"That was my birthday. I'd gone to the Monk's Den, my favorite restaurant, to celebrate. When I got home, I remember walking Rusty, it was about nine or so that evening and Margo and a man with slicked back hair were walking down the street and entered her apartment. She waved to me and I waved back. Rusty was being a bad boy and wouldn't go. We went back inside, and I tried him again right before going to bed. I walked down the street and crossed over to come back up the other side, Margo's side of Pine. Rusty seemed to be doing some serious sniffing. I was hopeful he was getting ready to go. That's when this man ran out Margo's apartment like his pants were on fire and bumped into me knocking me down. I'm lucky I wasn't hurt. He did help me up and apologized but hurried off without giving it another thought. I didn't feel as if he were sincerely sorry at all. Bastard. He sure did look a lot like Jack Nicholson in that movie that took place in an old Colorado hotel. You know, they were snowed in and the boy kept seeing redrum."

"Yes, I remember the movie, 'The Shining,' and I know to whom you're referring. Do you remember what time you had this collision with Tommy Harris?"

"Yes. Rusty peed just after that and we crossed over to my house and went in. I'd left the television on and they were just starting the eleven o'clock news."

I thanked Ms. Weaver for her time and help and slipped her one of my cards in case anything else came to mind.

As I walked back to my car, I reviewed all that she told me and decided I needed to speak with smug Mr. Harris again. It seems, he hadn't told the police or me the truth about his last date with Margo.

I wondered if they had sex. Was that why he was in such a hurry to depart her apartment, or was there some other reason?

I called Scanlon Financial and made an appointment with Tommy Harris. My ex-wife would've loved their parking lot. She could have gotten a lot of steps as every chance she got, she parked as far out as possible to force a long walk. It was huge and once again I seemed to find the only spaces at the outskirts of the lot, the frontier. I hoofed into the main office at a rapid pace and didn't wait too long before I was once again ushered into Mr. Harris' office. He didn't seem pleased to see me.

"Mr. Harris, I have witnesses who'll testify that you lied. You lied to the police and you lied to me. You left Spots well before half past ten and didn't drop

Margo off at her apartment around eleven o'clock. In fact, you arrived at Margo's flat on foot together a little after nine and you left shortly before eleven, the time you claimed to have dropped her off. You had sex with her, didn't you?"

This Main Line creep turned at least three shades of red and if looks could kill, I'd have been six feet under. He stared at me, as if he could make me disappear. But I sat there staring back at him. He wasn't any David Copperfield.

Finally, he replied with a question, "What if I did?"

"Her body was found with fresh semen and I'd like to pin down whose semen it was. I think it was yours. I'm wondering if you killed her, fled the scene, knocking down an elderly lady walking her little dog in the process, and then went back later to dispose of the body."

"You've got an active imagination, Bridge, maybe too active for your own good." Maybe this was the schmuck that put Mutt and Jeff on my tail.

"I just want the truth. You were the last person to see Margo alive, except for the killer, but then, maybe you did the dirty deed. Maybe you shot Margo in the back of the head. Fled the scene. Thought better of it and came back for the body, cleaned up the apartment, gathered any incriminating evidence and then dumped the body on Christian, nude save for a pair of argyle socks."

"No, I didn't do it," he snapped. "I left in a hurry, and I didn't go back again. She was alive when I left. And yeah, we had sex. She fucked my brains out. She did everything and anything I wanted. Afterwards, I was really sorry she told me that was it. It was over. No more Margo for me. She made it even worse by telling me what we had just done was a pity fuck, because she felt sorry for me. The bitch. I was so angry I could've killed her. I would've enjoyed slapping her around right then, and that's why I left in such a hurry. When I ran out, she was still smiling that cold and vicious smile she could get at times, but listen to me, she was alive and breathing when I ran out. Don't think you can pin her murder on me, you've got to believe me. I'm no murderer!"

That was one hell of an admission. It was very convincing. Either he was telling the truth, or he was the best actor since my man, Humphrey Bogart played Philip Marlowe in the "Big Sleep," and said, "My, my, my! Such a lot of guns around town and so few brains! You know, you're the second guy I've met today that seems to think a gat in the hand means the world by the tail."

If he was telling the truth, it explained the semen, but it didn't explain who killed Margo or why. He seemed sincere enough, but I wasn't convinced to cross him off my suspect list just yet. I'd met too many liars who were so convincing they could pull the wool over the eyes of a polygraph machine and operator. My list certainly included a lot of men who didn't measure up to a mother's standards for their daughter's potential husband. One would think an apparently nice girl, and good looking too, would have little trouble finding a great guy. That contemplation was way over my pay grade.

Chapter 13

I called it a day and drove back to my place. I wasn't paying much attention to the traffic behind me as I mulled over the state of my investigation. But the closer I got to my apartment the more the traffic thinned out. That's when I noticed I was being followed by a Cadillac. I couldn't see at first, but after slowing down and making a few unnecessary turns, I could see my buddies, Mutt and Jeff, were back. I finally arrived at my street, and after I turned onto it, I could see in my rearview mirror they continued on. I still took precautions parking, moving to my building, and checking out the elevator prior to entering. I was also exceedingly careful inside my apartment, checking out every nook and cranny before relaxing and feeling safe. I remained puzzled by the role of Mutt and Jeff and who hired them. Were they supposed to keep tabs on my movements and the progress or developments in solving who murdered Margo?

I wasn't up for cooking. I grabbed a Stouffer's macaroni and cheese out of the freezer, slid it in the oven, and turned the knob to 350 degrees. I cut up some carrots and celery and took the blue cheese dressing from the shelf in the door of the fridge. In about thirty minutes I had a passable meal.

After I finished eating and did the dishes, I sat down at my desk and reviewed all my notes. I had to visit with Jimmy again, the McKay's family friend, to ask a few questions about the sisters. I had a few questions I had to ask Detective Andrews. And I wanted to stop at the public library and do a bit more research on Mr. Martin McKay, the real estate tycoon.

I made myself a Jameson on two cubes and sat down and read the "Inquirer." The Eagles were beginning training camp and were optimistic for the coming season to be the best one in a long while. I'm from Missouri – "show me." The Phillies were still in last place and were beginning to talk about a variety of young talent they got in the draft and how the future looked bright. Bullshit. Talk is cheap. If you're going to talk the talk, you better walk the walk. I'm still from Missouri, the Phillies still needed to show me.

I watched the ten o'clock news and hit the sack. I hadn't realized how tired I was.
I couldn't have been awake for more than four or five minutes. I slept hard for a while, but then the Margo dreams kicked in and it was a restless early morning thereafter. She had really gotten into my head and infected my mind with scary dreams and lurid scenes of her with strange men. For some reason, fatherly instincts were surfacing.

I awoke bright and early. The sun wasn't even up. I just made some buttered rye toast and coffee for breakfast. While eating, I decided to begin the day stopping to see my old pal, Andrews.

I arrived at the precinct and sure enough Lenny was at his desk, appearing to complete some paperwork, and there is an awful lot of that in police work.

"Good morning, Lenny. Have you got time to take a short break and answer a few questions?"

"For you Bridge I'll stop the whole operation, and even call in all the beat cops to do your bidding."

"Jeez, don't you think it's too early in the morning for such dripping sarcasm?"

"It's never too early, and never too much for you, Jack? So, what is it you want to know?"

"I assume forensics went over Margo's apartment with a fine-tooth comb."

"That they did."

"Any fingerprints?"

He grabbed a thick folder and opened it before he answered, "Yes, quite a few, but more smudges than clean prints. Most of the clean prints were the deceased's, but there were two we couldn't match."

"What about blood? Any trace of it in Margo's digs?"

"The apartment was tested from the living room through to the bedroom, and not one smidge of blood did they find."

"So, she was shot elsewhere."

"It sure looks that way."

"Anything out of the ordinary on the M.E.'s report?"

"No, but what did you have in mind?"

"She was suffering from some pretty severe headaches."

"I don't think the exam wouldn't have touched that aspect."

At this point, I filled Andrews in on what I had learned. I didn't share any info regarding the diary. I thought I'd keep that to myself for the time being. I also told him that Mutt and Jeff were still hanging around.

"Hanging around like a couple of maggots on rotting meat." The smart ass wanted to know how long I'd been dead and stinking up the city. Ha, ha.

I once again spent time paging through the mug books. After over an hour, I was about to give up when I spotted him. I was staring at Jeff and he was staring back. His name was Antonio Renaldi. His face was long and thin, horse-like, and he had short cropped brown curly hair. But it was his eyes that grabbed mine. They were dark, menacing, and if it's true – the eyes are the window to the soul – he had none.

I went back to Lenny with my find and after a few minutes on the computer, he filled me in on this bad boy.

"Renaldi ran with the Santucci mob from South Philly. His record was as long as a really tough day with many arrests, few convictions. He worked with Joey Santucci, the son of the mob boss, and his partner was one Reggie Vincenzo."

He brought up a picture on the screen and sure enough, I was looking at Mutt. His face was thick with a nose that had clearly been broken at least once. Again, it was his eyes. They had no soul either. These were two bad boys, probably with little or no empathy for anyone. But why were a couple of mob thugs tailing me? My friend, Lenny, wanted to know the same thing.

"It has got to have something to do with the death of Margo McKay and my investigation because my other work was simply some insurance fraud claims and a couple of family insecurity issues."

"Meaning?"

"Wives thinking their husbands were running around and me playing "peeping Tom" to get the goods on them."

"Yeah, you wouldn't think that would be enough to bring Vincenzo and Renaldi into the picture. Unless you've got a husband that took exception to your efforts and he knows a guy who knows a guy."

"I doubt that."

"You never know. Some divorces are pretty messy, and if a pile of dough changes hands..." He let it hang there for a minute like Michael Jordan on the way to the hoop. Then finished it, "well, you know what can happen."

"Yeah, your probably right, but I still think this has something to do with the murder of Margo McKay."

We shook hands and agreed I should stay in touch and inform the police of any further problems with the mob guys and to let him know if I broke open anything that would shed light on her death.

I was starving. I called ahead and made an appointment with Jimmy Malkovich. All the way to Kennett Square, all I could think about was a steaming bowl of mushroom soup. I wasn't disappointed. I parked on the main drag and walked to a restaurant and bar called the Fun Guy. Clever. The owner may have been a fun guy, I don't know. What I do know is all too often, as a detective, I feel like fungi, always kept in the dark under a pile of shit, just like all the mushrooms grown in this town. The mushroom soup was outstanding, in fact so good, I ordered and devoured a second bowl.

From the Fun Guy I walked to Jimmy's office. And once again the receptionist sent me down the long row of little pens to his office. The door was closed. I knocked and heard him say, "Enter."

I went in and he said hello and motioned for me to take a seat. He didn't offer to shake my hand as he was in the midst of blowing his nose, and it sounded gosh awful messy. My feeling of relief was huge. I had been dreading a repeat of the slippery dick handshake he gave me previously.

"What can I do for you, Mr. Bridge?"

"Do you remember a female friend of both girls while you were in high school?"

"Let me think about that for a minute. Yuck, yuck."

He sat in silence and I wasn't sure his eyes hadn't slid shut. And then his head came up and he said, "Yes, there was a girl in between them. I mean between grades. Margo was in ninth grade, MJ was a junior, and this girl, Sally, was a sophomore. Let me think about her name."

I waited patiently, shucks, I didn't have anywhere pressing to go. Although it wouldn't be a hard sell to go back and get another bowl of that great soup.

"Sally Porter," he blurted out at last. "She was Sally Porter, and the best of friends with both girls. They were inseparable. They had the nickname, "The Triplets.""

"Do you happen to know where Ms. Porter is today?"

"She's not Miss. She's Mrs. Ron Barrington. Ron and Sally got married right after high school. There was some scuttlebutt at the time that they had to walk the aisle. Supposedly Sally had one in the oven. And, sure enough, seven months later she delivered."

I asked Jimmy for her address and he grabbed a phone book from his desk drawer and looked it up for me. I thanked him profusely and made my escape before he could offer me his hand.

I had been in such a hurry to escape his clammy grasp, I hadn't asked for directions to her house. But my luck held. I saw a police officer coming out of a coffee shop near where I had parked and stopped him to ask him directions to Dawson Court.

He was very accommodating, and the directions were fairly simple.

I passed the high school, which sat on a hill and looked quite imposing with its brick edifice and tall, white columns, on my way to Dawson Court. They sure don't build them that way anymore. Now, they're all one-story with open courtyards and sometimes hallways to classrooms in those courtyards. What a stupid idea for an area with cold winter weather. I found Sally's house and parked. I rang the bell and almost instantly, as if she was waiting for me, the door opened and there she was. A blonde, not beautiful, but easy on the eye with a great complexion and big brown eyes which immediately engaged me, stood to the side of the door.

"You must be Mr. Bridge."

"Yes, and Jimmy must have called you to give a heads up about me."

"Indeed, he did. Please, come in and have a seat?"

I did as I was asked. It was a cozy house and the style and cleanliness marked her as a good homemaker. The smell emanating from the kitchen was incredible. The furniture was practical and comfy. The mantel was adorned with family photos and on the wall across from me, there was a child's artwork hanging in a frame. She definitely was a good homemaker.

"How can I be of help?"

"You were very good friends with the McKay sisters, "The Triplets" so I'm told, and I thought you might give me some background that might help me solve Margo's murder."

"Yes, we were the very best of friends. They treated me as if I were a sister, too. In fact, Mom and Dad treated me like a daughter. By the time MJ was a senior, there was some rivalry brewing for dad's attention between MJ and Margo. After we went off to college, it seemed to grow worse. MJ didn't want to share her father with anyone, not me, and certainly not Margo. She became tremendously possessive."

"Why do you think that was the case?"

"I'm not sure, but after their mom was killed in the car crash, it became even more pronounced."

"How so?"

"MJ would plan things with her father and not include Margo. I know Margo began to resent MJ's behavior.

I was beginning to think the sisters weren't so lovey-dovey after all. Maybe it was a love-hate relationship.

"What do you know about M. J. 's divorce from Lorenzo?"

"I know that MJ suspected Lorenzo of having an affair and then found out about the gambling. She was hurt and scared about the jeopardy he had put them in, and she was humiliated, MJ never failed at anything. But secretly, I believe she still thought Margo and Lorenzo were seeing each other. Margo never confided in me, but perhaps the rivalry between them might have stimulated her to take something that MJ valued. I don't know."

"Did you stay in touch with both girls after the divorce?"

"Not as much as before. Before that, we'd probably get together two or three times a month for lunch or dinner, whatever I could swing with my family commitments and responsibilities. After that, maybe we got together once or twice every five or six-months. MJ and Margo lived together, so I would meet up with them at Margo's place. Well I did, until things got tense between them and eventually MJ moved out."

"What do you know about the family company that Martin McKay built into a Philadelphia firm to be reckoned with?"

"I know Downtown McKay was growing rapidly. There was speculation in the papers that some underhanded, perhaps illegal, practices were used to build it so quickly, but nothing was ever proven. MJ didn't talk about it, but I sensed she was embarrassed by some of the stories mentioning her father."

"Was Margo involved in any way, did she comprehend what M. J.'s role was? Do you know, did they plan to work together in the company?"

"We never talked about that. I do know when she completed law school, Margo expected to gain a position in the company and be more of a force countering MJ."

"What happened after Martin McKay's heart attack and subsequent death?"

"The rift seemed to grow. Maybe all the stress was causing health problems for Margo. She was having frequent, horrible headaches."

"Did you notice any changes in her behavior?"

"What do you mean?"

"It appears as if she was becoming increasingly sexually active and her behavior was additionally very risky."

"I know very little, other than MJ was upset by some behavior Margo was involved in, and deemed it embarrassing to the family and the company. And MJ wasn't about to let anything interfere with Downtown McKay's success."

I was pretty much at a loss for words. I literally didn't know what else to ask. I thought it best to quit while I was ahead, and thanked Sally for her time and insight. I left her one of my cards and drove back to the office.

I spent about an hour updating my notes and thinking through all that I had learned. I put everything in the file cabinet and locked it. After that, I called it a day and drove back to my apartment. It was a messy drive as it had started to rain. It was one of those summer thunder showers with lightning lighting up the sky. You could smell the ozone. It made me think of when I was a kid and during a storm like this, sitting on the big front porch of our house with the whole family, including grandma, we could smell the chocolate from the factory all the way at the other end of town. What a great smell. Of course, it didn't hurt that my father had used cocoa bean shells for mulch underneath the bushes surrounding the sides of the porch. What great memories. Sometimes they're all you have.

Chapter 14

The next morning, I woke up with a slight hangover. One too many drinks the night before left me bleary eyed with a pounding headache as I went to the kitchen in search of coffee. Breakfast was a glass of tomato juice, two extra strength aspirins, and black coffee. I couldn't get over all that I learned the previous day from Sally. Her revelations opened up a whole new line of thought regarding who had motive to murder Margo, and what that motive might be.

After breakfast, I drove to the library again and spent some quality time with microfiche. I learned a lot about Martin McKay and his real estate investment business. I also learned from time to time there had been questionable business practices, and suspect persons involved with business dealings or overtures to unsuspecting victims or clients. Tony Santucci's name was prominent in a number of the Inquirer articles.

Did M. J. have knowledge and access to mafia sources? Could she have acquired a gun through

Joey Santucci or one of his associates and killed Margo? Could she have had Mutt and Jeff follow me and attack me? If so, why? M. J. hired me to find her sister's murderer. It didn't add up, but it seemed as if I needed to talk with Lorenzo and find out what he knew about connections between the McKay family and the South Philly mafia. I couldn't chance confronting M. J. yet. I was relieved I hadn't updated her totally. I hadn't revealed the diary, which ultimately could be more important than I realized, when I first discovered it hidden in the side table turned ass-backwards.

I needed to clear my head. I needed to rejuvenate my body. I needed to be ready to move the case forward. Thus, I spent the morning at the gym, purging my body of all the evil spirits and excesses. It did help. By lunchtime, I felt a whole lot better. Not quite ready to lick the world, but probably able to lick a butter brickle ice-cream cone.

After the gym, I stopped at this little Greek place off of second and had a lunch that was delicious. The Greek, as he was known, was to the kitchen as Scott Joplin was to a piano, or as Satchmo was to a trumpet. He was that good.
Whenever I needed to lift my spirits, all I had to do was visit the Greek's place. I usually got the lamb shanks, which were outstanding, but sometimes I got his famous skewers, which were very good, too.

The afternoon found me sitting at my desk thinking, trying to put into perspective all that I had learned so far. I picked up Margo's diary and began reading where I left off. Much of it was more of the same until I came upon an October entry.

Diary Entry – October

This week has turned out to be utterly riveting. I wasn't expecting it. Just the opposite, in fact. I was planning on working late all week because I have been having a hard time getting everything done for my boss, Jim Conover. It just seems like I can't work as fast as I used to these days, so I have catching up to do. Turns out, I'm not the only one at the office after hours. I was sitting at my desk slurping down wonton soup when I heard someone clear his throat. The noise startled me and as I juked a little, I spilled the rest of the container of soup down the front of my dress. It was Quentin, and now he was laughing at my predicament. Very funny, I boldly said to him. Now I'm a complete mess and a burn victim. I ought to sue you! I headed toward the bathroom to clean myself up, brushing lightly against Quentin's body as I passed him. A rush of excitement ran through my body. His looks are okay, say 7 out of 10, but his body is to die for. I have always wondered what it would be like to sleep with him. My heart was pounding, but I didn't let on. As I washed my dress in the bathroom sink, I fantasized about seducing Quentin. I imagined him looking me up and down, craving me, staring into my eyes, longing to hold me in his arms, captivated by the power I had over him. I looked in the mirror, standing there in my bra and panties and the silk stockings and garters I'd lately added to my wardrobe. I knew my twenties would be fun years, but I never knew how many men would want me, or how much I would enjoy toying with their lust, leading them on, playing with their feelings, using them for my own satisfaction. I checked myself out in the full-length mirror hanging on the wall. My curves were perfect, but my pumps were a little too corporate looking. In my mind I changed them to red stilettos, the kind that kill to wear but make men quake. And then I took everything off and threw on my gym clothes, a tight lavender tank top, black leggings, and sneakers. I threw my wet dress, bra, panties, stockings, and garters into my gym bag. It felt like a small rebellion to go commando at work – and I liked it! My mind turned back to Quentin.

Tonight's the night, I thought. Let the seduction begin.

This girl seemed to be on a mission to entice and manipulate men to satisfy her needs. It sure didn't sound like the younger Margo I heard about from Jimmy and M. J. I read on, and the next entry followed up on the scenario I'd just encountered.

Diary Entry – October

Back at my desk, I pretended to be entranced by my work. I ignored Quentin, which I knew would drive him nuts. His interest in me was so obvious. Sometimes, I like to get right to the punch, but this time, I wanted him to earn it. I could feel his eyes looking me over as he made copies of some briefs at the copier in front of my office area. After a few minutes of this, I looked up at him quickly with total lust in my eyes, a slightly opened mouth, made a motion like I was laughing to myself, and then returned to my work without looking at him again. Quentin walked past me slowly like he too was preoccupied but it was obvious that I was the only thing on his mind. I could FEEL him staring at my tits as he copied page after page. I didn't even have to check to know. Besides, let's face it. This certainly wasn't the first time I'd picked up on this vibe from him.

He went into his office which is catty corner to my cubicle and started moving stuff around and rustling papers. A few minutes later, I heard the sound of ice cubes being tossed into a glass, then Quentin came out into the hall again. "Care for a Scotch," he asked? "Works for me," I responded.

I joined him in his office, making myself at home on his brown leather couch (So buttery, my God! That alone could get the job done!). We clinked glasses, then downed our drinks in silence. Quentin retouched our drinks from a crystal decanter, and this time we sipped them and made small talk, which led to a third round of Scotch, which led to flirting, which led to polishing off the Scotch, which led to confessions of attraction to one another, which led to Quentin's arm around me, which led to him kissing me deeply, which led to more confessions of deeply-held feelings for one another. We made a plan to meet again like this toward the end of the week. About ten-thirty, we kissed one last time and parted with a drawn-out goodnight.

If this wasn't a stunning development. I was forced to read on to realize whether she succeeded in her quest to seduce this titan of the firm.

All week long, I felt like I was going to burst. Every time Quentin and I made eye contact, I got turned on. I could hardly wait until Thursday night, when we planned to stay late again. It seemed like it was taking forever for the days to pass. I received a few calls from random guys asking me out but didn't return any of their calls for a change. I wanted to save up all of my attention and energy for Quentin. The waiting period was making me want him all the more. All day long, all I could think about was how I wanted to feel his arms around me. Was I falling in love? Or was it the chase that was driving me?

At last, Thursday came, and there we were. The second we were alone, Quentin pulled me into his arms. We locked the door to his office and quickly helped each other undress. I lay on top of him, feeling his gorgeous, muscular body press into mine. He was suave, and smooth, and knew exactly how to kiss. I've been on a bit of a sex rampage recently, and I've had more than my share of men, but he is the REAL thing. He was possessed by a real hunger. I thought I was going to literally burst at the end. But it just kept getting better. I always like two rounds in the bedroom (or, in this case the boardroom), and Quentin, after a brief break for another drink, was up for the task. I don't know how it was possible, but somehow, he was even BETTER the second time. He seemed to intuitively know all the right moves. And what's more, I could feel how much he enjoyed making them. He is a freaking god!!! Right down to my fingertips and toes, every single part of me was alive and throbbing. Tears flowed down my face, and my chest and my cheeks felt flush with excitement. Amazing, amazing night!

I may never be able to concentrate at work again! I thought nobody could come close to Lorenzo, but Quentin has set a new standard. Wow!

Wow. Did this muddy the waters, or what? Now, I had another possible suspect. He could have been afraid of his wife finding out, or he might have feared a blackmail attempt on Margo's part. Maybe she did try to blackmail him, and he had to kill her or have her killed. Obviously, I was going to have to do a bit more digging.

I went back to the public library, and on the way stopped at my favorite Jewish delicatessen, Fleishman's Deli, for cream cheese, lox, and onion on a sesame bagel. I washed it all down with a Pepsi.

I wanted to find out more about John Baxter. Again, I hit the microfiche and immediately hit a treasure trove of information. Baxter had been involved in a number of real estate deals with Martin McKay and Downtown McKay a number of years back. As I researched more current information, I discovered that Baxter was still doing deals with Downtown McKay, but not with dead daddy anymore, now, it was M. J. running the show. The more I learned about the McKay sisters and the more suspects popped up with a motive for murdering Margo, I began to see the case to be as murky as the tap water in Camden after a bad storm.

I drove back to my place and parked my car. As I got out, I noticed a shadow or figure slip around the hedge running along the sidewalk to my apartment entrance. I approached as if I was unaware, and unsuspecting. When Mutt and Jeff came at me in the lobby, I was ready. I got Mutt first with a chop to his throat and while he was bending over, gagging and wheezing, as if hit by tear gas, Jeff moved on me. I was ready for him too. I let him grab me around the throat, but instead of allowing him to pull me back and choke me, I lunged forward and down and threw him over my shoulder to the floor. By this time, Mutt was recovering. Not for long. I kicked him in the balls so hard they shot up into his eyes, which appeared to be exploding from his puffy face. Before Jeff could regain his composure and come at me again, I backed up and stomped, as hard as I could, on an exposed hand lying on the tile floor. I heard the sound of cracking and wondered was it his hand or the tile. Just as I was contemplating another go at Mutt, one of the other tenants, Mrs. Call, came out of her first-floor apartment and in a shrill voice none of us could miss hearing, screeched, "I've called 911, and the police are on the way."

Sure enough, we all heard the siren closing in on us. I thanked her for her help and turned to see Renaldi and Vincenzo escaping out the lobby door. I watched them hightailing it, if you could call it that with a limping gait, to a Cadillac at the end of the lot and ride around the back of the building. No sooner had they made their getaway, then Philadelphia's finest rolled up to the front of the entrance.

I went outside to speak with them. I told them, "Two guys tried to mug me. One was tall and thin, and the other was short and pudgy. They got into a Cadillac at the end of the lot and took off around the back of the building. I didn't get a plate number. I'm okay. No harm, no foul."

I sent them on their way. I was sure Mutt and Jeff had ironclad alibis. It would have been a waste of valuable street time for these two to deal with this in any greater dimension. I assured both I would visit Detective Andrews the next morning as he had helped me with these two thugs before.

Feeling really satisfied with myself, I returned to the lobby and assuaged Mrs. Call's fears. I told her the apartment house was safe, she was safe, and they were not thieves or muggers looking for easy pickings. I left her with the impression it was a personal thing, they were after me. I did give her one of my cards and asked her to give me a ring, if she saw them hanging around again. She smiled bravely, took the card, and nodded her head so vigorously I thought it might fall off. Watching her made my head hurt.

I rode up to my floor and after entering my place, kicked my shoes off, got a
Jameson on two rocks, hit the remote for the news, and sat back in my easy chair. I was still floating on cloud nine for my success in the lobby. Payback can be so gratifying. I thought about who said that and decided I did. I chuckled at my own joke. I was well

aware however, I couldn't be two cocky. Like a debt collector chasing a client behind on their payments, I knew these two thugs were probably going to turn up again, and the next time, I might not have a harbinger of their arrival and intent to do me great bodily harm like I did today.

I went to the kitchen and took some chicken thighs from the fridge, a box of brussels sprouts from the freezer, and some leftover home fried potatoes from a recent breakfast. In no time flat, I sautéed the thighs with a diced shallot, and heated the home fries and sprouts with a little butter. Along with a glass of cabernet, my dinner was exquisite, if I say so myself. And who else was there besides me to say it? The chicken sure as hell wasn't going to give me a thumbs up, maybe the bird, ha, ha.

I read for an hour or two, then watched the ten o'clock news, and went to bed. Maybe the Jameson and wine kept the dreams at bay. Maybe I had consumed too much, over my limit so to speak? I didn't know, but again I slept soundly through the night, and didn't have all the tossing and turning that had been haunting my nocturnal efforts. That was a "good thing," thank you Martha Stewart.

Chapter 15

I sat at my desk the next morning drinking my coffee and outlining a course of action. If Margo wasn't murdered in her own apartment, where was she killed? Could Lorenzo shed any light on the relationship between M. J. and her sister? Did Margo's homicide have anything to do with Downtown McKay and dealings with John Baxter or the Santucci family, Tony or Joey? I'd discovered some things, and ruled some possible suspects out, but there was still much I didn't know. And even though she hired me, I wasn't sure how open and aboveboard M. J. had been with me. It seemed the more I discovered, the more confused I became. Somehow, I needed to check off some of my suspects and narrow down the field to only those with means, motive, and opportunity. Easier said than done.

I drove into South Philly hoping to find Lorenzo on duty at the diner. I found parking and went in to the Meet and Greet Diner and took a seat at the counter. A waitress with a name tag reading Jane approached me and took my order for a cup of coffee and a sticky bun. When she returned, I asked her if Lorenzo was working. She said he didn't usually arrive before ten o'clock, depending on how late he stayed the night before.

It was nine-thirty. I decided to wait, but in the meantime, I told Jane I'd be right back to finish my bun and coffee and went outside to a row of boxes selling newspapers. I found the "Inquirer" box and proceeded to feed it quarters. Eventually, I had pumped in enough, three bells appeared on the screen, the door opened, and I won the jackpot – my very own newspaper. I strolled back in and resumed my seat at the counter. Jane came over and poured more coffee. She was the friendly sort and she maneuvered the conversation toward my interest in Lorenzo. She was pretty in a sharp featured kind of way, but she had very sharp features, the kind some men found sexy. Not me though. I was thinking maybe now that Lorenzo was an ex-husband, he was expanding his partnership horizons. Maybe Jane was a new dawn, or he was chasing a Dawn or a Debbie, or who knows who else. I guess you'd call this South Philly Don Juan, a lothario.

I finished my bun and left the coffee dregs in the cup. A suave looking fellow with dark, swarthy features came in and the staff seemed to snap into greater efficiency. I imagined this must be the infamous Lorenzo I read about in Margo's diary.

He took a seat at one of the tables near the register and began to peruse the Racing Form. I took note he hadn't changed his ways very much after the breakup with M. J.

I walked over to the table and sat down. He looked up at me over his thick black glasses, and spat out,

"That seat is taken."

"I hadn't noticed. Are you a toddler who has invisible friends?"

"Are you some kind of smart ass looking for trouble? Because if you are, you've come to the right place. You've found trouble, with a capital T. Now, get the hell out of my face before I kick your sorry ass."

I was shaking in my boots, but I calmly replied, "Not looking for trouble, just looking to talk to Lorenzo about Margo."

That brought him up short. He rubbed his cheek with his hand, put the paper down, maybe buying time, and then said, "You must be the dick MJ hired to look into her sister's murder."

"That I am."

"I got nothing to say to you."

I tried another one of my techniques to extend conversations when my interviewee wanted to stone wall me.

"Why?"

"Because I don't know a thing, and even if I did, I wouldn't lift a finger to help either one of those conniving McKay bitches. Neither one of them was any good for me. Spoiled brats, that's what they are."

"I wasn't under the impression you were cruel or hardhearted."

"If you got that from Mary Jane, she done dropped a load of shit all over you."

"How so?"

"When it comes to our divorce, it wasn't pretty and I'm still sore about it."

I tried to catch him off guard with a real change in the line of questioning.

"How well did M. J. know Joey Santucci?"

That stopped him. He lowered his head and I thought I heard a soft chuckle.

"You've been nosing around a lot, haven't you?"

"I'm just trying to be thorough and earn my fee. Could she have gone to Joey for favors?"

"What kind of favors?"

"The kind that tip toe on the line between legal and illegal, and sometimes just boldly cross that line."

"She knew him well enough, but if you want any more, ask Joey."

"Do you still owe Joey gambling debts of six figures?"

"Not that it's any of your damn business, but that slate's clean." He got this smarmy look on his face, gave me a thin-lipped sneer and said proudly, "Why it's as clean as one of my tables after it's been bussed."

I had noticed a few of the tables on the way over to his from my perch at the counter, and now I was looking at his personal table. I didn't know what kind of bullshit he was handing out, but I wouldn't have laid my buttered bread down for fear of contracting some kind of salmonella or botulism germ.

"How did you manage that?"

"Clear out, I'm done talking to you, buddy. Just watch your step, Mr. Bridge. That's all I'm saying."

I sat for a minute more and we did a fast eye tango. I closed my eyes, shook my head from side to side ever so slowly and took my leave.

I got in my car and sat for a while watching the diner. I could see him through the window and wondered if Mutt and Jeff were working for him, and what the motivation would be.

I started the car and while in South Philly drove a few blocks to a warehouse. I had discovered, when researching Downtown McKay at the library, the company had this building. I thought it might be a good idea to check it out. I parked my car about a half a block from the address and decided to walk around the block and come at the building from the opposite direction. My surveillance revealed a twostory brick building with a front door on the street and a driveway on the right side blocked by a chained fence. The driveway led to a rather large door I assumed to be on wheels. The door was large enough to allow a midsize truck to enter the building. I wondered what M. J.'s company used this building for, and who had keys to it. I went around the block again trying to look like someone getting exercise through brisk walking, and lots of arm swinging. I thought I seemed pretty convincing. That second go-round paid off. On the left side of the building almost at the back was a window slightly ajar.

I made it to my car without too much huffing and puffing, got in and drove off. I had already decided I needed to check out the inside of the warehouse and this discovery confirmed I should, but at a later time, a much later time, when it was dark and most everyone was sleeping.

I drove back to my apartment for a little R. & R., on the way, I stopped at a Home Depot to pick up some "C" batteries for my flashlight. I was in luck; they were on sale, two packages for the price of one. It's hard to pass up a bargain that good. My mother taught me that when I was about twelveyears old. We were in the men's section of a department store in Lancaster and she found a cashmere houndstooth sport coat on sale for ten bucks. Mom made me try it on and of course it hung on me like a cheap floozy at the Dead-End Watering Hole. But she was convinced it was a great bargain and I would eventually grow into it, she bought it. It hung in my closet until my senior year in high school, and I still wear it once in a while, although I don't button it anymore because it's little too tight for that. She was right, it was a fabulous bargain – too good to pass on. Got to snap them up whenever you can.

Chapter 16

I was rolling around and sweating profusely. Mutt and Jeff had caught me unawares and they both had guns and were shooting at me. I was hit and fell down, down, down, and then I woke up in one piece, thank God. I had set my alarm for eleven o'clock and was still in that fuzzy half-awake mode when it went off, and I realized the sheets were soaking wet with sweat. It was obvious the case was getting to me big time. Maybe taking this case was pushing it for me; and I was getting nervous that I was out of my league. Plus, the empathy I was developing for Margo raised the stakes even higher. It wasn't my style to give up or pull out. I was going to see this all the way to the end. I just hoped it wasn't my end. I needed to shower, then dressed in a black pullover, black slacks, black socks, and sneakers. I was the man in black, a reincarnation of Johnny Cash. I wasn't planning to sing "I Walk the Line." In fact, I was planning to walk a very careful line to avoid getting caught for breaking and entering.

I took a couple of cans of Campbell's clam chowder out of the cupboard and heated them up, crumbled several saltines into the bowl, and ate the mixture quickly. Then, I emptied the batteries from my flashlight and reloaded it with my new purchase. I tested my work and the results told me I was as ready as I was going to be.

I drove to the warehouse in South Philly and parked fairly closely to my spot earlier in the day. It was a little after midnight. I decided to walk around the block as I had done before. There was no one on the street. A black cat crossed my path; I hoped it wasn't a bad omen.

When I came around the block, I took note that the street lights did not reach to the side of the building where I had seen the window slightly ajar. I took a quick look over my shoulder and scanned both sides of the street in front of me. Not a soul to be seen. Like a jack rabbit, I hopped the fence and clung closely to the side of the building. I could feel the rough edges of the brick through my pullover. Slowly, I crept along the wall until I was below the window. After regaining my composure, I reached up and was able to leverage the window higher. With a bit more effort, it was wide enough for me to crawl through. I hoisted myself on the sill and allowed the upper half of my torso to slide through the opening with gravity taking over pulling me to the floor. I hunched into a crouch looking out the window to see if anyone had taken note of my entrance. Negative. I spun around on my hunkers and checked the interior, at least as far as I could see in the darkness. Nothing. I was very quiet and not moving for several minutes. Again, nothing.

Not a sound. So far, so good. I reached up behind me and pulled the window down to its approximate starting place. Pulling the flashlight from my back pocket, I turned it on with my hand over the face of the beam. At this point, I moved into the center of the room, which was piled high with numerous cardboard boxes. I couldn't tell what was in the boxes, but the ones I could readily see, were labeled "Dynamics Corporation." There was nothing else visible in the room, but there was a door at the end of a row of the boxes and I headed for it.

I carefully passed through the door into a very large room. At the far end of the room was the big door leading to the driveway outside, which would be the right side of the building. I took note of the front door, and to the right and left of it, a number of pallets filled with more boxes. Some of these boxes were labeled "Downtown McKay." I wanted to look inside, but as far as I could tell, they were all sealed.

I scanned the other side of the room and the light fell on some kind of workbench beside another door with a glass window to its left, made my way cautiously to that corner, and flashed my light around. Starting with the top of the table which had some clipboards holding what appeared to be invoices, I scanned slowly and thoroughly. There were several drawers underneath the top, but I tried each one, they all were locked. When I beamed back to the office door, there was a brief, but bright flash. My eye caught something shiny at the base of the bench partially hidden behind a stubby leg. I bent down to examine what it was. To my surprise, it was the end of a gold chain. I bent down and reached for it, grasping it and carefully sliding it towards the open floor. I was stunned. I was looking at a gold charm bracelet, which appeared as if it had been broken, and one of the charms was a gold locket. I opened it and there was a very clear colored picture of a younger Margo and a woman, I assumed was her mother. I scanned the area letting the light play along the base of the bench and up and down the legs. Something was on the back leg. It was some kind of stain. I reached down and found it wasn't tacky, but it looked to be dark, maybe blood. I lay on my stomach to get a closer view. It looked reddish in color, and my mind jumped to a splatter of blood. I took out my pocket knife and scraped some of it into an envelope I had in my pocket. I wondered aloud, "Was this Margo's murder location?" Someone had been in a hurry and had not checked everywhere carefully. I suppose when she had been stripped nude, the bracelet fell to its hiding place behind the stubby leg. I carefully placed my finds in the side pocket of my pullover and pulled up the zipper so I wouldn't lose these valuables.

At this point, I tried the door to the office. It was locked, but after studying the lock, I felt I could pick it, but I'd have to come back with the necessary tools to do so. I flashed my light through the window pane and saw a desk in the center with a bulletin board behind it, filled with papers and a few pictures of buildings. To the right was a row of five file cabinets, each with four drawers. I could only wonder what secrets they held. Obviously, I would have to come back again. I didn't want to overstay my welcome. Now, was not a good time to be caught. Not that there was a good time. I retreated to my window of access. I pushed it up far enough for me to get the upper half of my torso through and then let gravity do the rest. I came to rest on the ground and furtively scanned to my right and left. Nothing. I was relieved. I stood slowly and maneuvered the window into a position that was negligibly ajar. It was so slight, I would need something the next visit to act as a lever to pry it up. Probably a ruler would do the trick. With that, I could slip it up enough to afford my fingers room. The rest would be a piece of cake, just like tonight. I moved in a crouch back to the fence and after proper and thorough surveillance, taking note that no one was in the area. Then, I climbed over and was back on the street. I walked briskly to my car, unlocked it, got in and started the engine. I pulled out from my spot, drove a little way, and then turned on the headlights. A quick glance at

my watch told me it was almost two a.m. I drove back to my place. The adrenalin which was pumping throughout my break-in was expended. But it had made me exceedingly tired. I couldn't wait to get home and hit the sack.

When I entered my apartment, I hid my evidence under a loose tile under the sink in my bathroom. I didn't even stop for a quick Jameson. I undressed and slid under the sheets. They were cool and felt ever so good. That luxury was the last thing I remembered. Sleep came easy for me and lasted until the first light of the new day.

Chapter 17

Sunlight streaming through my window awoke me with a start. I glanced at the clock. It was eight o'clock. I had overslept. Time to get moving. Lots to do and so little time to do it.

I made a breakfast of scrambled eggs and buttered rye toast, and ate quickly, showered and dressed. Then, I retrieved the envelope with what I assumed to be Margo's blood and drove to Andrew's precinct. He was at his desk.

He greeted me, "Not you again?"

"I may have something that will help move this case along."

"Oh, and what might that be." "I

have a sample of what I'm pretty

confident is Margo's blood." I

handed to him.

"Where did you get this?"

"I'd rather not go into that until you verify, I'm right."

"Why all the mystery?"

"The manner in which I discovered and obtained it would be somewhat questionable."

"Here we go again. You were on the wrong side of legal, weren't you?"

"Let's not go there now."

I filled him in with what I had learned since the last time we met. He thanked me and told me to keep him informed and warned me against committing any further crimes.

As I left, he resumed his paperwork.

I drove into South Philly to building marked Santucci Enterprises. I wondered how many of them were illegal as I approached the door. I opened it and entered a reception area. A pretty blonde was seated a shiny metal desk with a computer and a phone. A ruby red mug held a passel of Ticonderoga pencils. In this modern age of technology, I thought I was the only one still relying on such an antique.

She looked up from her typing and inquired, "How can I help you?"

I flashed my ID, and replied, "I'd like to see Mr. Joey Santucci regarding the murder of Margo McKay, but I don't have an appointment."

"I'm sorry, but you can't just walk in here and expect to meet with him. You will need an appointment."

We dickered back and forth and finally arrived at an after-lunch time for the following day.

I got back in my car and pondered my next move. I still needed to check into John Baxter's activities and how they might tie in with Margo's murder, if in fact they did. I also needed a tête-á-tête with Tyler Quentin regarding the liaison he had with Margo on the couch in his office. I decided to pursue this avenue first.

I arrived at the firm's building after finding parking on the street around the corner, and took the elevator to the 38th floor, approached the receptionist and stated my need to see Mr. Quentin privately. She scanned an appointment book and found a time in late afternoon where he had a half an hour. I nodded my thanks and departed.

Next, I drove to Baxter's place of business, The Shelby Company. I was met by a tall, dark, and muscular secretary, named Rocco. He informed me that Mr. Baxter was in New York City on business and would not be back in the office for a few days. Again, I was forced to make an appointment for the morning he returned. I wasn't having much luck with the day's efforts so far.

On the drive back to my apartment, I picked up some Mu Shu Pork from the China Dragon. I decided to have a quiet lunch at home, watch the news, and maybe take a nap before my afternoon appointment with Quentin.

When I walked in the door, I knew right away something wasn't right. There were indentations where furniture had been but placed ever so slightly elsewhere now.

Without hesitation, I went right to my hiding place under the tile in the bathroom. The locket was still there. I now knew, I better carry it on my person. I returned to my living room and it was obvious someone had gone through the papers and files in my desk. I wondered if my office had been searched as well. After eating, I would ride into my building and check.

I drove to my office, parked, and rode the elevator up to my floor. I didn't know what I would find, but the office had been untouched. I unlocked my file cabinet and found everything as it should be.

I updated my files while I was there and checked my messages. A Mr. Robert Overmyer had called. He was positive his wife was cheating on him and wanted to hire me. I called him back and established a time for him to meet me at my office. In addition, I asked him to bring a recent photo of the little lady.

Then, I sat and thought about the break-in and search of my apartment. Were they looking for something specific or just letting me know they were still around and checking up on me?

After a brief nap on the couch and then set out for my meeting with Quentin.

The receptionist smiled at my punctual arrival or maybe she liked me and was angling for a date. I noticed there was no ring on her finger. She walked me back to Quentin's office and ushered me in to that great view.

Quentin was behind his desk but stood when I arrived. The red head was seated at her desk. I asked him if we could meet alone. He nodded and sent Red on an errand.

He was curious regarding my return visit, "Why did you want to meet with me alone?"

"I wanted to discuss some things I thought you might prefer stayed just between us."

"Okay, go ahead."

I hit him with a zinger right away, "Was Margo blackmailing you?"

"What in the world would ever give you that idea?"

"She was working late a couple of evenings on tax work for her boss. She thought she was alone, but you were there too. Then, you took her into your office, had a drink, or should I say a bottle of Scotch? The next night, you had another encounter after hours. This was of a more lurid nature – want a recap, because I could give you a really racy version of your close encounter?"

His facial expression collapsed, and he sat quietly examining his fingernail.

After deciding he didn't have a hangnail he replied with a question, "How do you know this?"

"It doesn't matter how, I do, and that's why you need to answer my question."

"No, she wasn't blackmailing me exactly."

"Meaning what?"

"She wanted to see me again. I wasn't sure I could handle it. I mean, I really enjoyed Margo, but I was terribly worried about my wife finding out. When I shared my reservations, she assured me we could be discreet."

"Then what?"

"I was afraid of being discovered in the office, so we went to a hotel. My wife and I were going through a rough patch and Margo empathized and seemed to anticipate my needs. She could be a really great listener."

Immediately my mind took a turn. Hell, you want someone to listen to you, pay a shrink or buy a dog. That made me pause and question which would be cheaper. You'd have to take into consideration all the vet bills, and expense of dog food.

"Did you end it or was it still rolling when Margo was killed?"

"You can't think I had anything to do with that."

"I'm not sure. I want you to convince me."

"We got together about once a week at first, but it became more difficult and my wife was getting suspicious. By the time she was murdered, we were seeing each other once every two or three weeks."

"I suppose you have an alibi for the night she was killed?"

"I went to bed early that evening."

"Can anyone verify that?"

"My wife was home, but we don't sleep in the same room. So, the answer to your question is no."

We chatted for a bit more, but I wasn't sure where to go with it. He seemed really desperate and part of me wanted to believe him. I shook my head ever so slightly as we shook hands. I felt sorry for Mr. Tyler Quentin.

As I departed, I couldn't help contemplating what really motivates behavior like his. His wife couldn't be that bad, shoot they had been together for more than twenty years, I would imagine. Wasn't the companionship, the friendship enough? Maybe his life was boring, too much routine. Everyone's life can get that way at times. Most guys with boring lives don't run around on their wife. They seek out new ways to spark the romance, the relationship. Oh well, human nature being what it is, I wasn't about to go down that rabbit hole. I had more pressing things to do.

Chapter 18

Mr. Robert Overmyer was a punctual man, and fastidious regarding his appearance, as his hair was perfectly coiffed. His suit was tailor-made with a chartreuse kerchief in his breast pocket, matching his tie. The shine on his shoes was so glossy, if I looked closely enough, I could probably see my reflection in them. Maybe, Mrs. Sandra Overmyer desired more impromptu behavior from hubby. He didn't strike me, just from a first impression mind you, of a romantic kind of guy who once in a while would surprise his wife with flowers, dinner at a cozy restaurant, or a weekend get-away.

We shook hands and completed all the formal salutations. After each of us took a seat, he flipped a photograph of his wife on my desk. Although middle aged, she was an attractive brunette with a wonderful smile.

"Bridge let's get right to the point dispensing with any bullshit. My wife is having sex with some guy, and I want to know all the particulars. I'm thinking of initiating a divorce and I'll need all the ammunition you can provide to my lawyer. Sandra's not going to take me for any ride, no way."

"What gives you the idea your wife's running around?"

"Once every two weeks, she's meeting with two lady friends. Sometimes it's dinner, other times a movie, occasionally a play, or they've even gone to wine tastings. Now, I got nothing against the little woman going out once in a while, but I play golf with Jerry, the husband of one of her friends, and when I mentioned the last activity they had planned and attended, a play, he was ignorant, didn't know a thing about it. That settled it for me."

"That's just one incident, and there might be a harmless explanation for it."

"Nope, a few weeks before that they'd gone to a movie. I happened to read a great review in the "Inquirer" critiquing a portion of the plot. When I asked Sandra some questions, her answers didn't jibe at all with the article. That's when I became really suspicious."

I laid out my fees and explained even if I got the goods in a day or two, he had to pay a minimum of one week, plus expenses. He never flinched, just nodded agreement or that he understood my conditions.

"I need the names and addresses of the two friends, and the husbands too."

He took a paper out of his inside jacket pocket and flipped it on my desk. He also took a checkbook from the same spot, and in short order wrote out a week's' worth of pay and ripped it from the book. That too he flipped on my desk.

I garnered his opinion of me wasn't too high, flipping his shit my way. I felt like flipping him the bird and telling him to take a hike, but jobs in my business come and go, and I couldn't afford not to take his business, flipping and all.

"I'll be in touch, give me a few days. You got a number where I can reach you?"

"Yeah, it's on the paper I gave you."

I thought, you bastard, you didn't hand me the paper nicely, you flipped it at me like I was some half-assed flunky. I was still pissed off. Thank God he got up and left, because I was on the verge of flipping, myself, flipping the fuck out on his sorry ass.

After he left, I read through the material. I decided the next morning I would tail Sandra Overmyer, if she left the house, and see where, or maybe to whom, she led me.

Lounging low in my Protégé wasn't easy. My back was getting stiff and the right leg was showing signs of an imminent charley horse. I couldn't completely extend it and was afraid I'd have to get out of the car.

That's when I noticed the garage door go up and a black Mercedes Benz back out. It definitely was Sandra driving. I couldn't help myself, jumping from the car and hopping on my good left leg striving to extend my right, kneading the kink, and wondering if I wasn't obvious to her as she drove off down the street. I could only hope she hadn't glanced in the rearview mirror and watched some lunatic doing the "Hully Gully" dance on the curb of her street.

Quickly as possible, I jumped in the car, started it, then drove the same route she had taken. Thank goodness the Mercedes was cruising just under the speed limit.

Following at a safe distance was a breeze. From time to time, it was possible to allow another car or two to drift in between us.

This trip was strictly shopping. She stopped at a dress store and a lingerie shop, and back home again. I sat on the house for a while, but no one came or went. I called the surveillance off for the day and decided to delve a bit more into the McKay case. I drove to the library. I was spending so much time there the attractive librarian had started calling me Jack, instead of Mr. Bridge. I hadn't noticed any ring on her left hand, maybe I could convince her to do a little research in the stacks. I'd look deeply into her beautiful eyes, as if I was staring at the microfiche, and she could read my lips with her glistening mouth. And maybe if that went well, we could do some more research after she got off work. That put a little giddy-up in my stride.

Chapter 19

My search revealed a picture of Mrs. Martin McKay, and sure enough it was the woman in the locket with Margo. I wondered if each daughter had a locket, or was Margo mom's favorite as it appeared M. J. was dad's favorite?

My research continued with a visit to Billy Coopersmith, an old friend who was a business whiz. He knew his way around a computer too. I wanted the dope on John Baxter, his company – The Shelby Company, and the company I found on the boxes in the warehouse, Dynamics Corporation. I also asked him to check if any of these names had any connection to Downtown McKay or Joey Santucci.

He informed me of his going rate and that this work would take several days. He had my number and said he'd call when finished.

I called M. J. to ask about Downtown McKay. She was obviously curious as to why I wanted to go down that road. I indicated it was to rule out any business association as a cause of Margo's murder. She gave me a name, a Sal Antiglioni, to see at the main office. Further, she'd give him a heads up to make time in the schedule for Mr. Bridge. I thanked her and headed to the main office.

After a brief repartee with the receptionist, I was escorted to Sal's office. He was a nattily dressed man in his fifties with hair on the sides and nothing on top. But it didn't detract from his imposing figure. He looked up as I entered.

"That didn't take you long. I only got a call from M. J. about ten, maybe fifteen minutes ago. Please, be seated. What can I do you for?"

What can I do you for? Humor, maybe, but bordering on the threat level. I know I wasn't amused. If I didn't keep my eyes on him, he just might do me. I didn't care for that thought. "Take me through the nature of the company's business dealings, if you would please."

"We buy some properties as a speculation. We feel a certain neighborhood will gain in value, we want in before it takes off. We buy old apartments, modernize them, and boost the clientele. We buy chunks of a neighborhood on the edge of gentrification and tear the old properties down and build moderate to expensive homes and townhouses. We're mostly in Center City, but we do have a few angles going in New Jersey."

"Do you have a construction staff to do the work, or is that work that's bid upon?"

"We have a few handy men, construction types, on staff, but most work is put out on bid."

"Can you think of anything with regards to the business that would be a motive or cause for Margo's murder?"

"Not really. She had little to do with us at Downtown McKay company. Plus, our business is pretty tame, not a lot of excitement in it, too gentile."

Gentile my ass. This guy was as slimy as the grease on his hair, but I didn't want to tip my hand, so I stopped while I was ahead.

"Thank you for your time Mr. Antiglioni. I trust, if it's necessary, I could stop by and see you again?"

"Sure thing, Bridge. You take care now, you hear?"

Yeah, I hear. I recognize a threat when one's sent my way. I left his office in not the best of moods.

Driving back to my office, I noticed a green pickup truck tailing me. I couldn't see, they were too far back, but I assumed Mutt and Jeff were back. They weren't particular about what wheels they stole. Of course, who am I to talk, Mr. Mazda Protégé himself. I needed to be on my toes, though. I'd been threatened by several people, my apartment had been searched, I'd been jumped twice, once with devastating results for me, and I was being tailed a lot. Who could be so interested in me? And why the circumspection, a word I just picked up doing the crossword puzzle in this morning's paper.

I spent an hour or so updating my files and trying to outline a strategy for the next day. I know I needed to return to the warehouse, but that was a night job. With all the tails by Mutt and Jeff, I had to be damned sure they weren't around when I burglarized Downtown McKay's building. If they caught me inside, I'd be a dead man for sure. They'd claim self-defense. Judge, he was trespassing, and he had a weapon (a gun they'd plant on my body). Case closed.

I drove back to my place and was exceedingly wary the whole way. I didn't take any chances until I was safely bolted into my apartment.

Some hamburger was thawing in the fridge from this morning. I took it out, added a few ingredients, and formed a meatloaf in a pan, placed some stripcut green peppers on its spine, and covered it all with a can of tomato soup. A baked potato served as my starch, and I ate a pretty hearty dinner.

I watched a little television, but nothing interested me. The case consumed my attention at the expense of everything else. I had a Jameson on ice and then, another one. I even considered having one more, but good judgment won out, and I went to bed. Yes, tomorrow was another day, thank you Charlotte, but unlike Rhett, I did give a damn.

Chapter 20

Seated at my desk playing with my pencil, my mind wandering, the phone rang. It was Overmyer relaying his wife's notification at breakfast of a girls' night out. They had planned dinner at Rose's house and afterwards, a gabfest. Further, it might be late, don't wait up.

I asked, "What time?

"She said she was leaving before I get home, which is usually about six-forty-five to seven."

I assured him I'd be all over it, as tight as a tick on a dog. And tight I was, only at the opposite end of the street when she backed out of the garage. I looked at my watch. It was six and still fairly light out. I hung back as far as I could without losing her. We weren't driving to Rose's unless she was killing time taking a roundabout route. We were driving into Jersey. We wound our way across the Walt Whitman and down 295. She finally exited at West Deptford, driving toward the river. We arrived at a place aptly named the Winds Restaurant on the Delaware, and I followed her in trying to blend into the crowd, which was easy as the place was packed. The bar itself was constructed in a huge kidney-kind of formation allowing plenty of seats to have a view of the river and the Philadelphia Airport with planes taking off and landing every thirty seconds, it seemed. She was seated at a table for two next to an expansive window on the other side of the bar. I moved to the end of the kidney where I could still see her, took a seat, and ordered a Cabernet. My wine was almost gone when he sat down across from her. He looked young enough to be her son. Not a stud, but easy on the eye, I suppose. This appeared to be heading for a long night which wouldn't mix with too many red wines, I switched to club soda.

I ordered a filet mignon medium with fries and asparagus. My dinner came with a house salad and ice cream for the amazingly low, low give away price of $19.95. The steak was cooked just right and deliciously juicy. I was surprisingly pleased, and full. I couldn't tell what they got. But after much hand holding and goo-goo eyeing of each other, they managed to finish their dinner, then left. I waited and then followed.

Sandra had gotten in his car and it didn't take long to arrive at a small rancher in a quiet nineteenfifties neighborhood. As I watched from a distance, he opened the door for her, a gentleman all the way, and arm-in-arm they strolled into the house. In short order, a light came on at the back. I took my camera and strolled around the block. The sun had set, and it was a moonless night. I dipped down and slunk along an unruly hedge separating his property from the neighbor and made it to the window. The blind was slightly ajar, and sufficiently so to take in all the action. Now I knew why she stopped at the lingerie shop. I had to admit, she was smoking hot for a woman of her age. You might say she was well maintained, but I guess a lot of money can buy that.

I watched and couldn't figure out why she wasted all that money to take off the pretties so quickly, discarding them to the floor like I would a pair of stinky socks. They had slipped into a demanding rhythm and I was impressed with both of them. She wasn't acting her age, and he was doing his best John Holmes impression. Oh, if I were only young again. Where oh where did my youth go?

I got all I needed photo wise and took note of the address upon returning to my car. In the morning I'd check out who he actually was so I could enter it in my report to Overmyer. I did feel sorry for Sandra though, she just wanted a little zip and zing in her bland life. Tonight, she looked happier than the other day. I guess you make your bed, and then you've got to lie in it. It would've been much better for them to have gone to a counselor, but not my problem.

The next morning after stopping at CVS to get same day pictures, I discovered the young man, Herb Winston, was the assistant golf pro at Mr. and Mrs. Obermeyer's country club. Surprise, surprise.

I called the stuffed shirt to tell him to pick up his "evidence" later that afternoon. I typed my report, and placed it, along with all the photos, in a large manila envelope. Then I sat around in a dismal funk until he arrived. I felt sorry for both of them, but I didn't think anything I could say would change his mind. I was bullheaded enough to go ahead and try anyway.

After he sat down, I launched into my sermon. "Marriage, particularly for as long as you two have been married, can get stale. You take each other for granted. I believe all Sandra wanted from you was a little romance and bit of mystery to rekindle the relationship. I'm not a marriage counselor…"

He interrupted, "No, you're not, and our relationship isn't any of your goddamn business."

I talked right over him, "…but you two should really try one before you give up and throw away all those years." I was really emphatic, but all for naught.

While I was pleading, he was writing a check, which, once again, he flipped on the desk. "Now hand over the envelope, and I'll be on my way."

What an irascible bastard. I could empathize with Sandra. Hell, if I was married to him, I'd probably be running around too. Well no, I wouldn't have married him in the first place. I finally did as he asked with great reluctance and felt like a real shit about it. Maybe scruples aren't a good thing to have in my line of work, kind of like a politician, at least the kind we generally have in Washington, D. C., who don't seem to have much of a moral compass to do what's right, avoiding the pitfalls of political expediency.

Chapter 21

It had only been a few days since the beatdown, but I was making a quick comeback. Not too shabby for a middle-aged guy like me. The pain was really just discomfort at this point and I could handle it. The Percocet wasn't necessary anymore. Good, I could drink Jameson again, oh yeah, that's right, I never really stopped. I have a pretty good tolerance to pain, just don't let me catch a cold. What a wimp.

After breakfast, waffles and sausage, I drove up Broad Street and found the building that housed the Office of Records for Philadelphia. I wanted to find out who owned some of the properties that Downtown McKay was developing or planning to develop. I stood in a short line and then was directed to the applicable ledgers. It was tedious, but necessary, research. After a couple of hours of work, I had a fairly extensive list of names. Now, all I had to do was locate these folks. Where did they go after they sold their property to M. J.'s company?

I rode to my office and spent the next couple of hours on the phone calling people whose names matched those on my list, and I thought the research at the Office of Records was tedious. I made successful contact with seven of the names on my list. Two weren't interested in speaking with me, two had died since the sale of their property, and the other three were willing to speak with me. I set up appointments and got directions to each new abode.

First stop, Mary McIver. She lived alone and was quite loquacious. I don't know if that was due to being by herself too much of the time, or whether I just had a way with people. Probably the first. She indicated to me that there had been a large number of muggings in her neighborhood and someone had left her threatening notes. She was particularly angry about the phone calls. They were terrifying, sometimes very heavy breathing, sometimes nothing at all, and occasionally the threat, "I'm going to get you, you bitch." After too much of this shit, she'd had enough. She sold to Downtown McKay and moved to an apartment in the Great Northeast.

I next visited with Dominick Del Rio and he sang the same song as Mary. The lyrics he sang were almost word for word what had been sung by Ms. McIver. It was a very sad song. But he was not only sorrowful, he was angry, too, for not getting anywhere near what he thought the property was worth, but he had enough and felt there was little choice for him but to sell and move on also.

On the way to the third person, actually persons, Mr. and Mrs. Dan Fitzpatrick, I stopped at a Burger King and picked up a Whopper and fries, which I ate in the car on the way. I arrived about fifteen minutes late for our agreed upon time. When they opened the door to their modest bungalow in Westville, New Jersey, after identifying myself, I apologized for my tardiness. They accepted and I was relieved, but I had been famished and really had to make the food stop.

We sat down in a small living room and I proceeded to ask why they sold their Philadelphia property.

Mrs. Fitzpatrick spoke right up, "Our neighborhood wasn't safe anymore, and Dan and I weren't safe either. I was knocked to the ground and my purse stolen just two blocks from home, and Dan was mugged right in front of our place. He had three broken ribs, a variety of lacerations, and a concussion. We couldn't take any more violence."

Her rendition of events was heart-wrenching. Anger and sorrow were overcoming my sensibilities. Who was behind this campaign to threaten and hurt, mostly senior citizens, until they gave up? Gave up on the neighborhood and gave up on the home that had been their refuge for so many years, selling out for less than the property's value. Someone with no scruples and no empathy had to be behind, what appeared to me, a consistent and coordinated undertaking to devalue real estate and then buy it up.

This didn't strike me as M. J.'s style, but I had no idea who was in bed with her. Was John Baxter somehow involved? What about Santucci, and son, Joey?

I departed the Fitzpatricks with a thank you and best wishes for a better, safer life in New Jersey.

Feeling tired and a bit sleepy, I headed back to my apartment. After a treacherous drive, I was surrounded by a very heavy fog that had dogged me all the way. I had to snap out of my stupor, knowing these would be ideal conditions to be jumped and put a hurting on my slowly recovering body. I parked and entered the building warily. The same could be said for the elevator, and my apartment. When satisfied I was safe, I locked up, kicked off my shoes, and fixed a drink. I watched the late news as I sipped my Jameson. It seems there rarely is any good news. Too many stories about shootings and murders, but they weren't my concern at the moment. I knew if I sat sipping much longer, I'd fall asleep in the chair again, so I went to bed. I hadn't even finished my drink. I left it on the kitchen counter for the next evening. It really went against my grain to pour Jameson down the drain, even watered-down Jameson. There's much wisdom in the trite old saw, "Waste not, want not."

Chapter 22

This morning, I thought to myself while eating a breakfast of Wheaties, hey, I am a champion too, Margo's champion. I received a call from Jeff Andrews asking me to stop at the precinct first thing. It sounded important, so I wolfed down my cereal and skipped another cup of coffee. I drove straight to the precinct and Jeff was at his desk. No cordial hello, just jumped right in.

"Bridge, I need to know what you know and what exactly you've been up to."

He wasn't going to be put off. I hadn't heard that much insistence in his tone since I screwed up a family insecurity case. I'd been peeping on the husband with his girlfriend. Later that evening, he went home and strangled his wife after beating her pretty thoroughly. It was ugly.

"I take it the sample I gave you was Margo's?"

"Yes, it was. Now talk."

I recounted what I'd been up to and some of my suspicions in relatively complete detail. I still didn't mention the diary, or the locket. Thought it best to hold on to them for now.

"I think Margo was killed in the Downtown McKay warehouse. I also believe the Santucci crime family may somehow be involved, and I suspect M. J.'s company may not be on the up and up. Possibly all of it ties together. Give me enough time and I'll present it to you all gift wrapped in a bow.

"I don't like it, Jack. Some of what you've done is highly illegal and could eventually jeopardize any case we can ultimately piece together. I can't have it. I won't be a party to it. It could cost me my career."

"Come on, Andrews. Just give me a few more days. I know I can pull it altogether. Give me a chance. I won't let you down and I won't put you in any jeopardy."

"You better mean it. Keep me posted every step of the way. I don't want any more surprises."

I escaped the precinct with a smile on my face and a song in my heart. But I knew, if I couldn't make some quick strides in this case, it would be out of my hands.

Billy Coopersmith left a message on my home phone which I had listened to before heading out to the precinct. He said that he had my requested research. I drove directly to his place and sure enough he had a thick file for me.

"Give me the gist, Billy."

"You were right. Dynamics Corporation is a dummy firm that was created in Delaware for one Joey Santucci. From what I could find, a lot of money is passing through this firm. You might have some money laundering going on there. As for John Baxter and the Shelby Company, they have a number of crossover connections and business dealings with the Santucci businesses. All this is further complicated by the many connections to the Downtown McKay company."

"Is there any direct evidence of say, fraud, or illegal activities?"

"The information I was able to glean from these companies is highly suspicious, but you'd probably need more paper and a forensic accountant to seal the deal." I paid Billy, thanked him, and suggested the possibility of more work.

It appeared time to revisit the warehouse. But first, I needed to make my appointment with Joey Santucci.

I drove to his South Philly office and was expediently escorted into a large room with a beautifully carved desk. He was not seated there, as I expected him to be. He was lounging on a sofa to the left side of the room. He waved me over and I took a seat at the other end.

"How can I be of help, Mr. Bridge?"

I shared that M. J. McKay had hired me to look into the death of her sister. I wasn't quite sure where to begin, "What can you tell me about the McKay sisters?"

"What makes you think I can shed any light on the family?"

"I know that you were friends with Lorenzo and at least, M. J. knew you."

"You do your homework. I like that in an employee."

I didn't quite know how to take that comment. Was it a compliment, or was he trying to establish some kind of pecking order with me?

"That really didn't answer my question."

"No, I guess it didn't." He looked at me over his glasses with a glare and I sensed he was not happy to have me interviewing him. "I knew the family. Once in a while, I did small favors for whoever might need one."

"Did that include Martin McKay?"

"Yes, it started with him."

"Do you have anything to do with Downtown McKay?"

"No, I'm afraid I have very little knowledge or experience with real estate."

He lied right to my face. I played dumb thinking it might be my healthiest approach to this confrontation.

"Do you have any ideas regarding Margo's murder?"

"And what do you mean by that?"

"Do you have any knowledge, if Margo had enemies, or are you aware of any reason why Margo would be murdered?"

"No on both counts. I'm afraid I can't really help you."

I pondered, can't help? or won't help? or don't want to incriminate yourself? He stood up, and I supposed this was my signal to leave.

I stood too and extended my hand which he gave a perfunctory shake. There was no reason to thank him, so I didn't.

I decided to sit in my car a block down the street from Santucci Enterprises. It wasn't long before he and one of his goons, built like Popeye the Sailor, came out and jumped in the truck. I followed at a safe distance and they stopped in front of the Downtown McKay warehouse. They hustled from the cab, unlocked the door, and in no time, the large scissor gate door on the side of the building rolled open and Popeye got back in the truck, and drove in. I waited for quite a while, but they didn't come out. I decided enough was enough and drove away.

Next, I stopped by the office and spent about an hour updating files and creating a list of things to do, and then I went home.

I read the paper while eating dinner. It was a Swanson frozen TV dinner. Turkey, mashed potatoes, and green beans. There was a muffin in the corner of the tray. I ate it, but it was nothing to write home about. I took a nap.

My alarm went off just as the eleven o'clock news was gearing up. I dressed as before, all in black. I retrieved the flashlight from my desk and a few tools to help me pick the lock on the office door. Arriving in South Philly just after midnight, I parked a few spaces past my previous spot. And again, I walked around the block as if I was out for the exercise. A jogger was running the street in front of the warehouse, so I went around the block a second time. The next time around there was no one. I jumped the fence, and having remembered to bring a wooden ruler, pried the window up enough for my fingers to gain a hold. I pushed it up enough for me to gain a purchase and pulled myself in letting gravity pull me to the floor. Quickly, I switched into a crouch and scanned the room. It was dark. I saw and heard nothing. I reached behind me and closed the window, then carefully moved across the room with the beam from my light. On the way, I stopped by one of the boxes marked, Dynamics. I peeled the seal and peeked into the box. It was filled with wooden blocks. The blocks, of varying sizes, seemed to be remnants from construction jobs, wood that normally would be discarded or trashed. I closed the box and attempted to reseal the tape, but it didn't look like it would hold.

At the office door, I took out my tools and in a view minutes it was swinging open. I moved to the desk and rifled through the drawers, but all I found were typical office supplies and a bunch of blank supply and shipping forms. There was nothing else of interest.

The file cabinets seemed the next logical choice to inspect. It took a minute or so pick the locks. The first two drawers contained information about potential properties and properties already owned by the firm. The third drawer contained reports about the maintenance of the properties. The bottom drawer had what I was looking for, bill of sales from Dynamic Corporation for all kinds of expensive equipment and supplies. Each form had a serial number that corresponded to a delivered package. I took three from the bottom hoping if someone checked, they wouldn't go that far back.

Back in the warehouse area, I found boxes marked Dynamics. Upon further inspection, I could see each box had a serial number, which I assumed corresponded to the bill of sales. It took another thirty minutes, but I found one of the boxes for the third bill of sale in my hand. I slit the tape and opened the box. The box was filled with varying blocks of wood. Probably scraps from a construction job. The bill of sale indicated machinery for the modification of certain construction materials at a cost of over $35,000. I was stunned. This couldn't be right. I searched again and in about ten minutes found a long rectangular box. It matched the serial numbers on one of the other bills of sale. It was supposed to contain some kind of girders, but when I opened the box it was filled with bricks. The cost of this package was over $15,000. I had uncovered two boxes, supposedly holding over $50,000 worth of materials and equipment, instead, all worthless shit. I decided it was time to giddy up. And giddy up I did. I went out the same way as before, after trying to make sure all looked the same prior to my arrival.

I escaped through the window and left it slightly askew. I jumped the fence, walked briskly to my car, and drove quickly back to my apartment.

I still had the forms and wondered what my next step should be. Maybe it was time to confront M. J.

On the other hand, maybe it was time to speak with Lenny again.

Chapter 23

I got up early and decided to call M. J. instead of my buddy, Lenny. My call woke her up. Tough shit. I wanted answers, and I wanted them right away. "We need to meet today," I demanded.

"My, aren't we in a testy mood this morning? Didn't you sleep well?"

"I slept just fine, but there have been some developments in the case, and I have questions that require answers. Plus, it's payday again."

"Oh, in that case let's do lunch at The Joys of Tel Aviv. I hear it's one of the best in the city."

We planned to meet at this very trendy Israeli restaurant at one o'clock.

I got there early and decided since she'd pick up the check to have a Red Breast on two cubes. She arrived and handed me an envelope as she sat down. We both looked over the menu and when the waiter returned, we both ordered the Tayim, which was a sample of various parts of the menu.

The hummus and laffa were really tasty. But it was time to get down to brass tacks.

"What connection does Downtown McKay have, or you, with the Santucci crime family?"

"That sure was blunt. I can't say you pull your punches. And the answer is none."

"We aren't going to get far; particularly, if you keep lying to me."

"I knew Joey through Lorenzo, that's it."

"He never did favors for you, or the business."

"Maybe on occasion I needed his help. Just small potatoes."

"Really? Did you ever stop to ask yourself, if he had anything at all to with the murder of your sister?"

"That can't be." Did I detect the flicker of a smile as she said it?

"Why not? How can you be so sure?"

"Joey really is a sweet guy. The things they say about him aren't true. He couldn't have had a hand in her murder."

Either she was putting on one hell-of-an act, or she was more naïve then I could ever imagine. I really didn't know how to proceed. Ward Bond like, I thought it might be best to circle my wagons. He always seemed to know when the natives would attack the pioneers.

I thanked her for lunch and my envelope and took my leave. I drove back to the office. I needed to review everything I had and plan another move. I needed something to shake things up, maybe loosen someone's resolve to whisper all the right words in my ear.

I got back to the office and unlocked the file cabinet. In the bottom drawer I had a safe. I spun the combination, opening the door to retrieve my Glock pistol and holster. I checked, and it had a full magazine with one in the chamber. The case had taken a nasty turn drawing grave concern from my inner voice. It was best to be armed, be prepared.

I listened to a few messages, but nothing pressing, at least no potential work for me.

I reviewed my files homing in on Anthony Santucci and Martin McKay. My extensive work in the library finally paid dividends. I remembered a fact from McKay's notes when scanning my research on Santucci. They both attended and graduated from St. Peter's Prep. Further, they had been in the same class. Questions, they had to know each other, the classes were too small not to, but had they been friends, and did that friendship carry over into adult life? Maybe Martin and Anthony planned Downtown McKay together.

Further study of my scribblings on Santucci revealed Sal Antiglioni had worked for him in the not-toodistant past. Coincidence? Bullshit, the Santucci mob was strategically placed throughout the McKay business. Obviously, Martin McKay was aware of the alliance and infiltration, but the imposing question was, did MJ know?

I sat, not stirring, for a long time, thinking it possible that dad, neither a psychic nor a fortune teller, had put the wheels in motion that would kill one daughter, and possibly put the other one in danger of a similar fate, when he lay down in bed with Santucci. I blanked everything out, but my brain kept repeating, "You lie with dogs, you get up with fleas."

I needed to update Lenny again, and I eventually needed to confront M. J. with all the connections I'd discovered between organized crime and her company. But I wasn't ready to make such a frontal assault, just yet. There were a few moves I needed to make first.

This was as good a time as ever to brainstorm steps I should be taking. I made a list:

- Set up a meeting with Jim Conover, Margo's boss regarding the tax case
- Find out more about John Baxter and the Shelby Company by an in-depth review of Billy Coopersmith's report

- Visit some of the properties owned/managed by the Shelby Company • Try to answer the question – What really was the role of Sal Antiglioni?
- Revisit the Downtown McKay warehouse at night
- Consider meeting with Anthony Santucci
- Check-in with Lenny Andrews at the precinct
- After completing all that, set up another meeting with M. J.
- And don't forget to read more of the diary

I called Margo's law firm and requested Jim Conover's secretary. She answered my call in what could only be described as a perky voice. She sounded small, but vibrant – probably a cheerleader in high school. We established a meeting for the following morning at ten. Next, while doing phone chores, I dialed the Shelby Company and spoke with a man, I assumed to be Rocco. Mr. Baxter would be in the office tomorrow. I asked for and got a time for my interview after lunch, one-thirty. I considered phoning for a meet with Anthony Santucci, but decided I wasn't ready for it.

My stomach began to rumble. It seemed a good idea to head up to the Tacony section of the city and pay a visit to the original Frankie's and Joe's for some mussels in red sauce and a few glasses of cheap red wine. I drove there with much anticipation but lost a bit of it looking for a spot in which to wedge my Mazda.

I found a really tight one that reminded me of a spot I got into when going to Victor's, the opera restaurant, in a couple of South Philly row homes on Dickinson.

The manager rings a bell and quiet descends upon the patrons, and then a waiter or waitress bursts into song, maybe an aria. I wouldn't know, but I love the energetic delivery and the haunting voices. The lyrics were a mystery to me, but I do know it brought tears to my eyes. I fondly remembered being there one time, sitting in the middle of the room, when this gal with rather large bulbous breasts began singing, and the next thing I knew she had draped a breast on each side of my head, which she rubbed enthusiastically. The other patrons loved the performance, but I know I had to have turned three shades of red. My embarrassment eliciting even greater laughter from the other patrons.

I again reminisced about my magnificent parallel park job that had about four or five inches to spare in the front and rear, and it was another masterpiece parking near the mussels joint. I strode into the bar proudly and got a small table on the second floor. A waiter arrived and took my order right away, no hemming-or- hawing for me. Like Frank Rizzo, former Philly Police Commissioner and Mayor, I was a man of decision. Although many of his decisions weren't too popular, now that I think about it. Maybe I should've thought, like George S. Patton, I was a man of decision. As I recall my U.S. II, he was one decisive son-of-a-bitch.

Three glasses and a bowl of maybe fifty or so mussels later, I was satisfied. I left a good tip with money for the bill under my plate and walked down the steps into the darkening evening.

Getting out of the spot was a bit more difficult than settling into it, and required much backing and wheel turning, then pulling forward ever so slightly, and repeating the whole process, again and again. I was out and on my way down Frankford, when out of nowhere a beat-up, old Charger pulled beside me, rode level for a block, and then swerved over to hit me. I saw it coming and reacted quickly but drove up on the sidewalk to avoid being hit. Thank God there were no pedestrians. The maroon Dodge continued on down the street. I didn't get a plate number, because it happened all too fast. I sat collecting myself, not moving, but aware of their possible return, I finally began to function again.

Exceedingly careful were the watch words for the remainder of the trip to my apartment. I arrived without further incident, made my way into the building, while carefully scanning my surroundings. Once in the locked apartment, relaxation was possible and directed me to pour a Jameson on two cubes. I sipped and thought. Thought and sipped. I must be getting close to something or someone that's a no, no. I assumed Mutt and Jeff had been in that Charger. I wondered whether it was Mutt or Jeff driving and thought Frankford Avenue was a good place to hold a Demolition Derby. How wrong was that, it wasn't the Schuylkill Expressway. I knew I'd best let Lenny know what happened over the phone. I wasn't planning for a face to face just yet. I wasn't ready. I still had some loose ends I wanted to tie together. I made the call and he wasn't very happy. He lectured me for a few minutes but agreed I must be getting close to something or someone.

Chapter 24

After a couple of blueberry muffins and black coffee at Dunkin Donuts, I arrived for my appointment with Conover fortified and inquisitive. I didn't wait long until I was ushered into his office. He stood as I entered rising to a height, I would guess, of six-six or thereabouts. We shook hands and his was a firm grip with his big meaty hands enveloping mine. Conover was in his early thirties. A dark mustache dominated his face. He asked, "How can I help, Mr. Bridge, with your investigation of Margo's murder?"

"I wondered if you aware of any activities either here in the office or outside work that could have led to her being shot in the back of the head?"

"What we do here is pretty tame stuff. I'm not aware of anything at all which might be motive to kill her."

I fudged facts a little bit, when I put forth, "She was helping you with tax forms, paperwork, for one of your clients, John Baxter. It was a delayed filing and I gather had some irregularities."

"You know I can't discuss a client's business with you. Attorney-client privilege is sacrosanct."

"I realize that. I was just curious why a relatively young member of the staff was involved with such a high priority client?"

"Well, to be honest with you, Margo had an extensive background in tax law in her undergrad course work. She was skilled in organizing and prioritizing, separating the chaff from the wheat, so to speak. Besides, he asked for her, and the client always get what they want."

I'm glad he told me what he was about to say was the truth, the whole truth, and nothing but the truth, but I was shocked. I tried valiantly to keep a poker face as I thanked him for his help. I think I did a pretty good job, but to make sure, I spun on my heel and strode across the room then out the door as fast as possible.

Once outside, I stood blocking the sidewalk, contemplating the bombshell, Baxter asked for her. One had to contemplate, why would a big-time business man ask for a newbie to work on such vital documents? The leads being developed by my investigation were "Twilight Zone" strange. I had to be Rod Serling and pursue them, even to the "Outer Limits." I chuckled at my own joke.

It was time for lunch and even though it was out of my way, I had a hankering for a slice or three of Bilenza's New York style pizza. It was sacrilege to support anything New York due to the rivalries with the Giants, the Mets, the Nets, etc. But I couldn't help it, Bilenza's was great pizza. Hell, maybe hatred of the Big Apple didn't apply to food. I could hope that was the case.

Three slices and a Pepsi later I was feeling pretty pleased with myself, and also a bit drowsy. I had to snap to, I'd need my wits for the next interview. I drove to the Shelby Company building and slid into a spot in the parking lot which had a white sign, boldly printed in red, Visitor.

Mr. Baxter didn't make me wait until my appointed time. He came out to the reception area, glad handed me like we were old college chums and led me into his office where we sat in a couple of plush chairs facing each other.

He began, "And you're here to see me, why?"

I explained how M. J. McKay had hired me to look into her sister's murder.

"How can I help? I knew M. J., but never met Margo. I wouldn't know her if she walked in here now."

That stopped me from nodding. It was like a splash of cold water right in the old keister. If he didn't know her and never met her, why was he requesting she work on his company's taxes?

I took a different approach, "How does your company fit in with McKay Downtown?"

"We're a subsidiary, that's it. We really don't have much to do with the company and developing properties."

I nodded like it made sense to me, then played dumb, "What does your company do?"

"We buy, renovate, and manage apartments. It's pretty standard stuff."

I asked for examples and he took the time to lay out the particulars of where, how many, how profitable, for a few of the complexes.

"I guess you can't really be of any help to my investigation but let me give you my card. If I have any further questions, I trust I can set up another appointment?"

"Most definitely."

We had kind of a touch shake which he initiated, and it made me feel like I was in some kind of secret club. Declining membership in his secret society, I left.

I drove back to my office and proceeded to update my files from all the notes I'd taken and then, considered further actions. Maybe it would behoove me to visit some of the properties he laid out for me. That would be a good project for the morning. I left for home and was exceedingly circumspect, until safely ensconced in my recliner with a Jameson on two cubes.

On the way home, I stopped at a little Mexican restaurant for take-out, a little place called Juanita's. I ordered, didn't wait too long, got the food, paid for it, and drove home. At home, I bolted the door behind me, and ate while watching the news. I read a little bit and watched a cop show on TV but sleep rapidly overtook me. I went off to bed.

In the morning after a little fruit salad, I headed to the first apartment property he had given me. It was a series of four brick buildings five stories high. From the size, I guessed each housed maybe fifty apartments. I tried building A, which was locked, and buzzed six apartments before someone responded. She sounded elderly and when I explained who I was and that I was gathering some background information to assist my investigation, she told me in no uncertain terms to go to hell. So much for building A. I tried B next. After buzzing five apartments with no responses, I moved to C. My mother didn't raise a fool. If at first you don't succeed, don't try again, try something different. At C, someone was entering as I arrived, and I followed them. I rode the elevator to the second floor to avoid any consideration from the gentleman I followed so closely. I looked like I belonged there. On the second floor, I knocked on a door marked 203. An elderly gentleman, way above eighty, answered, "Can I help you?"

I showed him my P.I. license and he invited me into a very warm combination living/dining room. We sat on a couch together. He leaned in when I spoke. I assumed he was hard of hearing but saw no aid.

"I'm doing a little background research on a case I'm working, how are things here at your building?"

I don't know what I was expecting, more fishing than anything.

"Apartment 205 has many men coming and going at all hours, but mostly at night, after dinner. I think they're paying for sex. 205 is a two-bedroom apartment and two young women live there. They are pretty. I've seen them, but only in the afternoon. Believe me, after dinner you can't go to the laundry down the hall or the snack room just past that, which has all the vending machines, without running into these guys. I called the police and complained. They came and spoke to me, claimed they'd look into it, but nothing really happened."

"Were they detectives or patrol officers?"

"They were in blue uniforms, I guess that means they were patrol."

"I know this would be a huge imposition, but could I come back this evening and see what's going on for myself, Mr., sorry, I don't know your name?"

"My name is George Wentworth, and I don't know about coming back."

I tried to sell it. "Maybe I can do something about your problem, put an end to it."

He thought about it and surprised me, "That'd be swell. You know you ought to talk to Ms. Zeller over in building D. She's in 306, I know because we play Bingo together at the Clubhouse in the rec room on Thursday mornings. Kate will tell you the same thing I'm telling you. She has the same problem."

We made arrangements for my return after dinner. I drove to the other two properties Mr. Baxter had described. After a few hours of similar spying done at the first complex, I discovered a couple of other dwellers who were noticing the same problems with many men coming and going at all hours at their complex. They had called the police too. Coincidently, all were in the same precinct and the descriptions of the patrol officers sounded eerily similar. I wondered if any reports were even filed on these police visits, or if a few bad pennies were on the take from a prostitution ring.

I drove home and fixed an easy dinner. I took leftover chili out of the freezer and heated it up. It was filling and would have to do.

Following dinner, I was back at Mr. Wentworth's, parked, and rang his buzzer. After identifying myself he zapped the door. I rode the elevator to his floor and when it stopped and the doors opened, a man in a hurry almost knocked me down as I tried to step out. He was disheveled; his shirt wasn't tucked in and his tie had a slipshod knot. He said nothing to me, not even, "Excuse me." I assumed he was a john as I watched him scurry away like a rat fleeing an alley cat. If he only knew.

I rang the bell and George opened his door and let me in. We sat and talked for a while. He suggested that I mosey on down to the snack room. Before I left, I swallowed an airplane bottle of Johnny Walker Red (the liquor shop had no Jameson – darn it, just my luck). If I encountered anybody, I wanted them to smell my breath. Down the hall I went. It was a little after half past nine.

I cruised the hall and the snack room for the better part of an hour when I bumped into a fella leaving 205 and headed for the elevators. I deliberately bumped into him and gasped right in his face as if he knocked the wind out of me. Actually, I wanted him to smell my breath.

"Shay boddy," I slurred, "swhere's a guy go to get laid in dis joint?"

He looked at me, laughed, and hooted, "205 buddy, if you aren't too drunk to get it up."

He moved down the hall, and I called after, "Shanks pal."

George was waiting for me when I returned. I recounted the events of the hallway. I assured him this would get my full attention, but I'd have to come back another evening. I needed Billy Coopersmith to help me with some high-tech gizmos and photo equipment.

I drove home and without incident hit the sack, but before doing that, I called Billy and we made plans for the following evening.

The next afternoon, we reconnoitered at his place, loaded all the equipment in his van, and drove to Wentworth's place. We stopped on the way at a pizzeria called Luigi's and I bought a large pepperoni pizza for the three of us. Arriving at the apartment complex just before dinner, it was pretty quiet, not a lot of activity. We carried everything in and made two trips to do it.

Once inside, I let Billy do his thing. He went down to the snack room which was across the hall from 205 and set up his miniature cameras with a relay to George's apartment. He would be able to record all comings and goings with sound. The camera had a very sensitive mike. It just amazed the two of us, George and me, how small it all was.

When Billy was satisfied and returned to the apartment, he wired me. After testing everything to make sure all was working well, we dove into the slices. It was pretty good pizza, but not up to snuff with a Luciano pie.

All the time we ate, we watched the monitor to see what action might be occurring down the hall. There was little activity. I pulled out another airplane bottle of Jameson and drank it down and then stumbled down the hall to the prostitutes' place.

I boldly knocked on the door, which was opened by a stunning blond with large, in-your-face, breasts. She also had on way too much makeup for my taste.

I slurred, "Shello dare, baby. Hows bout inviting sme in?"

"Well hello there, big boy. Are you sure you can handle me in your condition?"

"Sures enuffs. I wanna have aah good time. Was'it cost?"

'It's five-hundred bucks for around the world, and two-thousand for all night."

I pulled out my wallet and fanned it open so she could see as I counted two one hundred-dollar bills.

"Sorry buddy, but you'd do better on the Admiral Wilson boulevard in Camden with that chump change."

"Oh, I'll be huh back ah tomorrow night wit more money," I stammered.

She closed the door on me, and I staggered down the hall to George's.

"Did you get it all, Billy?"

"Indeed, I did."

We watched and recorded for about three more hours, and then we got lucky. Pay dirt. Sal Antiglioni showed up with Rocco as a companion and used a key to enter apartment 205. Not ten minutes later, two patrol officers arrived on the scene, knocked on the door, which opened just enough for us to tape Sal handing an envelope to each of them. The door closed and the one cop was stupid enough to open his envelope and count the money, which we filmed as well.

We certainly had enough evidence to tie Sal, Rocco, and possibly the Shelby Company and Downtown McKay to a prostitution ring in at least one of their complexes. My bet it was more widespread than that.

It seemed obvious to me, a lot of illicit money was flowing through what appeared to be a legitimate real estate enterprise. I wondered what other illegal activities flowed through M. J.'s company? I hoped I could find out.

We packed up, thanked Mr. Wentworth for his cooperation and urged him to be patient. I explained it might take some time until I could make the D. A.'s office and the police aware of what was going on. But I assured him, eventually it would be closed down.

After we got back to Billy's, I helped unload all the equipment, paid him, and drove straight to my office with the evidence. I stashed it in the safe at the bottom of my file cabinet locking both the safe and the cabinet, locked my office door, and went right home.

The day's events, hell the evening's events, required careful consideration and reflection. That meant it was time for a Jameson. Sometimes it helps lubricate my thought processes. Most of the time, it just helps. Running things around in my head, so many ideas over and over, was too much. I undressed and crawled under cool sheets and into a comfort zone that cast its spell, making me sleep hard until the dreams pushed out the REM sleep with terrifying scenes and images. I couldn't shake the night fears and stirred about three-thirty. A pee would be good, I thought, and made my way to the bathroom. Relieving myself felt good, and once in bed again, warm fuzzy thoughts and feelings helped me slide into a more relaxed snooze. Maybe all the progress I was making on the case, was helping me to sleep through the night. I wasn't sure, but I was sure I wanted the good night's sleeps to continue.

Chapter 25

In the office early the next morning, I reviewed everything I had garnered from my investigation to date and tried to put it into an organized and chronological order. Not the best of typists, it took a while, but I finally finished everything up, printed out two copies and locked one in my file cabinet safe along with all the evidence I'd collected. I wasn't quite ready to take everything to Lenny Andrews. I was contemplating one more visit to the McKay warehouse. A strong gut feeling was telling me I missed something important, something that might help me put a cap on the case.

M. J. called and informed me she would pick me up at my office around eleven the next morning. She refused to answer any questions. The only thing she would reveal about our meeting was that we were taking a road trip and I would be pleasantly surprised. I had much to do the rest of the afternoon and evening.

I drove to a number of the other properties managed by the Shelby company. At each one, I got pretty much the same story from people who were home and would speak with me. Lots of men coming and going at all hours, but mostly evening, and no help from the police. I estimated about a dozen brothels were part of Baxter's operation. They had to be generating thousands of dollars every week from their illegal enterprise. Somehow, they were laundering this illicit money through Downtown McKay.

I got back to my place about dinner time. I took a couple of chicken thighs out of the fridge and placed them in a Pyrex dish, combined a package of dry onion soup into a bottle of red Russian salad dressing I had emptied into a mixing bowl and then poured it over the chicken. I put the dish in the oven at 325 degrees for a half an hour and then dumped it all on a plate of crispy Chinese noodles. It was delicious and tasted authentically Asian.

After eating, I dressed in my Johnny Cash outfit, although I prayed, I wouldn't be singing "I Walk the Line" later. I hoped my luck would hold out and I'd be alone, again, in the warehouse.

I sat in my recliner and dozed, catching a needed forty winks. At about eleven I got up and gathered my tools, a ruler, and my flashlight. Then, I drove to my preferred spot past the warehouse and followed my routine from the two previous visits.

All went smoothly, and twenty minutes later I was inside. I moved stealthily to the workbench outside the office. Lying prone on the floor at the far end of the bench away from the office door, I was able to play the light into the recesses of darkness at the back. Sure enough, I had missed a piece of evidence. It was almost impossible to see lodged against the back-corner leg. It had nestled up against the leg, and because it was dark, looked to be a part of the leg. I used tweezers to extract it. Thank God my arms are long, a thirty-six-inch sleeve. When I examined my trophy, it was as plain as the Mennonites I grew up with. It was a chunk of fingernail painted a navy blue with a few sparkles dotting the end. Actually, it was those sparkles that revealed its hiding place. I turned it over carefully and noticed what appeared to be a tiny bit of skin with maybe a dab of blood smear at the center. I slid it in the envelope I took out of my jacket pocket.

Once again, I picked the lock to the office door and roamed through the files as quickly as I could. Most seemed to be stuffed with requisition forms and bill of sales, but one file in the last drawer I opened held correspondence between the Shelby Company's John Baxter and Sal Antiglioni of Downtown McKay. It was some kind of code and I knew I didn't have time to decipher it. I took the last letter in the file and stuffed it in my pocket with the envelope safeguarding the fingernail and zipped the pocket to make sure I didn't inadvertently lose anything.

On the way out, I retraced my steps and left the same way as I had on the two other visits, but this time Mutt and Jeff caught up to me. As I reached my car, I heard the shot, dove in and started it up. Thank heavens no one parked in front of me and I drove with my head as low as possible, but not so low I couldn't see my passenger side mirror. It was clear, and I peeled out as fast as my Protégé would go. Recklessly barreling down the street I glanced in my rearview and saw they were about ten car lengths behind but gaining fast. I made a quick right and took a hair-raising two-wheel left. The car straightened out and I made it to the next block with no car visible in the rearview mirror. I sped up and took another right and raced through an alley at high speed, then took a left at the end and killed the lights, parking between two large trucks. I ducked down, pulled my gun and waited. I sat still looking for lights. Nothing. I sat there for another ten minutes. Still nothing. I was sure they were cruising around looking for me. I had to hope they thought I kept going and got away, and then gave up their stalking and expected kill leaving the area to depart for my apartment or office.

Another ten minutes passed, I put the car in drive and edged out of my spot. Driving back streets and side streets, I made it to civilization where there were lots of lights and other cars. Watchful and exceedingly careful, I made it to my office. I parked and entered the lobby. There was no one there and the elevator was open and clearly empty. I guessed they thought I would head to my apartment. I unlocked the office and went right to my safe in the file cabinet. Without hesitation, I emptied the contents of my zipped pocket into the safe and spun the dial several times to reset it. I locked the door and took the stairs two at a time, almost stumbling in my haste to exit the building, the handrail my savior.

I must have been living right because there was no one there. I made it to my car and drove to a motel across the river. It was a Deep Sleep Motel in Oaklyn. Once in my room, I relaxed and fell on the bed. I was shivering, but it wasn't because of the air-conditioning as there wasn't any. What could I expect from such a cheap dive? I hoped the sheets were clean. I also hoped the name of the motel wasn't an omen. If Mutt and Jeff had their way, I'd be sleeping the deep sleep. I couldn't help but think, I'm getting too old for this dangerous shit. I was drained from all the excitement, but the adrenaline was still pumping, so sleep took a while, a long while, and when it did come, it was fitful, to say the least.

Chapter 26

I woke the next morning in a sweat. The room was hot and stuffy, and felt confining. Since I paid cash when checking in, I just left after leaving a Lincoln for the cleaning lady. She wouldn't have much work to do, just change the bed, if that was ever done in this dump. Hell, I hadn't even used a towel.

I drove back to my apartment, circling several times on the lookout for Mutt and Jeff. They were nowhere to be seen. I parked and entered the building safely, navigating all the way to my apartment untouched and unhurt.

A quick shower and a change of clothing made me feel like a new man, not a superhero – I'd need a suit of Kevlar for that feeling. I took the stairs down to the ground floor and exited the back. The sun was beginning to peak at me over the horizon. Maybe this was a good sign.

I slid into my car and drove to the office. Circling the block several times, I saw no sign of Mutt and Jeff, but I did notice Rocco sitting in a green Plymouth van south of the entrance to my building. It was evident they had pulled out all stops and were tag-teaming me. Not to be out-done, I parked a block behind my office and walked in through the back. Again, I took the stairs and was out of breath before I made my floor. I stopped, leaned against the wall, shook my head and said out loud to no one in particular, "Damn, I really am too old for this shit!"

I laid low in my office and ate a breakfast bar, hoping I'd be safe there until more people would be out and about and M. J. would pick me up. I pondered the mysterious way she had presented the day to me. A road trip, but to where and why?

Eleven o'clock couldn't come fast enough. It was like watching the grass grow during a soccer match. I kept looking out the window and finally noticed Rocco was gone.

M. J. strode into my office and forcefully stated, "You'd better be ready to go!"

"I am, but where to?"

"Ask me no questions, I'll tell you no lies," she chortled. I guess she thought she was being funny and still mysterious, but I couldn't help but wonder how many lies she had already told me.

We got into her Corvette, well, she slipped in gracefully, but I had a tough time manipulating my body into such a low and tight space. The engine roared to life and away we went.

She drove like a bat out of hell to 95 and headed south. We drove for quite a way without conversation. She had the radio on and was singing with each tune. Her voice was melodic, and I almost fell asleep, but her driving kept me awake.

We crossed into Delaware and passed Wilmington doing seventy-five. Her driving was erratic, with tailgating a specialty. I was afraid for my life, again. After turning off the radio, she opened up.

"You could never guess where we're going."

"No, I'm sure of that."

"This is going to be a fun day. I love where I'm taking you. I have so many fond memories of spending time there with my father." "That's not much of a clue," I offered.

Coolly, she responded, "It wasn't supposed to be. I like to keep you in the dark." I could only imagine what that meant.

We crossed into Maryland still doing seventy-five. She zig-zagged in and out of lanes like she was Mario Andretti, almost sideswiping a Honda Accord, and then almost rear-ending a Cadillac. If we got to wherever we were going in one piece, I'd fall out of the car, because I probably wouldn't be able to get out any other way and kiss the ground and thank the Lord.

In a little while we approached Fairhill. I knew a little history, and I knew that this was the former estate of William duPont Jr. It was a large and beautiful tract of land, 5600 acres, if I recall correctly. Now, it was home to the Fairhill Racecourse, home to cross-country steeplechase racing. This concept of racing had begun in the United Kingdom whereby jockeys and horses would race cross country from church steeple to church steeple.

I must say, it was a lovely day for such an affair.

We pulled into a parking lot and, I managed to scrape myself from the seat and fall out into a crouching position. Maybe I should've leaned down and kissed the ground. Instead, I just said a silent prayer of thanks to God, and asked him to keep watching over me, please.

We approached a large crowd of people gathering for the races. I was reminded of Saratoga and Churchill Downs on Derby day. There were brims and feathers everywhere. The colors were a kaleidoscope of hues most bright, pinks, violets, yellows, oranges, and greens. The dresses women were wearing were expensive looking and seemed to be better suited for a formal dinner dance. She led me to a tent where champagne was being quaffed at a copious rate. We joined in and then she led me outside where we could see the racing.

I had noticed the leather bag over her shoulder, but

I thought it was a pocketbook. She retrieved a pair of binoculars from it and handed them to me. I held them to my eyes, adjusted the focus, and could see many mounts in a paddock area, and jockeys in scintillating uniforms of many hues. Sharp.

She gave me a program. "Do you want to place a bet? We'll find a tout over there where that boisterous crowd is circled and purchase a ticket at that stand.

"Sure, why not?"

Although I didn't know a thing about horses, other than they eat hay, I placed a bet on a horse called Rose of Shannon.

In a few minutes the jockeys were mounted, given a leg up by the trainers, and trotting to the starting line. I thought it was about to begin; however, they rode out and back several times. I guess like all athletes; they too needed to loosen up.

They finally were arranged in the semblance of a line, followed by a second and third group, and then the flag went down and off they went. They sped over the grass kicking up sod in huge clods, and their hoofbeats sounded like drumming. Over the course they flew and into the first jump over a row of bushes. Rose of Shannon was fifth over the jump but landed quite well and was gaining on the leaders as they rounded a bend. I watched with the binoculars M. J. had so thoughtfully provided for me.

The second jump was a fence and one of the lead horses clipped it and fell and two more horses behind it stumbled over the fallen horse and went down too. Rose of Sharon had been on the other side of the jump and avoided this catastrophe pulling into second place. After running another furlong or two, there was a jump with a pond on the other side. Graceful beauty, these fine animals made it look easy. By this time, the crowd was frantic, and the screaming and shouts directed at horses and jockeys urging them on was comical to me, as if they could be heard that far away, and would it matter even if they were heard?

After two miles of running and jumping, the horde came around the final turn. Rose of Shannon was neck and neck with another called The Dean of Dublin. I found myself shouting and urging her on. Thirty yards from the line, they were still deadlocked with each jockey whipping flanks and pushing heads as if their lives depended on it. Neck and neck, they flew to the line. It was so close, I couldn't tell who crossed first. Whoever won, won by a snot.

M. J. leaned into my ear and shouted, "You won!"

It was such a close finish, I couldn't imagine how could she tell?

"Are you sure?" I think I screamed it at her, I was so excited, and the adrenaline was flowing as fast as the champagne in the Phillies locker room following a clinching victory in the World Series. "Definitely, her nose was down at the wire."

M. J. was right. After a few minutes, the judges posted Rose of Shannon the winner and I went and collected twenty-five dollars. I was ecstatic having won my first ever bet on a race. Winning sure beat tearing up the ticket, which is what my companion had to do.

We stayed for the remainder of the card and then drove to a place called the Country House Restaurant. It was nestled into a grove of trees in a farm-like setting.

We ordered drinks. I asked for a Jameson on two cubes as per-usual, and M. J. a Bloody Mary. The drinks arrived and I noticed her Bloody Mary had a toothpick floating on top spearing several plump olives. I wondered if my racing luck would hold and I could win one or two of those tasty balls from my hostess. That's when she interrupted my reverie and went right away to pumping me for information on the case. I was very careful how I responded and thought about each fact I related to her. I wasn't prepared to give too much, yet.

Both of us ordered the crab cakes and I can say without a doubt, they were the best I ever tasted, and all jumbo lump crab meat and little, if any, filler.

Over dinner, I steered the conversation to the day we had.

"That was a nice surprise," I said. "And I ended up winning eighty dollars. What a great day."

She laughed. "Yes, it was fun, and reminded me of the good times I had here with my daddy."

After dinner, we drove back to Philadelphia pretty much the same hair-raising way we drove to Fairhill. I was frightened and held the seat with a grip of steel all sixty-five miles. But she did deposit me safely in front of my office building. I thanked her profusely for such a wonderful time and she looked at me and leaned slightly toward me as I was offering my thank you. Maybe she was offering her lips to be kissed, but I didn't take her up on the offer. I needed to keep my wits about me and like George Washington, I had to beware of foreign entanglements. I opened the door and she said in a voice that sounded disappointed, "Don't forget this."

She handed me my envelope and bowing slightly to thank her again, I closed the door and she drove off.

I went up to the office and sat at my desk for a few minutes thinking maybe I had misjudged her.

Chapter 27

It was time, well past time, to delve into Margo's diary. I had been remiss in continuing to examine all the ruminations her writing revealed. But that would have to wait just a bit longer. I had to respond to a message I'd received as it probably meant another job.

When I got to the office this morning, there was a message for me from Fran Diffenderfer of the William Penn Insurance Company. I returned her call and she asked me to stop by to see her about an insurance fraud job she had open. With nothing else on my plate for the moment, I swung over to Market Street, parked in a way too expensive garage, and rode the elevator in her building up to the 17th floor. Her office was just down the hall and I only had to wait to see her for about five minutes. She came out to the reception area, gave me a hug, and walked me back to a beautifully decorated, but functional, office.

She handed me a folder, then replied, "Mr. Duffy Coughlin-Murphy had an accident on the job at

Liberty Lumber Company and claimed disability. Our company covers Liberty and our doctor, after examining Murphy, truly believed he was a slacker and trying to defraud the company. He, on the other hand, has a medical report countering our doctor's findings. We need you to get evidence, preferably photographic, that Murphy is committing fraud."

"I see. Are you okay with my standard rate and expenses for this job?"

"Sure thing. In fact, if you can wrap this up quickly and save us court time and legal fees, there'll be a nifty bonus in it for you."

"That sounds great. I'll get on this today. But just so you know, I won't be able to devote a whole day every day to this case as I've got another big one on my plate. I assure you I'll do my best like Larry, The Cable Guy, to "Get her done!""

She thanked me as we shook hands, and I left her with a promise to get back to her by Thursday.

I rode back to the office, reviewed the file, and took out my camera with a telephoto lens, then drove to Murphy's neighborhood. I drove around the block once and parked at the end of the street with a view of the side of his house and the front yard, which had a tremendous slope, possibly a six-foot drop, to the sidewalk. I held up the camera and zoomed in with the lens. It was pretty sharp, and I realized the side window had no shades, blinds, or curtains and I could view his living room.

I sat stoically in my car for over an hour. The neighborhood was dead. No one was out and about. I guessed this was a working-class neighborhood, ergo, people were working and not at home eating bon-bons.

Everyone except Murphy who had just come into view of my lens. He was carrying what appeared to be a very full laundry basket down the stairs on the far side of the room. It was an impressive feat of strength for someone dealing with a severely damaged back. I know backs can be tricky. Hell, I pulled something in mine a few weeks back just lifting my golf bag into the trunk of my car. But I didn't claim disability or miss any work. In fact, I was up and at 'em the next day. Jameson has tremendous healing power, well, maybe just plain power.

I snapped a series of photos coming down the stairs and passing through the living room. I imagine he was headed to the basement where he might keep a washer and dryer.

I hung around for another hour but didn't see him again. It started to rain, and I drove back to the office in a downpour. On the way home, I dropped the disc from my camera at a CVS and filled out the form for next day service.

The next day, I returned to working Margo's case.

On Wednesday, I borrowed Billy Coopersmith's van and drove to parking location at the opposite end of Murphy's street. I had a partial view of the backyard and an unobstructed view, other than a very low hedge separating yards, of the front. I moved to the back of the van and through a side portal-type window I watched. Late morning there was activity. I saw his head briefly moving farther into the backyard. Then nothing. Maybe five minutes passed when I heard the roar of the engine. In short order, Murphy came around to the front pushing a lawn mower. He proceeded to work that Toro up and down the slope, as if it were child's play. Needless to say, I was snapping away, and I had my phone out taking video as this grasscutting scene played out. Mr. Lying Faking Coughlin-Murphy had a starring role in a Bridge production that would save William Penn Insurance Company's ass.

I packed everything up and drove to the CVS. I paid for my pictures which were ready and dropped off the new batch with a same-day request. I was told by a clerk with a pitiful case of acne to come back after four. He assured me everything would be ready.

I killed some time at a non-descript Mexican joint, called Fran Diffenderfer at William Penn and set up an appointment for the following morning. I had purchased an "Inquirer" at the CVS, so I killed time reading it while eating a couple of soft tacos.

At the appointed time, I drove back to the CVS and retrieved my photos. I couldn't help but think, a drugstore such as this would have some kind of product to help the boy who waited on me. Acne that bad must have some impact on this poor kid's self-esteem and confidence; particularly, with the opposite sex. Oh well, it really wasn't my problem, as my grandpa used to say about small problems or problems that weren't his, "I've got other fish to fry."

Fran and I met the next morning and she announced how exceedingly pleased she was with my work, she felt sure court would now be avoided. Fran stated matter-of-factly, "Mr. Duffy CoughlinMurphy, after seeing what you got us, will be extremely anxious to cut some kind of deal."

We made small talk while her secretary ran an errand, and when she returned, I was given a mighty satisfactory check for my services.

I thanked her and departed after a nice hug. It's always reassuring to know your efforts are appreciated.

Chapter 28

It was back to Margo's musings. I sat at my desk and opened her confessional paging to the spot I had marked with a three by five card. I read slowly, not wanting to miss any detail, any possible clue, and then I got to this entry.

Diary Entry – November

All of the excitement of the past few weeks has been eclipsed by my headaches, which have gotten exponentially worse, and more frequent. Dr. Chow has referred me to a neurologist and ENT for scans and a workup to see if there are any additional issues at work here. None of the prescriptions she has given me can cut through this godawful pain. I've been calling out of work more often than I've been going these last few weeks, and I may have to go out on disability if this keeps up much longer.

I couldn't begin to imagine what she'd been going through, but I thought she was a real trooper for the way she handled it.

On top of this, MJ and I are no longer on speaking terms. Since Dad died, she's been an entirely different person. She actually had the nerve to tell me that I'm out of my mind if I think I'll ever work at the company or get a penny's profit from the business. As far as she's concerned, I don't even deserve to have the same last name. She called me a cheap whore and said it's a good thing our parents are deceased because they would be so ashamed of me. She suspected I had a fling with Lorenzo. I did, of course, but I wasn't going to own it. No way. I can barely believe I did it myself. I insisted she was delusional, but she knew I was lying, and she said she never wanted to see me or speak to me again. We haven't talked since. I feel guilty, but I also feel mad. Aside from the screw-up with Lorenzo, I've been a pretty good sister. She should give me more credit.

That M. J. is a hard-hearted woman. I suppose she could've found out that Lorenzo and Margo had an affair. I guess, in this case, that old saying "blood is thicker than water" didn't hold water.

It's all jealousy. All of it. I can't help she's letting her anger get the best of her. Nobody told her to get married to the first guy who came along and showed interest in her. I tried to snap her out of all those wasted days mourning him when he left. God knows I did my best to cheer her up, but she doesn't want to get over Lorenzo. She can't face the fact he's a degenerate gambler and womanizer. He wasn't worth all the tears. She should get out and meet someone new. She doesn't want to do that. Oh well, that's her choice, but I have a right to live my life the way I want, too! If you ask me, this isn't about Lorenzo at all. It's about DAD. She's jealous thinking I was dad's favorite. Again, NOT REALLY MY FAULT, MJ! Maybe he loved me more, maybe he didn't. Frankly, there were many times I thought MJ was his favorite. Does it matter now?

I took a child development class in college, and I do remember reading in the course text, fathers had a huge influence in the growth and maturation of daughters; particularly, in their relationship with men.

After all, wasn't I there for MJ when her world fell apart? I took her in and shared my double bed and small apartment with her. And when Dad died, I took care of making all the arrangements because she was so devastated, she was helpless, almost a complete basket case. The way she carried on, you'd think she was the only one who lost both parents. I'm dad's daughter too, and I have as much right to the family business as she does. And if she thinks she's going to keep all the money from Downtown McKay without giving me my fair share, she's got another think coming. I'm going to ask Quentin and see what I can do, what legal options I have. I am all alone in the world, just like MJ, and there is no way of knowing if that status will ever change. I need the money to provide myself just as much as she does. I don't understand why she has so little concern about me, when all I have ever done is give, give, give.

This certainly revealed a huge rift in the sisters' relationship. Why didn't M. J. come clean to me about all this? Was she embarrassed? Did she feel guilty about treating Margo so shabbily and want to make amends? I didn't know and nothing I'd learned so far could answer my questions.

Okay, now I am REALLY confused. I just walked past Conover's secretary's desk and saw a file labeled Downtown McKay. I couldn't open it and look as Rita came back and sat down at her desk before I had a chance. I said hello and kept moving. What the hell is going on? I tried calling MJ, but she didn't answer or chose not to. Is Downtown McKay in trouble? Is MJ up to the job, if there is real trouble? Is she trying to pull a fast one on me? I'm lost.

In my mind, Margo seemed to be a lost little girl. Maybe my fraternal instincts were surfacing. I wasn't sure, but I thought taking another run at Lorenzo might be a good idea. Maybe, if I worked him right, he might let something slip. As things were developing, I needed something to help me push through this morass of contradictions.

Chapter 29

I drove to the diner, and sure enough Lorenzo was ensconced in his booth bent over the Racing Form studying all the numbers intently, as if he could make any sense of them.

I sat down across from him and he looked up.

"Not you again. I thought I made myself clear the last time."

"I'm a slow learner."

"At least you're honest and own up to being stupid, I'll give you that."

All he was giving me was a raft of shit. I wanted some substance, so I threw him a curve ball.

"So, Lorenzo, tell me, how was Margo in the sack?"

I thought I detected a bit more color in his swarthy skin. I know his eyes narrowed to slits.

"How'd you know about that?"

"I'm a detective. I learn things." I thought he was stalling, so I threw him a slider this time. "Was she better than Mary Jane?"

It took him by surprise and before he thought he let it slip, "She was a hellcat." Then he caught himself and told me to get lost.

"I've got one more question for you."

"Shoot."

"Did M. J. ever get you a position with the firm?"

"Yeah, I worked for Downtown McKay for a few months."

"Doing what?"

"I was the manager of the warehouse and records."

I stood and he gave me what I took as a hairy eyeball. I left shaking in my boots.

As I drove to the office, I contemplated his slip of the tongue and his work history revelation. The diary and Lorenzo both confirmed the affair. Lorenzo had a key to the warehouse.

Sitting at my desk updating my files, I couldn't help but ask myself out loud, "Did Lorenzo, at some point, out of hatred for both sisters, confess, or more likely, brag, about his affair with Margo? How else could she have known? Lorenzo had a key to the warehouse. Did he despise Margo? Had she broken it off and he wanted it to continue? Or perhaps more likely, had she threatened to tell all to M. J.? Any positive answers to my questions would certainly give Lorenzo motive to murder his sister-in-law. He struck me as being capable of violence. Shit, he'd threatened me with it.

Chapter 30

There was a message on my phone from a Mrs. Katherine Demuth. She sounded hoity-toity as I listened to her plea to discover who her husband was dating on the side. I called the number she left and got a hold of her. I apologized to her for declining because I'm a one-man firm and my plate was full. I did recommend a friend of mine, who probably could use the work. She thanked me and hung up.

I retrieved the diary from my safe and took a whack at December until I came to this passage.

Diary Entry – December

I don't know if I can even write down what I have to say, but I must. It's a real burden and writing about it in my diary will hopefully help ease the shock. There's nobody in the world I can talk about this with, so I've got to collect my thoughts, and then write them down, get them out. I'm just so numb.

Wow, this sounded really intense. My curiosity was piqued, to say the least.

The ENT didn't detect anything, but the MRI scan explained my headaches. It explained everything, really – the fainting, the clumsiness, the difficulties concentrating, the headaches, and my intense sex drive – everything. I have a malignant brain tumor. The neurologist, supposedly the best in the city, said nothing could be done about it because it's in a bad spot, and it is way too big. It's too far along.

The doctor told me to get things in order, spend time with loved ones, look into hospice. It won't be long before I will need full-time care. I'm going to die.

I took my handkerchief from my back pocket and wiped my eyes. I wasn't sure I wanted to read on, or if I could read on. But after pausing for a while, I did go on.

It doesn't feel real. It can't be, I'm only 25 years old. I'm too young to die. I don't have anyone to turn to, either. I sure can't or won't go to MJ with this. Forget looking at a bright side, there is no fucking bright side.

My life has been a joke. I have accomplished nothing. All I have cared about has been pointless, stupid vanity. Nothing is real. I have nobody to talk to, nobody to share my life with. I have no parents. My sister wants nothing to do with me. My friends are all just idiots, really – just people I party with. The men, oh for God's sake. I don't even want to think about it. I feel like a fool. There will be nobody to mourn me. Not even a dog. Just a couple of losers at the bar who will talk about what I was like in the sack. What a legacy. I'm going out for a drink. No, make that a lot of drinks. I'm going to get plastered.

Holy shit, what else could I say. I was stunned and drawing a blank – my mind was numb and overwhelmed by a deepening melancholy. It was hard to fathom her death at such a young age, and with so much potential left unfulfilled. I didn't know quite what to do next. I continued my reading. Again, I was stopped short when I turned to this entry.

Diary Entry – January

I know I don't have much time left and I'll never have children. All I have is my sister and I don't even have her, but at the very least I want to know what is going on with Downtown McKay. I know something hinky is going on with the family business. I came across some forms in Baxter's tax records that indicate some kind of connection between the Shelby Company and Downtown McKay. What the hell's going on?

The next entry demonstrated not only was she inquisitive, she was resourceful too.

When I was confident everyone left the office for the evening, I searched Rita's desk. In the bottom drawer was the file I'd seen, but when I picked up, it didn't seem nearly as thick as the first time I'd seen it. There were a few documents which pointed toward a close working relationship with the Santucci family. It could only mean one thing, that the mob was taking over our business. Did MJ know about this? I can't go to her, but I can go to the police. I heard someone coming down the hall. I stuffed the file back in the desk, but not in time. Jim Conover entered the room and saw me. He asked what I was doing. I thought quickly and made up a story about running out of a form I needed to complete my work and thought maybe Rita would have those forms in her desk. I don't think he believed me. I left the office as quickly as I could. My heart was racing.

Was Conover in cahoots with organized crime too? Did he rat out Margo to Joey Santucci and then either Mutt, Jeff, Sal, or Rocco was provided with a key to the warehouse, and given marching orders to pick her up and kill her, from either Anthony or Joey? It seemed plausible it could have gone down that way. Did I need to speak to Conover again? Or maybe it was time, way past time, in fact, to take all I had to Lenny Andrews and let him sift through the whole mess. I certainly had unearthed enough evidence to bring multiple charges against all of them, if not a count of murder. The police might just do a better job from this point on. Maybe I was in over my head? I decided to sleep on it and go with my gut in the morning.

Chapter 31

In the morning, I mulled over the whole case while I hate a bowl of oatmeal with honey, raisins, cinnamon, and milk. It was time to take everything

I had to Lenny Andrews and let the police department and the district attorney sift through it all.

I drove to the precinct and met with my buddy reminding him I had promised he wouldn't be disappointed. After I explained all and showed him the tapes, I had of the prostitution ring in the apartments managed by the Shelby Company and the payoffs to the two patrol officers, he was duly impressed and quite thankful. I left knowing I had performed a community service.

I swung by George Wentworth's place and shared with him that all the evidence was being thoroughly examined by the authorities and his problem would soon be solved.

I drove back to my office and checked the messages. One of Fran's insurance friends had called, Wiley Banner with Independent Insurance, to enlist my help with a bump and back scam. I called and made an appointment to see him that afternoon.

I drove to Gino's and had a steak sandwich and fries. Not a very healthy lunch, but a most satisfying one, I must admit. The place was mobbed, and I had to wait in a long line. I thought I might be late for my meeting with Banner, but I caught a break with traffic and lights and made it with ten minutes to spare.

After identifying myself the receptionist, whose name plate read Pamela Nussbaum, showed me into Mr. Banner's office. He stood and after all the formalities he came around and sat next to me. He handed me a yellow folder and indicated, "We became suspicious and regarded this as a scam when it became apparent the same doctor and lawyer were involved with so many rear end crashes and claims of back and neck injuries filed against us. We need you to look into this and see if you can get evidence to prove it's a scam."

I explained my fees and he seemed okay with them. Probably Fran had filled him in when she recommended my services.

"I'll get started on this immediately, and hopefully, I'll let you know something by the end of the week."

I drove to the doctor's office and parked just down the street. Scanning the file while I sat and monitored traffic in and out of his office, I made note Dr. Harold Sanders wasn't very busy. I held my stake out position for over three hours, and in that time, he had but one patient.

The next move was to drive to the lawyer's office and I again parked a little less than half a block away. Mr. Leonard Lewis, Jr. wasn't very busy either. I sat on him until dinner time and he had only one client. But I did take note it was the same client from Sander's office earlier in the afternoon.

As he left the office, making a snap decision, I followed him. He was a Hispanic male, about five eight or nine, and looked to be in his mid-twenties. He drove an old blue Toyota pickup truck that showed some hard use with many dings and a bent back bumper. I tailed him into North Philly beyond the Temple campus. He parked outside a row home, got out, saw a neighbor several doors down and walked to him and held an animated conversation. I made a note of both addresses and copied down the license plate numbers for the pickup.

On the way back to my apartment, I stopped for some Chinese takeout, General Tso's chicken. I consumed most of it, but what I couldn't eat, I'd have for breakfast in the morning.

After reading the "Inquirer" from cover to cover, I completed the evening by watching a few shows. Then, I called it a night.

The next morning after my leftover breakfast, I visited the yellow folder again and realized the neighbors were involved in one of the lawsuits. Mr. Orlando Reyes, the Hispanic male I'd followed yesterday, had been rear-ended by Mr. Saquan Brown, his neighbor from three houses away.

I continued my research of these two men and discovered they were both unemployed and collecting unemployment insurance. I knew times were tough, but to resort to fraud was really desperate. I wondered if I put a little heat on them, would they melt?

I once again headed into North Philly, fairly close to an area Frank Rizzo, a hardnosed Philadelphia Police Commissioner, referred to as "The Badlands." They were sitting on Brown's porch each drinking a beer. I identified myself as I approached their cozy gathering and launched right in to Independent Insurance's evidence that some serious fraud was being perpetrated by Sanders and Lewis, and if they insisted on keeping quiet, they'd be going to prison for their role in such felonious behavior, too. "But," I stretched that word out so far it would've knocked me unconscious if it snapped back like an elastic band, "but," I said it again for emphasis, "if you two help the insurance company put an end to this fraud, no charges will be brought against you."

They looked at each other and eyed me up and down, and then Brown said, "Okay."

I loaded them into my car, and we rode to the Independent offices. Wiley Banner was glad to see me and brought in the company lawyer, Kathy Delano, to handle the case from there. Banner took me to another office and a cute petite brunette cut me a check. Everyone was pleased. I decided to celebrate and stop for a fancy dinner at the Abbey on Front Street. I really splurged with a big ass steak and a bottle of expensive cabernet. The bill with the wine and a most generous tip came to one-hundred-thirty-five dollars. I must confess, I was worth every penny of it.

Chapter 32

Next day, the shit hit the fan. The Inquirer reported the police making numerous arrests in conjunction with co-conspirators Anthony Santucci, Joseph Santucci, John Baxter, Sal Antiglioni, Rocco Matarazzo, Antonio Renaldi, and Reginald Vincenzo in a real estate ring to defraud senior citizens of their properties. Additionally, this same crowd faced a number of counts regarding the prostitution rings within the apartment complexes managed by the Shelby Company. Of course, Downtown McKay was prominent throughout the story. Another article related how the company was being used as a conduit to money launder the illicit funds from all the brothels. There was an article at the bottom of the page suggesting that Margo McKay, who had worked at the law firm Barrow, Nickerson, Smythe, and Fuller and who had been murdered the previous January, may have discovered a paper trail that led to her demise. Several articles mentioned the search warrants police obtained for searches of the offices of the Anthony and Joey Santucci, the

Shelby Company, and the Downtown McKay warehouse. A whole host of evidence was utilized to prove probable cause for the warrants, including a copy of an e-mail message written in code, which the police deciphered, implicating many of those who were recently indicted with a variety of RICO crimes. Stephen Stetson, the District Attorney, shared a prepared statement with the press, "This is a real win for Philadelphia, my office, and the office of the Police Commissioner. Taking so many members of organized crime off the streets will make our city a safer place and legal entrepreneurs will be free to conduct their affairs without fear of competition or threat of violence."

My friend, Lenny Andrews, received a lot of good press and was mentioned throughout all the stories as being a vital cog in the discovery of key evidence and ultimate arrests and charges. Jack Bridge was not mentioned at all. That was okay with me. The only reason I would have wanted any press, it might've garnered me a few clients; otherwise I preferred to keep my anonymity.

There were follow up stories and new angles reported the next day. It seemed as if one of the lesser members could be broken, they might pin down who gave the order to hit Margo McKay, and who carried it out.

I needed to call M. J. and set up a time for her to come to my office. I really wanted to wrap things up and be done with the whole thing, although I expected my discoveries about Margo and my compassion for her would always stay with me. From this point on, probably no day would pass without me giving a thought to her.

EPILOGUE

I called M. J. to let her know my report was finished asking her to stop in to my office so we could go over it and settle up for all my work. We set a time for ten the following morning.

It was a long twenty-four hours. I was more than ready to be done with Margo's murder case and my investigation. I probably should have gone with my inclination to decline her offer on that first visit. Hell, this case almost got me killed, not once, but twice.

The day before our meeting, I put the finishing touches to my report. I read it through, then reread it. The second reading allowed me to proof for errors, which popped out and made me wonder how I could've made so many simple mistakes. Finally, the report was complete. I printed out two copies, stapled them, and placed one in my file cabinet, and one in the top desk drawer.

On the way home, I stopped at the precinct to ask Lenny for a favor. He was just leaving but assured me he would do it. After all, he owed me big time for all the great press he got making so many arrests of really bad actors. He even thought a promotion might be in his future. That assuaged my doubts and made me happy.

Dinner was a couple of cans of Campbell's New England clam chowder and too many Trenton crackers, all washed down by one Jameson after another. I didn't make it to the bedroom or a soft, inviting mattress. No, I fell sound asleep in the chair.

I woke up early, took a very hot shower, and dressed in my best sport coat and slacks. I wanted to be early for my meeting with Mary Jane McKay. On the way to the office, I picked up a bacon, egg, and cheese on a plain bagel and black coffee at a Dunkin Donut. I consumed the meal seated behind my desk. I looked at my watch, it was nine-fortyfive. Waiting was interminably exasperating and difficult. It was like Christmas Eve and I was the kid trying to fall asleep quickly so Santa would drop off my gifts and Christmas could arrive.

An eternity later, there was a knock on the door. It flew open before I could respond. In swept M. J. like a tidal wave rushing the shore. She strode confidently to my desk and sat down opposite me.

Then, her piercing eyes found mine, and she said, "It was great that you were able to expose all the mob related activities in my company, and the police were able to gather enough evidence from you and elsewhere to convict them all. You saved my company, and even though you failed to identify which of these hoodlums killed my sister, you saved my Downtown McKay from their greedy hooks. I can't thank you enough."

She laid a rather fat manila envelope on the corner of my desk and informed me it contained a very generous bonus. She drew out the word generous pushing those bright red lips towards me, as if they would underscore her point.

I opened the top drawer of my desk, took out my report, and handed it to her.
Then, before she could read any of my tome I had so exactingly prepared, I said, "Not so fast, M. J., I didn't fail."

I emphasized DIDN'T and drew it out for a beat or two. I couldn't help myself. Call it personal pride, call it disgust, call it what you will, but I couldn't explain my motivation for such inhospitable behavior.

She arched a brow and through clenched teeth said, "What do you mean? You DIDN'T identify Margo's killer!"

Two can play the game and usually do. She emphasized the word DIDN'T too. Only her version sounded derogatory and degrading.

"Oh, but I did identify Margo's killer, M. J." I revealed, "I got really suspicious when your sister's direct boss, Conover, let it slip that Baxter had requested Margo to work on his tax problem. On my first visit to your warehouse, I found a charm bracelet with a locket. The locket contained a picture of your mother and sister. I also discovered dried blood on the office-side back leg of the workbench standing just to the right of the doorway. That blood was Margo's. She was murdered in your warehouse, but there was a struggle, a partial piece of fingernail split and broke off sliding all the way to the back of the bench up against the far side back leg. It too was your sister's. I discovered it on my last visit to the warehouse. There was a small piece of what looked to be skin clinging to the underside of that nail. Both items are safely ensconced in plastic bags with proper markings and identifications in my file cabinet ready to be turned over to the police. I'm confident the DNA on the bracelet and the DNA from the skin stuck to the nail will be identified as yours, Mary Jane."

She tried to interrupt. I stopped her by raising my hand like a bold crossing guard in a school zone. I may have even pushed the palm toward her for greater emphasis.

"My pal, Detective Lenny Andrews, gave me permission to speak with John Baxter while he was still in police custody, before being sent off to prison. I had just one question for him, why did he request Margo? He had to know she would discover the mob's connection to Downtown McKay going through all the paperwork and tax forms. He told me why." I paused for effect. She seemed to lean forward in her chair. "You, Mary Jane McKay, directed him to do so. Why? You wanted it to look to me, and the police, as if Margo discovered the infiltration of the company by Anthony and Joey Santucci and all their underlings, and we all would make the assumption one of them murdered her to shut her up about the money laundering, fraud, strong-armed tactics, and prostitution being employed in all the companies associated with Downtown McKay."

At this point, her face lost all its beauty and turned into a hideous mask of rage and hate. I had never seen someone's demeanor change so quickly. That first time she entered my office, the impression I had was right on. This was one hardhearted woman. Hurting cold, like a 7-11 slushy brain freeze cold.

I went on, "I'm sure, when the D.A. offers Joey a deal, he'll rat you out so fast, it'll make your head spin. Yeah, he'll sing like a bird about how you came to him for a gun. A gun that had been used in a what was classified by the police as a mob hit. This would add to the impression one of the hoods shot your sister in the back of the head, execution style, to keep her from going to the police."

I paused briefly one last time to catch my breath, and she smirked and said, "Go on, Bridge. Don't stop now, it's just getting juicy, go ahead, tell me all the lurid details."

"You had a key to Margo's apartment. You knew it was time to make your move. You were waiting for her when she came home from Grumpy's. You talked her into accompanying you to the McKay warehouse or you forced her with the gun you bought from Joey. You had that key too, after all, it was your building. You unlocked the door, and again she either went in freely or you threatened her, but somehow once inside, she made a move to defend herself. Maybe she sensed what was coming. You had a brief scuffle, and then you got the best of her, but not before Margo's finger nail was torn and scattered to its hideaway under the workbench. You forced her to turn around and murdered her in cold blood. You shot her in the back of the head to make it look like a professional hit, then you stripped her naked, save for the argyle

237

socks to muddy the waters, making it appear to be a possible sex crime. Stripping her hastily, you didn't see the torn bracelet as it fell to its lodging place beside the back leg of the workbench. After dumping the body and weapon at St. Paul's, you came back to the scene of the crime and tried to clean-up. You thought you were thorough, but you weren't thorough enough. I have just one question for you. Why?"

"You're too clever for your own good, Mr. Jack Bridge." As she said this, she brought a gun, probably slipped out of her purse while I was talking, up above desk level pointed at my chest. Her hand was as steady and unmoving as a snake sunning itself on a rock. There was no panic. I was thinking, maybe she was planning a scenario like this the whole time I was working for her. I was also thinking, how embarrassing it would be right now if I lost control of my bladder. She went on, "I was counting on you to expose organized crime's role in undermining my company. After the D.A. would finish proving all the charges against the Santucci family, Downtown McKay would be free and clear of them all. It would be all mine, and I wouldn't have to share it with my oversexed foolish sister who slept with my woman-chasing husband. She didn't think I knew, but I did, and I could never forgive her in a million-years. I hated Margo for it. That little bitch deserved what she got."

I couldn't help myself, "I guess it's true."

She bit, "What?"

"Revenge is a dish best served cold! And there's no arguing you're a cold-hearted monster."

She was holding the gun and presumably all the regular cards in the deck, I wanted to be the joker showing the last laugh was on her, not on me. I couldn't help myself.

"You didn't know, because Margo didn't share it with you, but she had an inoperable tumor. It was very large, the size of a tangerine, and the pressure it was causing on her brain was responsible for the changes in her personality and her sexual appetite. She couldn't help her behavior with all the men, even with Lorenzo. Margo had no control of it. The prognosis the doctor gave her was three months, which meant she'd be dead by February. Ironic, isn't it? You didn't have to kill her. Nature would've done it for you in another month."

This information stopped her in her tracks. She pursed her lips, hesitated, looked up at the ceiling momentarily, but there wasn't time for me to make a move.

Without batting so much as an eyelash, M. J. pressed on.

"That's too bad for her, but now, it's all too bad for you, Jack. Too bad you're not going to spend any of that fat envelope I just gave you. This gun came with the other one Joey sold me." As she said it, she waved it toward me. I knew she meant business, but she didn't have to flaunt it and scare me even more. "This too was used in a mob hit,

and the serial numbers have been filed off and treated with acid. And detective that you are, you'll notice, I'm wearing gloves." She laughed at this. Was she impugning my talents as a sleuth? I wanted to protest but thought better of it. "There are no witnesses, and the dumb cops will run ballistic tests on the bullet that kills you, and then blame the mob. I guess I get the last laugh."

Just then, from behind her came the bass voice of Lenny as he stepped out of the closet, "Not so fast Ms. McKay. Drop the weapon or I'll happily shoot you where you sit. Believe me, it would give me the greatest pleasure."

She sat perfectly still. I suppose she was contemplating possible actions, possible choices, while I contemplated whether or not I had just peed myself, or was I just sweating profusely in my boxers. She was staring Hobson' choice in the face – a choice which is really no choice at all.

The look on Lenny's face, was it hunger or longing in his eyes, made me think he was hoping she'd try to spin around and shoot at him.

Pausing a bit more, she dropped the gun on my desk. I gasped as I grabbed it, "Great timing Lenny, I was really starting to sweat it. I trust you got it all on tape?"

"You bet I did, Jack. The D. A. will have an open and shut case, and I hope she takes this broad all the way to the death penalty. This conniving manipulator doesn't deserve life, sitting her ass in a cell for the next fifty or sixty years."

He cuffed her in what might be described by the ACLU as an aggressive manner, and forcibly marched M. J. McKay from my office for the last time. It was obvious Lenny was enjoying himself, and I sure got a kick out of watching him in action.

After they departed, I checked the contents of the envelope, twenty-five thousand in cash. I wondered if M. J. would want a refund. I hoped not, because I didn't plan on giving her one.

This case had been a real can of worms, and Mary Jane McKay, who thought she controlled the characters, the plot, including the climax, had misjudged this sly old bird. If she had done her homework, she'd have known I was the proverbial early bird, and I'd get ALL the worms, including her, and justice for poor sick Margo McKay, the girl in the argyle socks.

The Boy with the Gold Nose Ring

- Introduction

- Prologue

- The Teacher

- The Guidance Counselor

- The School Aide

- The Administrator

- The Juvenile Detective

- The Mother

- The Girlfriend

- The Father

- The Friend

- The Artist

- The Associated Press News Release

- Epilogue

Introduction

First came a tall one, all legs and very little body, then a short one, followed by one in a print dress her hair in pigtails, and then one in boxer shorts with cutoffs underneath and all of it semi-covered by a baggy sweatshirt. There was one with ripped jeans, and one with holes in the seat of his pants. Another one came with a pixie cut, followed by one with spikes of hair sticking up in a most unusual configuration. A few wore t-shirts advertising bubble gum, "Blow Me," while a couple of others had designs and messages equally inconceivable for their age and offensive to many, but not all, adults. Then, there was a kid with slicked back hair and one with no hair at all. No makeup on some of the girls, yet others with so much makeup they reminded one of birthday cakes, minus the candles. On many, there was no visible jewelry, while others displayed ears with more earrings than fingers. Some had bright eyes and shiny smiles of carefree joy, while still others looked like extras from a Blevel horror flick with Kool-Aid dyed hair and eyes so dull and lifeless they were perfect casting for the role of Zombie the walking corpse. They came in all imaginable shapes, sizes, and designs. But they came.

Some came running, chasing after one another, kite tail chasing the kite. Some were walking and talking in shrill staccato bursts, excitement personified and uncontained. An avalanche of adolescents cascaded from big yellow buses onto the cement pavement fast becoming whirlpools, little eddies of cliques tugging some children this way and others that way. Others coursing across streets inside and outside the crossing lines, rippling over curbs racing down sidewalks only easing as they approached the smiling adults greeting them just outside the front doors of the building.

The air was filled with anticipation for another year, another challenge to be met and conquered, or to be met with apathy, or outright anger for having to be there ending a summer of fun, listlessness, grand adventures, or too many disappointments. Yes, they came with the morning sunshine radiating energy. They came in a bubbling, boisterous anticipation of rediscovery, last year's friends, familiar smells, and the building, or reserved hopefulness of discovery, a new fun teacher, an enjoyable class, or discovery of a new, or hidden, talent.

The school stood in brick splendor. It was a lifeless monolith save for the memories. Past moments, past experiences lingering in hallways and classrooms, waiting to be reborn and then erased by imminent, hopeful ones yet to be made, to be lived. There were happenings, some wonderful, some not so, awaiting their grand entrance with an aura of urgency. The building, a haven to some, to others a hell, stood with its own sense of anticipation, and waited their arrival.

Some would find it a safe place to explore dreams or construct new ones, some would not find that to be the case. All would labor there. It was a place of struggle and meant to be so. It was a place to seek, and maybe find the how and why of life, and yet, not fully master all the answers to many significant questions. It was a place to extend the limits of self, yet remain in shadowy confines superimposed by others, or at times, by oneself. It was a place to stretch and grow, to take three steps forward and, at times, slide back two. It was a place to become, or simply to be.

In the cities where the smokestacks had belched their smoke and smog, where the machines had turned raw resources into finished goods and products, where the human tide had been tamed and harnessed like so much fodder for the economy, where the children's grandparents had built a nation and won a war, the children were changing. In the suburbs where split levels became tracts and tracts of Sunny View Meadows, and Trace Willow Runs, where America stretched itself and grew mall after mall, and light industrial parks, one after another, where the children's parents chased a dream and lost a war that almost tore the country asunder, the children were changing. In the rural lands where small farms once reigned supreme, huge combines and conglomerates were swallowing those homesteads, or the land was being sold at exorbitant, too good to pass up, prices to feed the housing frenzy sprawling over the countryside which ancient peoples had subdued; the children were changing. America was changing.

At first, some of the professionals working in the building saw it and were dismayed, unsure of what to do. Then, other adults began to notice subtle, and not so subtle, differences. The children still came to the building, but they weren't like the others, the ones who had come before. These children coming now weren't the same as their ancestors. They had changed, and were still changing, evolving, into what? Who knew? Who could predict? But the adults couldn't pinpoint all the contrariness and doubts they were feeling or sensing. It was exceptionally hard to get a handle on the elusive personalities of this new generation. Not knowing, not understanding such evasive change to the way it had been made concerns turn to doubt. Doubt turned into anxiety, and that anxiety grew a little larger and a little deeper.

Few spoke out, fewer communicated freely, and so the silence hung heavy like moist humid air clinging to lungs gasping for breath after some sweat-producing exertion. Not talking about the changes taking place made the adults feel a little lonelier, and their worries and concerns became a bit more ominous and imposing.

Many adults were perplexed by, and distrustful of, what the future might bring as it unfolded. As children, hadn't they faced all the challenges, joys, and disappointments of growing up? It hadn't always been fun. They didn't always get what they wanted, even though many of them had worked long and hard. They did develop a sense of purpose, a sense of being useful and responsible. Hadn't their adults made it tough on them? Lectures about life had frequently been drummed into their heads until it seemed they might explode from overload. The lectures had been tainted by lessons from a "Great Depression," hard times, and a most horrible, unthinkable, war. But these lectures had led them to set goals for themselves, and eventually a strong work ethic grew and became a vital and vibrant driving force in their lives. It was a power that propelled them to become mythical Americans. American citizens who adhered to the system which started with working hard, moved on to getting ahead by making a lot of money, and then, spending it on the good life. Hadn't they superseded their parents? Hadn't they been giving their children a far better life than they had known as kids or ever imagined possible? Hadn't they given their children everything? And then they wondered, how could this alarming change be happening? They asked themselves, how could our children be such a collection of ungrateful, self-centered human beings? After all, wouldn't you think these kids would worship the ground we, as their parents, walked on, for all that we've done for them, and for all that we've given them?

Not so. Now it seemed as if things had changed without the adults really knowing when, or how, it happened. Times had surely changed, children had certainly changed, and maybe some of the variations were a result of subtle changes in how the adults interacted with the kids. Was it the people who were ultimately responsible for the children's upbringing who wrought these changes? Maybe permanent disturbing growth had developed unintentionally because of doting parents. Is it possible the children learned these self-centered behaviors ...? No, it couldn't be true.

Adults who had always been driven achievers, growing up competing with peers every waking moment, filled their days and nights with a burning quest to succeed, and measured their achievement by the quantity of expensive toys collected, and large beautiful homes purchased. After all, wasn't that what life was really all about? Acquiring all the marvels of a modern age for home and family became an end all. Underneath this affluent veneer they crafted an inferior substratum of childhood expectations that this is what the good life is and would always be a constant cornucopia for them and their prodigy. Their children had everything and all by whim with the least effort necessary. Personal accountability had been replaced by the angle, manipulation, unrealistic presumptions, short cuts, and high-tech driven lives. And the children, empty sponges, were soaking it up for fare-thee-well. The important relationship, the lifeline connection between effort and reward had been smashed beyond all recognition. Parents, who either had to, or felt they had to, worked more and more to maintain lifestyles that didn't afford time for their children. They abdicated their parental responsibilities to television, tech games, or, in many instances, school.

In a highly mobile society, chances are grandparents were too far away to make an appreciable difference or positive impact. Dad was replaced by the latest sneaker fad, gold chains, while technology became an alternative for mom. In some instances, television became a pervasive substitute for parents creating an even bigger demand for things, possessions, not significant life experiences to foster positive growth. The media truly did become the message and the pitchman made the puppet children dance his tune, just like the Pied Piper of Hamelin. Terms like "latchkey children" crept into the vernacular as dad, and increasingly mom, chased the almighty dollar. Unfortunately, the missing quality family time and togetherness were non-existent in the lives of too many children. Kids were left to their own devices. Adults forgot or ignored the truism that idle hands are the devil's workshop.

Some resourceful kids fulfilled their emotional needs in the school building, but some turned outside the building to poor role models or gangs for unmet inner demands. Others found nothing to satisfy needs and withdrew inside themselves. Occasionally, a few turned on each other, turned on their parents, or turned on themselves, committing suicide.

While too many adults had too little time for children working to maintain the lifestyle, others just outright indulged in excess and cheap fleeting highs, alcohol or drug-induced. These adults turned from their children to themselves, to whatever vice appealed to them, with some temptations costlier than others. Mostly, they were disappointed as what they truly sought was never found in their chosen pursuit. Social services and agencies were understaffed and overworked. Countless atrocities were recorded and recounted, but still the children suffered.

Although the next generation had everything, they had nothing. The parents finally knew something was amiss and the headlines screamed it; this caused adults to be afraid. Some hoped what had been done so badly could be undone. They wanted to believe it so much, they willed it to be so. The inevitable march of time often travels in the guise of the unexpected, and sometimes marches boldly, but sometimes quietly, into our lives, yet, it always arrives. All too often, we are surprised by its viciousness and cruelty, but we really shouldn't be. Today is always conceived in yesterday, and we do reap what we sow.

The children were a compilation of all those yesterdays, both the good and the bad. They were a product of parental successes and failures. They were a fruition of the past and an emissary of the future. Each child entering the building was a living, breathing story with varied plot lines unique to

their own lives, but all shared the common thread of change. They represented incomplete struggles with an inevitable conclusion. Many would aspire to greatness, and some would manage to achieve it, the lucky ones. Most would somehow muddle through. And for a few, like Johnny Beasley, the last chapter, life's climax, was all too sudden and all too final.

Johnny was a kid who lived a life fraught with one disappointment after another, undue setbacks to his plan, and too many infrequent successes – a disheartening, and short-lived tale, all too familiar as the nation rapidly approached the end of the twentieth century, and the dawning of the millennium.

The TEACHER

"One of the things you learn from history is that every generation of men is always going through a period of painful, critical, and destructive transition." – Frank Underhill

The building was like many of the time, a place of bricks and cement blocks painted an off white from ceiling to head level and from there down a coffee milkshake color. The terrazzo floor, though worn from millions of steps skipped, walked, and jumped upon it, had a keen shine that spoke of custodial pride and care. Posters and signs adorned the walls providing both direction for expected behaviors, and information regarding upcoming events. Some were a reflection of inspiring thoughts and catchy slogans of the period. Although the building was erected a quarter-century before, a little over twelve-hundred youngsters between the ages of ten and fourteen had left their mark upon its newness, slightly more than half that approached the beginning school year now. As in any typical September, the building smelled of a conglomeration of fresh paint, disinfectant, polish, floor wax, old books, new texts, and a sundry of unidentifiable odors. It was not a pleasant, nor unpleasant air that greeted each visitor's olfactory senses, but a familiar, to be expected remembrance of previous days spent in the school. It was as if to say, "Yes, that's right, that's as it should be." The familiarity was comforting to most children and adults.

Each room had been arduously and carefully prepared prior to the opening day and the building was awake and animated as if the listless days of summer hibernation had never been. Bustling children on their way to becoming students again, greeted friends and former trusted teachers. Soon the bell, precursor to regimen, schedules, rules, class activities and lessons, and homework, would sound, violating the kinship of the hallway, extinguishing the catching-up, reminding all of their impending appointment with homeroom. The unwelcome invitation to be followed by a somewhat chaotic exodus from dalliance with the past and on to a new beginning.

Reporter: "It's my understanding, Mr. Warren, you had Johnny Beasley in your eighth-grade homeroom and then in your social studies class. Think back to the beginning of the school year. What was it like? How did you first encounter Johnny? What were your impressions of him? How did you get along with him? What was your relationship like?"

I knew I had to get to homeroom. I just couldn't be late on the very first day. I sure didn't want to set a bad precedent for my young charges; after all, punctuality was important. Too much summer reminiscing in the faculty lounge and that second cup of coffee almost cost me a tardy appearance. But I slipped down the hall with a, "Hi, how're you doing?" here, and a "What's happening, kiddo?" there. I couldn't forget all the salient points of yesterday's faculty meeting. I ticked them off in my head as an outline to conduct the business of homeroom. Lord help me if I got the new attendance procedures, reduced and free lunch forms, insurance applications, free condom permission slips, and by all means the sacrosanct information/activity permit cards (to be filled out in triplicate), all botched up. I didn't want to start the year off in the administration's dog house.

Excuse me if I sound a bit jaded, as if I don't really care about homeroom or that I'm a lackadaisical professional when it comes to meeting responsibilities. Before you start thinking I'm overpaid and underworked, let me explain. It's just that I've been doing this routine for so long, it's pretty much second nature by now. In fact, I could probably do all that's required in my sleep. I'm highly organized and move these tedious, but necessary, activities along so I can interact with my young charges in a fun way. Get to know them, or at least a little about each of them early on. Things do change, but in many ways they don't - not really. That's a paradox for those on the outside looking in, I know. At any rate, some might call me a battlescarred veteran, but I don't care for that analogy. It sounds as if I'm in a war zone, or that I should've retired before developing a case of PTSD. That I can't give up the smell of charcoal, and sulfur, and all the blood and guts splattered on the chalkboard. I prefer to think of myself as sapient, perhaps "crafty" would be more apt, due to all my years of experience. I like the kids to feel welcome and their natural curiosity piqued right out of the gate. I want them to know I'm interested in each one of them and that I really care about them all.

But no! The administration's first initiative is with forms, forms, and you guessed it, more forms. Of course, that's all after the flag salute and any announcements emanating from the box on the wall to the right of the American flag, our voice on high. On the other hand, it may be a dose of practicality for all the students' form-filling years to come when they're adults. But somehow it just doesn't sit quite right, not with me, and not with the students, either. For practical considerations, and both students and teachers can be practical, we all put our true feelings aside and completed the required rituals of the paper trail.

In case you haven't figured it out, I'm a teacher who loves what he does, and for the most part does it well. I've been a middle-school history teacher for over two decades. The interaction with young people is a joy and truly a rewarding experience; particularly, when you see a light bulb go off in their eyes, or they write you a note from the heart describing the impact you've had on their lives and how much they appreciate you and what you do.

As I looked around, checking on the progress, or lack thereof, completing these homeroom tasks. I noticed one student was simply sitting at his desk staring at the ceiling. I checked my seating chart, which I set up as they entered the room. It helps me to learn their names quickly. After a week or so, once I know everyone, they will have a choice of seats. The chart identified that Johnny Beasley wasn't completing any of the work. In fact, it appeared his preference was to work on his dexterity and aim snapping wasps, tightly-folded pieces of paper propelled by a rubber band which can sting if the aim is true, at a couple of pretty girls sitting in front and to the side of him. He was focused on Brenda Zoppa, and the look in her eye revealed she wasn't thrilled by his attention.

I said to him, "Johnny, that's enough with the wasps. Move to a desk up here by me, and hand over the shooter and any wasps you have left."

Johnny's face was long and narrow with a mantel of greasy golden locks falling over one of his eyes set deep and half-closed peering at me. There was a gold ring in his nose. He cocked his head to the side, as he bought some time to size me up with both eyes; his hair fell to the side of his head exposing the other eye. He sneered, "What did I do? I didn't do nothing," which came out in a nasal whine. And that was all he said.

It was enough. Cut me some slack. Were we really going to do this dance on the first day of school? This young Darrow-want-to-be decided to test the water by sticking his foot in up to his mouth. I chose to ignore his denial and repeated my instructions, as if he hadn't heard me, "Move to the desk up here, and hand over the shooter and any wasps you have left."

The room became look-out-here-it-comes quiet. Twenty-five pairs of eyes left their work on forms to check out the surly young man's next move. Would he continue striving to pass the bar exam, arguing further, or would he comply with the direction given in an even-tempered matter-offact tone? He glared at me and I glared at him, and the outcome of this mini-battle of wills was suspended between us, a wishbone ready to snap from pressure applied to each side of it. The class was waiting, poised on the brink of their seats, eyeballing us both and waiting impatiently to see who would snap off the biggest piece of the bone, getting their wish.

It was over before any crack of the bone could cut the air like a smelly fart. Johnny stood up, shuffled to the front of the room, slapped two wasps and a rubber band in the palm of my hand, and took the assigned seat. He was muttering under his breath. I thought I caught the word "prick." A teacher can always take the high road with muttering and pretend it wasn't heard; particularly, an older veteran, such as myself. Or all too often, a teacher can take the low road of confrontation, getting down in the dirt with an unruly student, and watch the class descend into a quagmire of roads less traveled. I, being of sound mind, chose the high road, not so much because I'm really an astute teacher, but why make a scene embarrassing either one of us, or both? Silence once again settled in and the class resumed working on the compilation of data on the given forms. Even Johnny finally participated in the effort. The last minutes of homeroom passed uneventfully and in an unnoteworthy fashion. I collected everything and sent them on their way as the bell sounded. As a professional it is important, no, make that vital, to manage the class from bell to bell. Down time, or "learning fallout," is the nemesis of any professional, usually the newbies. Free time opens up Pandora's Box of bad things, which can only leave the teacher hoping for the best. It doesn't generally work out too well; everything hinges on hope.

The remainder of the day passed routinely and quickly, but eighth period, the last one for the day, found me renewing my relationship with Mr. Beasley. I had him, along with twenty-three other thirteen and fourteen-year-olds, for eighth grade social studies. I introduced the class to social studies through a packet I had created around the seven social sciences. I thought it was a nifty opening lesson designed to maximize student participation in both small and large group settings. In small group, I moved about the room monitoring and adjusting as needed, and then led a class discussion of the material. It went well, but any good activity needs to move to another after ten or fifteen minutes to maintain student interest and focus. I had another handout, which I had distributed during small group, a great timemanagement technique regarding notebook maintenance for assignments, returned homework papers, and student initiated or teacher-given notes. This packet had a number of helpful hints on writing an essay and provided some credible examples modeling the desired outcome. We completed the lesson with a closure activity on a slip I provided, students writing the most important thing they learned and what would be most helpful to their success in the course as their "exit ticket." These were collected at the door as my class filed out to go to their lockers and then, to the buses parked out in front of the building, awaiting their arrival. I was pleased there were no overt challenges to my authority and Johnny's resistance to the lesson was minimal, as he participated throughout. That didn't mean I had succeeded with him, however. Throughout the lesson he chose to give me the low-down sullen stare, but I'd seen a whole lot better in my many years of service.

After school, I made my way to the guidance office to glean any background information I could about Johnny Beasley from his counselor and records. I hoped to find something which might help me better understand and address his needs. His counselor was a woman named Sally Pitts, who had been successfully guiding young people for more years than she'd ever admit or want you to mention. She was seated behind her desk when I poked my head around the corner of the jam, and asked, "Hi, Sally, got a minute for me?"

She looked up from notes she was making in a folder, gave me a pleasant smile, and said, "Sure thing. Have a seat and fire away. What's on your mind?"

Her office was child-centered with a few beautiful posters of children, animals, colorful hot-air balloons with encouraging captions. A shelf contained some knick-knacks revealing a bit about some of her interests and a number of books. Student notes, essays, drawings and work adorned a bulletin board to the right of her desk. I felt comfortable and knew why the students liked her and felt good seeking her advice or help with some matter or problem. Sally maintained a demeanor that put students and adults, too, at immediate ease.

"I trust you had a relaxing summer break?"

"I did, but from the look on your face, you didn't come in here to hash over my summer doings. So, what gives?"

"I need some information, background, on one of my eighth-grade boys, a young man named Johnny ..."

Before I could finish, she exclaimed, "Beasley."

"Yes, it seems we got off on the wrong foot during homeroom, and while he ultimately cooperated and I had no problems with him during eighth period, I see trouble brewing on the horizon."

"He's somewhat new to our school. He came at the end of last year from a city school where his academic and behavioral record wasn't too good. I met with his parents prior to his start. They told me they've moved a number of times, but now own some kind of store, which they live over, and are desperately hoping this is the last change. I gather from some things they didn't spell out, Johnny was a reason for so many different residences, and schools."

She went to a file cabinet and retrieved a folder, presumably with records. She opened it, quickly scanned the first few pages, then said, "He tests in the high range. School work should be no problem; however, his grades are mostly C and D with comments such as, "Doesn't complete assignments, fails to cooperate, frequently off task, misbehaves, and so on, and so on."

"What about IQ?"

"His most recent score in sixth grade was a 125."

She continued to pour through his records and then noted, "It seems with all the changes, he's had a difficult time adjusting to new surroundings, and fitting in with his new classmates."

"Anything else?"

"A disciplinary chart from his last school indicates he was suspended three times last year. One was for insubordination, another for leaving school grounds, and the third was for possessing pills, his mother's prescription for Valium. It doesn't say whether he was taking or selling them. Just that he had them in his possession."

"I figured his record might look something like that. I was hoping it wouldn't, but I guess you and I have our work cut out for us trying to reach this one."

"Looks that way."

"Well, thanks for your help. You have a good evening. I'll see you tomorrow. Hopefully, it will be a better day for Johnny."

Prior to departing, I made copies of "A Baker's Dozen: Letters to My Students" that I'd been utilizing for a few years. I believed they helped my students better understand me and perhaps, would inspire them in some positive way. In the past, some students had written me letters of thanks;

particularly, during their high school years. Once in a while, I'd even get a note from one of my students while in college or even after that. I planned to distribute my letters in class the next day, have the students read them for homework, then, the following day discuss the letters in small groups of four before holding a debriefing session with them. If I didn't handle it this way, I was afraid the letter packet would end up in the bottom of a locker, or, even worse, in a trash receptacle.

I was really excited for the next day and had trouble sleeping that night. It's funny. Sometimes you get a great idea for a lesson while you're trying to fall asleep and you write it down and develop it over the next day or two and then you implement it, occasionally successfully, but more often than not, something goes wrong and it's back to the drawing board. Once in a while, a little tweaking is all that's necessary, but because the original idea was a good one the lesson is worth rebuilding. Rarely it cannot be saved, and you just have to scrap it. There is always a great deal of anticipation how the students will respond. If your delivery is vivid and you're adept at selling yourself, usually the students buy into the plan. I confess, that's really a great feeling – to know your lesson was engaging, informative, useful to each student, and well received. That's why a lot of us, educators, go into teaching. Obviously, it's not for the money.

A Baker's Dozen: Letters to My Students by Mr. Warren

My Rationale for Writing These Letters to You

Dear Students,

I did not sit with pencil and paper in hand to write some lengthy discourse on the wisdom of the ages. I merely intended to share some thoughts about important things in our lives not to influence your opinion, but to initiate thought and reflection regarding issues that influence the quality of our lives. I would hope that you'll take the time to read these little pieces and contemplate the message, but more importantly to take away what may be important or significant to you and may have some positive impact on your life.

I have devoted almost 25 years to educating young people and while the great carpenter can see his finished product and admire his work, it is hard most of the time, for a teacher to see, to know what impact, what results they have created. Students are ever changing and growing, and the efforts of a teacher may not be witnessed for years.

I can only pray that in all my years of teaching I have been able to reach, to influence a number of my young charges to not only be better students, more successful students, but to be better people, more successful people.

Sincerely,
Mr. Warren

From Letters to My Students # 1
Dear Students,

John William Gardner once wrote, "The society which scorns excellence in plumbing as a humble activity and tolerates shoddiness in philosophy because it is an exalted activity will have neither good plumbing nor good philosophy: neither its pipes nor its theories will hold water." I can remember my father telling me over and over again as I grew up, if a job is worth doing, it's worth doing well. And he always said what he meant and meant what he said. Those sentiments were embodied in my Saturday morning chores. If the job wasn't done right, I had to do it all over again. We lived on the corner of a rather large property. I had to sweep the sidewalks and gutters every week and he would check my effort when completed. I didn't learn soon enough that I might as well do the job fully, correctly the first time. Many a Saturday afternoon I spent muttering nasty things about my father under my breath, but today I thank God that he cared enough to instill in me the appreciation for a job well done, and the desire to do the job to the best of my ability. This approach has stood me well in the world of work.

I share this childhood story with you hoping to focus your attention on your current job, the job of student. You probably don't think about the future that much and certainly don't dwell on the connection between such and the educational record, knowledge, and skills you are currently building, but when you don't do well in school, you are closing doors to your future and possible opportunities. Your whole approach to work and life is reflected in your homework. Those assignments which are sloppy, hastily done at the last minute with little thought or concern and are generally incomplete reveal an individual who will most likely take the same approach in the adult working world. Those assignments which are neat, conscientiously complete, and demonstrate a real interest, a curiosity to learn and know reveal an individual who will most likely approach work and life in the same steadfast manner. And I would argue that these are the people who will be successful and have a satisfying life. But don't take my word for it, just look at what Coach Keely has done with our football team. During practices the boys had to move from one area to another.

This move involved either the sidewalk or cutting across the grass. Keely punished his players for cutting across the grass and his rationale made a lot of sense to me. "If you take shortcuts in practice, you'll take them in the game." And one could flip a paraphrase of his message by saying, "Do it right in your formative years and you'll do it right in life!"

So much of life becomes routine and is based on habitual behaviors. I can't emphasize enough how important it is to develop good solid habits while you are young. If you initiate positive procedures in your life now and build upon them as you grow and mature, you will have laid the foundation for happiness, contentment, and success. And you too will have learned and earned the rewarding feeling of a job well done, whether it is some menial task around the house such as painting the woodwork, or the most important case the firm has ever handled.

Sincerely,
Mr. Warren

Somebody said that it couldn't be done
But he, with a chuckle replied, "maybe he couldn't," but he would be one who wouldn't say so till he had tried. So, he buckled right in with the trace of a grin on his face. If he worried, he hid it. He started to

sing as he tackled the thing that couldn't be done, and he did it. – Edgar Guest

From Letters to My Students #2

Dear Students,

It has been said that friendship gives great value to life. I have been married for a little more than twenty-one years to a woman who has been my best friend. And while I value the love that we have shared, I believe I value our friendship even more. Paraphrasing Sarah Dressen, at times, life can be an awful, ugly place to not have a best friend. There have been difficult times, challenging times, sad times where a friend makes all the difference. The strong bonds of friendship lift one's spirits to soar above the mundane to recognize friendship is permanent, while the problem is only temporary, and it too shall pass. As Jon Katz took note, friends are part of the glue that holds faith and life together. Powerful stuff is this condition of friendship to say the least. Good friends who share with you all the bright and happy moments that life brings make those times extra special.

William Shakespeare even weighed in on friendship when he wrote, "A friend is one that knows you as you are, understands where you have been, accepts what you have become, and still, gently allow you to grow." Early relationships can be lasting ones. I grew up in a small, rural town and several of us from elementary through high school shared that experience helping to foster lifelong friendships. We still communicate regularly and strive to get together during the year and every summer to relive old memories and create new ones. And this is true despite the fact that we are so far flung from Panama City, our home town. Now we are scattered across the country from Georgia to Washington to Pennsylvania to Florida. During my working years, I have again had the good fortune to find several people who have become close friends. These relationships are invaluable providing timely counsel and advice, help when needed – an ear to listen, or proactive behavior, and perhaps most importantly, acceptance. Moreover, these priceless acquaintances in our lives make all the memorable occasions that much more so.

Having eight dogs grace my life, I know what unconditional love is and how much it can mean to an individual. A true friend shares a dog's love with you. But to have a friend, you need to be a friend. Friendship, without a doubt, is a two-way street.

Having grown up with a mother and father who were avid gardeners and individuals who appreciated the beauty and serenity of plants and flowers, I recognize the potential positive impact that flowers can provide for a human spirit, very similar to the gift of friendship. Alfred Tennyson stated, "If I had a flower for every-time I thought of you ... I could walk through my garden forever." And I, whenever I think of my buddies from my school days, or my friends from work, or my lifelong companion, Susan, I am in the most beautiful garden that buoys the spirit from the doldrums and lifts my heart to rise above the disappointments of everyday living. Without a doubt, friendship gives great value to life.

Sincerely,
Mr. Warren

"We're born alone, we live alone, we die alone. Only through our love and friendship can we create the illusion for the moment that we're not alone. – Orson Welles

From Letters to My Students #3

Dear Students,

Ben Franklin believed that one should "either write something worth reading or do something worth writing." Good writers strive to communicate in an interesting and exact fashion something of importance or entertainment value. Obviously, they want to catch the reader's attention and hold it throughout the text, but they also want to impart a message or messages precisely and perhaps to ultimately influence the reader's thinking.

Sadly, too many student answers, essays and papers are filled with vague innuendoes and generalizations. The final product does not demonstrate a real familiarity with the material or even a rudimentary knowledge of the facts. Don't just write that the early twentieth century was earmarked by reform, go on to demonstrate a greater knowledge by indicating the progressives, who were comprised of many college-educated women, supported three reform presidents in Roosevelt, Taft, and Wilson at the beginning of the twentieth century in an attempt to rectify the shortcomings of society as exposed by the muckraking journalists of the day. Then, expand on the various journalists and the problems with which they dealt. But don't stop there satisfied with your work, go on to indicate the specifics of what was done, and what impact it ultimately had on American society. One of your writing missions is to strive to be inclusive and complete.

Author of *The Scarlet Letter,* Nathaniel Hawthorne, once said, "Easy reading is damn hard writing." And if one takes the time to do the job properly, the merit in his thinking becomes apparent. There is a craft in writing that seeks and selects just the right word to convey just the right mental picture or thought.

I consistently ask you, my students, to give me stuff, not fluff. It is imperative in our society to communicate clearly, fluently, and efficiently. If one does not make an effort to develop and hone writing skills in all subject areas, a great opportunity has been squandered. Writing is an instructional responsibility of every teacher, no matter what their discipline. In addition, it is the responsibility of every student to develop in writing, at a minimum, a proficiency in constructing a composite answer, a cogent line of thought, or a proof of supposition, or thesis statement.

In the sexist 1960s, IBM took a full-page advertisement in *The New York Times* boldly announcing, "Send me the man who reads." Why, you ask, were they clamoring for men who read?" Reading exposes one to a variety of writing styles and techniques, and sufficient amounts of reading would almost ensure that some of the good writing approaches would rub off on the reader and help establish developing better writing habits and results. Moreover, reading helps to build a more versatile and well-rounded vocabulary. To be a better writer, try reading more often, which forces me to make a paraphrase of the IBM ad: send me the student who reads.

Sincerely,
Mr. Warren

"If you don't have the time to read, you don't have the time (or the tools) to write. Simple as that. – Stephen King

From Letters to My Students #4

Dear Students,

Robert Brault wrote, "Every lie is two lies – the lie we tell others and the lie we tell ourselves to justify it." There may be times you feel trapped and the only way out is a lie. There may be times you feel the only way to get ahead is to tell a lie. But Brault's insight was keen as you try to rationalize the lie as necessary you only end up lying to yourself. And too, once a lie passes through your lips, the next lie slides by more easily than a Rita's water ice sliding down your throat on a hot summer's day. A lie has a life all its own.

And you may get ahead or evade consequences for a time, but once the lie is out there, it can never be captured, you can never take it back. It's kind of like putting a nasty picture or thought on the internet. Once it's out there, it's out there!

Bill Copeland warned, "When you stretch the truth, watch out for the snapback." That exaggerated truth, that lie you told has a way of coming back ghostlike to haunt you and at times terrify you. Truth fears no questions, but a lie has trouble standing up to an inquiry and often folds like a cheap tent leaving the liar gasping for breath and the next lie.

Trust is an important bond between two people. It is strong enough to be the glue holding us fast during difficult times, but a lie weakens that trust and too many lies can destroy the bond altogether. Michael Josephson said, "Honesty doesn't always pay, but dishonesty always costs." And all too often the price it exacts is so much higher than can be afforded. It could be the loss of a friend, or a loved one.

O. Henry wrote, "There is no well-defined boundary between honesty and dishonesty. The frontiers of one blend with the outside limits of the other, and he who attempts to tread this dangerous ground may be sometimes in one domain and sometimes in the other." It is a more precarious perch than the one a tightrope walker takes. Few, if any, have the necessary balance, dexterity, and skill to walk a line so fine.

While some may believe truth is beauty, others will recognize that the bald truth can be downright ugly. And I'm sure, depending on the truth, a whole range exists between. No matter how it looks, however, the truth is always best. When an individual is stripped of money, possessions, and other worldly items what is left is character. Honesty and truthfulness are key components of quality character. When you look in the mirror, can you honestly say you like and respect the person you face? If not, perhaps you need to be more honest, more truthful. Try it, you'll see positive results, and you'll feel much better about yourself. Hey, I wouldn't lie to you! Trust me!

Sincerely,
Mr. Warren

"The Guy in the Glass" by Dale Wimbrow

When you get what you want in your struggle for self, and the world makes you king for a day, then go to the mirror and look at yourself, and see what that guy has to say.

For it isn't your father, or mother, or wife, whose judgment upon you must pass. The guy whose verdict counts most in your life is the guy staring back from the glass.

He's the guy to please, never mind all the rest, for he's with you clear to the end, and you've passed your most dangerous, difficult test, if the guy in the glass is your friend.

You may be like Jack Horner and chisel a plum, and think you're a wonderful guy, but the man in the glass says you're only a bum, if you can't look him straight in the eye.

You can fool the whole world down the pathway of years, and get pats on the back as you pass, but your final reward will be heartaches and tears, if you've cheated the guy in the glass.

From Letters to My Students #5

Dear Students,

Is it important today whether one has manners and the will to exercise them on a regular basis? Does it matter whether or not you're polite? I'm told that the common courtesies are a thing of the past. Maybe that's true. I do remember a time when the expectation was to treat one's elders with respect. I can remember my parents emphasizing the need to treat everyone with

politeness, even those who were rude to me, not because they were nice, but because I was.

I cringe when I hear how some of you respond to an adult. The body language is defiant and challenging, the tone is disrespectful, and the look is classic death ray. Somewhere along the line those of you who persist in such bad behavior missed the lesson about catching more flies with honey than vinegar. It's bad enough that this rude behavior is directed towards another, but when it's an adult I believe that's abominable. Yet, it is even worse when I overhear one of you speaking to a parent as if they are servile drones ordering this or demanding that.

Emily Post believed manners to be a "sensitive awareness of the feelings of others." People readily talk in the theater disregarding those around them. People answer a cell phone in a restaurant and carry on a conversation interrupting the dinner and conversations of those around them. People operate their vehicle in the passing lane at fifteen or twenty miles per hour under the speed limit and seem oblivious to the many close calls which occur as other drivers try to weave in and back out getting around the miscreant

driver. Too many people seem unable to put

themselves in the shoes of another, to see a different perspective, to feel what another may be feeling. Why?

Is it that all too often you see politicians argue with one another, sports team managers argue with officials, and maybe you even see nasty disputes carried out in your own home, setting a bad precedent for you? Our society seems to have forgotten the wisdom of Barry Goldwater who said, "To disagree, one doesn't have to be disagreeable."

All of this self-centered offensive behavior says to me that it's time for a change. It's time for parents and perhaps schools to re-emphasize courteous behavior. The mission of our time then is to actively seek, find, and utilize greater civility. Ralph Waldo Emerson believed that life wasn't so short that one couldn't find the time for courtesy.

There really is something to the old saw "what goes around, comes around." It behooves us all to remember the golden rule to treat others the way we wish to be treated. Remember, karma's only a bitch if you are.

Sincerely,
Mr. Warren

A Little Manners Poem

Wait your turn -don't interrupt.
If you use it, pick it up.

When you need some help, say, "Please." Be
kind and loving - never tease.
Say "hi" when meeting someone new and be a
friend whose words are true.
If you win a game, don't gloat.
To thank someone, write a note.
Don't be piggy when you eat.
And clear your space so it looks neat. These
manners are the perfect start to showing
friends you have a heart.
--Anonymous

From Letters to My Students #6

Dear Students,

**A former administrator in my middle school,
liked to welcome his students to the new school
year during an assembly. One of the points he felt
obligated to make was that it was so important for
us to remember the three R's. No, not readin',
'ritin', and 'rithmetic.   But Respect Yourself,
Respect Others, and Respect the Facility.**

**It is important to conduct oneself in such a way
as to always think and act in a manner resulting in
positive outcomes for self. This includes actions
that reflect a quality of character based upon a**

mind-set that clearly understands the morality, the right and wrong of any given situation. Some might go so far as to add, avoiding actions that are detrimental to not only the human spirit, but the physical body as well.

This approach to self should also carry over to others. Every human being deserves to be treated in a polite and humane manner. The Golden Rule requires that we treat others the way we wish to be treated. You never know how far a little kindness will go in the life of another. Respecting others truly is a reflection of the respect we have for ourselves.

Finally, the students were fortunate to have such a wonderful facility in which to spend a good part of the waking hours. It behooves one to make the effort to treat the building, the furniture, and all the elements of the facility with respect. Trash belongs in a trash can and not on the floor or school grounds. Spills may be accidents, but we should be responsible enough to clean up after ourselves and not leave the mess for someone else. Marking the desks or walls with graffiti is disrespectful from many vantage points and creates extra work for the custodians. Disposing of chewing gum is a real nuisance; do not stick used gum under a chair or desk, wrap it in a tissue and then throw it out in a wastebasket or garbage can.

These three R's require such little effort. But they do guarantee a school that will be a happy caring community. Further, they guarantee a place where students, teachers, other personnel, and administrators enjoy and look forward to conducting the daily commitment to lessons and learning.

When you step on the grounds of our middle school, strive to remember to bring along the three R's. Respect Yourself, Respect Others, and Respect the Facility. Not only will you build esteem within yourself and your colleagues, but you won't need Aretha Franklin spelling it out for you, "R E S P E C T, find out what it means to me!"

Sincerely,
Mr. Warren

Respect:

Respect is a lesson that everyone should learn

Respect must be given before an expected return

Respect is something that's given for free

Respect is about us and never about me

Respect is the basis on which relationships are founded

Respect is the anchor that keeps a person well grounded

Respect builds the character and defines who we are

Respect sets the standard and raises the bar

Respect is magnanimous and helps to fulfill

Respect is the partner that sits with good will

Respect is like honey so sweet it's perceived

Respect a taste to savour for when it's received

-- Anonymous

From Letters to My Students #7

Dear Students,

Warren Bennis believed that, "Leadership is the capacity to translate vision into reality." Bennis reiterated thoughts found in the Bible in Proverbs 29:18, "Where there is no vision, the people perish." Obviously, to be a great leader, one needs a vision, a picture of what can and needs to be. But one may ask, "How does a leader see and grasp a vision to follow?" Great leaders are proactive. They are constantly looking ahead, attempting to forecast, to see what change may bring and what dangers may lurk, and then they

plan accordingly. Once a vision is in place, a plan is required to reach the established goal. This is followed by the necessity to generate sufficient enthusiasm and commitment to persist and push on to achieve the goal, no matter how easy or difficult.

Much can be accomplished with an active and vibrant leadership. Margaret Mead recognized, "Never doubt that a small group of thoughtful, concerned citizens can change the world. Indeed, it is the only thing that ever has." This insightful anthropologist realized history contains countless examples whereby an individual or small group exhibiting leadership qualities changed the course of history. John Maxwell understood that people buy into the leader before they buy into the vision.

A leader needs to be able to sell himself to the people, to his constituents, to sell his leadership before they will buy into his vision. Harry Truman identified that, "Men make history and not the other way around. In periods where there is no leadership, society stands still. Progress occurs when courageous, skillful leaders seize the opportunity to change things for the better." Some believe that great leadership rests as much on luck as it does on skill. But I remember reading somewhere that luck is when opportunity meets preparedness. So, seize this time, this opportunity to hone your leadership skills, remembering that if you aren't the lead dog in the sled team, the scenery never changes. If instead you are content to be a follower, if you are better suited to be a follower, at least develop the ability to recognize a skilled leader with a great vision to follow. And then, pull for it with all the might you have.

Sincerely,
Mr. Warren

"A leader is one who knows the way, goes the way, and shows the way" – John C. Maxwell

From Letters to My Students #8

Dear Students,

Martin Luther King, Jr. described faith as "everything we see is a shadow cast by that which we do not see." In other words, it's a lot like electricity. We can't see electricity, but we can see the light when we flick on the switch. Fibonacci Numbers appear so frequently in nature, for example in the number of petals on a flower and the arrangement of those petals, there must be something we cannot see influencing such a rational approach to things of nature. Nature casts a huge shadow with its many mysteries and beauties. And perhaps the nature of mankind casts the largest shadow of all. Faith can make a difficult, if not impossible, task possible. "A person's faith when activated," according to Renner, "sets in motion supernatural power that enables that person to do what normally he would never be able to do." Certainly, Martin Luther King, Jr.'s faith empowered him to engender enthusiasm within his followers to persistently protest in a nonviolent manner until their goals were achieved.

The bride and groom have faith in each other and the sanctity of marriage. They believe in love and all the good things which evolve from a loving relationship. They may be unable to see the future, but they maintain a blind faith that their relationship will stay strong and see them through no matter what.   They reproduce believing what is to come for their child will be as good, if not better, than the life they have experienced. In fact, they frequently believe they have the power to make it better for their children.

Faith never denies evil, for it certainly does exist in our world, but sees around it to the possibilities on the other side. Faith is confident and optimistic. Faith never denies evil, for it certainly does exist in our world, but sees around it to the possibilities on the other side. Faith is confident and optimistic and never shows anger or impatience. Martin Luther wrote, "The whole being of any Christian is faith and love. Faith brings the person to God, and love brings the person to people." The faithful are outward bound after their inner reflection seeking to overcome the challenges of daily living.

Elizabeth Barrett Browning recognized "Whoso loves, believes the impossible." But I have found that love, tempered with strong elements of faith, hope, and charity, conquers the impossible. One doesn't have to look way into the future be it clear or translucent, one simply must accept God at His word and take the next step.   Faith provides light to our footpath of life and guides us through the beautiful passages as well as the rough spots, lost ways, and dead ends. Faith denies worry which Corrie Ten Boom suggests does not empty tomorrow of its sorrow but empties today of its strength. So, keep your strength, by keeping the faith, and taking the next step.

Sincerely,

Mr. Warren

"Optimism is the faith that leads to achievement. Nothing can be done without hope and confidence." – Helen Keller

From Letters to My Students #9

Dear Students,

Christopher Reeve who played Superman in the movies prior to a devastating fall that left him a paraplegic never complained about his accident and its consequences. He merely put a smile on his face and went on to make the most of what life he had left spending quality time with his wife, his family, and friends. He once said, "A hero is an ordinary individual who finds strength to persevere and endure in spite of overwhelming obstacles." Certainly, one could view Reeves as a hero based upon that definition.

We all need heroes in our lives giving us someone to emulate, qualities to admire and copy in our own lives. This is particularly true for young people. But there is a danger that youth may be drawn to false heroes. Young people can be influenced easily. It is vital that you are careful when identifying those individuals who you deem worthy to idolize, to strive to follow in their footsteps.

When I was coaching soccer, I frequently heard people make the claim that "sports build character." I beg to differ. In my opinion, sports reveal character. This brings to mind the old saw, "when the going gets tough, the tough get going." Bob Riley was clearly in agreement when he wrote, "Hard times don't create heroes. It is during the hard times when the 'hero' within us is revealed." Each and every one of us has the potential to be a hero. We just may not always recognize the opportunity or the role we might be playing in someone else's life.

Perhaps it behooves us to strive to build the qualities, the attributes of those we most admire, our parents, recognizing that frequently when it didn't look like there was a light at the end of the tunnel, our parents kept digging anyhow. They didn't give up and kept after things to make them right for family, friends, and those less fortunate.

Our middle school is a school community that through service projects believes it possible to make each and every one of you heroes in your commitment to those around you. You should feel fortunate that not only are you receiving a quality education, but your spiritual well-being is of paramount priority to the staff and administration. You will graduate as both a knowledgeable individual and in touch with the God-like qualities harbored within your heart. Remember after all, we are our brother's keeper. Step up and be a hero for those who desperately need you to be their keeper. Live by the lyrics made famous by the Beatles and "Still Bill" Withers, "He ain't heavy, he's my brother."

Sincerely,
Mr. Warren

"The Hero Within"

Limit yourself to the easy
And the difficult you'll never try. Easys
need live on the fringe of the world
grubbing for nickels and dimes, claiming
that life has dealt a cruel blow; crying:
the fault is not mine.
Heroes need training to do the grand deeds
that earn them a hero's acclaim. It's
setting your eye on the hero inside,
knowing you're fair to the game.
Knowing you've got what it takes to be tough no
matter how rough life may be.
I'm a hero, I know it! When my actions show it
it's because I'm a hero to me. – Adeline Foster

From Letters to My Students #10

Dear Students,

Tennessee Williams, noted author and playwright, described life as "all memory, except for the one present moment that goes by so quickly you hardly catch it going." He does raise a valid point that the present is so fleeting. It seems impossible to truly grasp and hold the present in any other form than a memory. If true, much of our life, perhaps both the best of times and the worst of times exist in the past, and it makes me sad to think the happiest moments become memories so quickly supporting the old adage that time flies when you're having fun. And if true, it of course demands that our memory be vivid and accurate to fully capture all our experiences. Perhaps the things we forget are just not vivid enough or do not have any connections to our remembered experiences. These perceptions of memory might explain why soldiers who lived through an emotional incident can be so handicapped by post-traumatic stress disorder, being unable to perform daily responsibilities, and suffering from debilitating night sweats and dreams.

A thing learned is a part of us. It is always within the grasp of our memory and is so strong and vivid due to those connections made within the past. But how does this have anything to do with me, you inquire? Some things which you need to learn, need to know, may not be so graphic and may prove to be difficult to find memorable connections. At this point, perhaps another approach to remembering the necessary or required information would be a mnemonic device. These are tools which may contain the essentials in a little phrase or rhyme which will help the memory bank work more efficiently. An example would be the many situations in mathematics where it is important to remember the order of operations. Of course, the proper order is parentheses, exponents, multiplication, division, addition, and subtraction. Many a student has utilized "Please excuse my dear Aunt Sally" to recall the proper order and complete assigned work in a successful fashion.

Socrates, when preparing for the delivery of a speech, realized that he knew the layout of his house like the proverbial back of his hand. Using the house, he could attach segments of the speech to the familiar. The introduction he would associate with the entrance way and foyer. Various points to be made in this portion of his speech would be associated with items located in this area of the house such as a plant, a vase, a table. Each point would begin with a small thing and build to larger and larger items. In his mind he could stroll through his house passing from room to room recognizing key features and delivering each segment of the speech with all the substance he intended. And his impressive speech and presentation were made possible by the utilization of a memory device.

If you have to give an important speech, then practice using the various points of your own house to recall the elements of your speech. Stand before a mirror and practice your speech over and over, making sure to make eye contact with yourself. Look to the left, then look to the right. Your audience, each and every one of them, wants to feel as if you are talking to them – make eye contact with as many people in the audience as possible. Keep it short and sweet, always on point. You'll be surprised how much you can remember and deliver in an efficient manner.

So, wrap that rubber band around your wrist and when you look at it, and remember how to maximize your memory.

Sincerely,
Mr. Warren

From Letters to My Students #11

Dear Students,

A very close friend once told me "You cannot change the things you aren't willing to confront." Today, our nation sinks in a quagmire of indecision and inaction on the part of our leadership. The executive and legislative branches continue to avoid the hard choices, the unpopular choices, because re-election is a more desired result than fulfilling the duties of the position. Their unwillingness, inability, or fear of confronting things that need changing will unfortunately leave a legacy to you and your children that will be at the very least, challenging, and at the worst, difficult to, if not impossible to, overcome. It is sad to contemplate that you may be the first

American generation not to exceed the living standard of the previous generation.

As in all things there is a life lesson to contemplate and react to within the headlines and news clips of our day. Some qualities or shortcomings about ourselves we don't like, or we recognize as a weakness, and these are things we'd like to avoid. In fact, we generally do avoid them, much to the detriment of our well-being. You may take note that you don't like to read, and you may even recognize that it's probably based on the fact that you're not a skilled reader. But reading is like any other acquired skill which needs practice and repetition. If avoided, then no improvement will develop. Just as politicians avoid taking the hard course whereby no solution will be implemented to solve our nation's huge and looming deficit, if you continue to avoid taking action regarding your personal disappointments, no change, no improvement can occur.

Frederick Douglas realized no change comes without struggle. He knew the road to equality was not paved and was, in fact, filled with numerous potholes and pitfalls. Black militant leader Eldridge Cleaver recognized too that "if you're not part of the solution, you must be part of the problem." If you are unwilling to make a commitment to change, if you proceed with the status quo, even though it may create dissatisfaction within you, you are part of the problem.

Many of you need to hone and refine your writing skills before you go off to college and join the world of work. But when assistance is provided, when advice is offered to facilitate said improvement and you make no effort to embrace that assistance and advice, you are hindering, if not disregarding any chance of making the necessary progress. Your writing skills will remain limited, and limiting, due to your lack of effort. Without effort, the desire for growth can only be that, a desire.

It is never too late to take an inventory of positive and negative attributes, to visualize what changes you would like to make in your life, and to develop a plan to reach those results. The most difficult step of any journey is admittedly the first one. However, a step once taken generates a kind of momentum to help with the next step and each and every succeeding step. So, slip into and lace up your Nike walking shoes now knowing success, better yet victory, is just steps away.

Sincerely,
Mr. Warren

From Letters to My Students #12

Dear Students,

William Buechner once said, "The simplest explanation is that it doesn't make sense." He must have taken a test or two in his day. One of the key components of solid test-taking skills is common sense. You need to ask yourself, "Does this answer make sense?" Perhaps one of the most valuable cognitive tools available to any student is that question, but in my many years of experience it is a tool rarely utilized.

Test taking can be and should be a challenge; however, it is also an exercise in critical thinking. One needs to reflect upon the sensibility of an answer. If the question given asks, "Which *northern* city had the most trouble dealing with busing to solve de facto segregation and the integration of the public schools?" it doesn't make much sense to answer Birmingham or Montgomery or Little Rock as none of these cities qualifies as a <u>northern</u> city. If the problem given asks, "When a number three times itself is cubed equals twenty-seven, what is the number?" Knowing the five times table as you do, you remember that five times five is twenty-five, times five again is over one hundred. Therefore, you know that an answer greater than five does not make sense. Or this multiple-choice question:

Secretary of State Dulles pushed for treaties such as _? _, which impacted Vietnam by attempting to contain the spread of communism through a series of pacts and treaties. Most students narrow the choices down to a. SEATO (Southeast Asia Treaty Organization) or b. NATO (North Atlantic Treaty Organization). I am amazed by the number choosing answer b. Common sense dictates that a treaty that impacted Vietnam which is in Asia would be a treaty with the word Asia in the answer, not North Atlantic.

Albert Einstein recognized the importance of common sense and asking questions when problem solving when he said, "I am not a genius, I am just curious. I ask many questions, and when the answer is simple, then God is answering." Many problems faced on an examination or assessment really do have a simple answer. Frequently, students create real difficulty that doesn't exist.

Another important concept to remember and utilize would be that many times the test or exam contains clues if not outright answers to other questions. If one is looking and asking the right questions, it is possible to ferret out those bits of information that will help answer another question or solve another problem. Even short essay questions can incorporate facts gathered from other areas of the test in order to construct an essay with "stuff" rather than "fluff." Always use the information available to you on a test to your own advantage.

Piers Anthony once wrote, "All things make sense; you just have to fathom how they make sense." So, the next time you are confronted by a difficult homework assignment or an assessment that seems impossible, put your mind in scuba gear and dive right in without hesitation or trepidation. While things may seem murky at first, the answer will ultimately make sense. Hey, it makes a whole lot of sense to me.

Sincerely,
Mr. Warren

"Without memory, there is no culture. Without memory, there would be no civilization, no society, no future." – Elie Wiesel

T ake time to reflect and ask questions.

H ave a complete understanding of the problem or question.

I nstitute a rational plan to follow.
N ever just give up and state, "I can't."

K eep plugging until it's solved or done.

-- Anonymous

From Letters to My Students #13 Dear Students,

When facing obstacles, I often think back to a quote from an unknown author, "I complained that I had no shoes till I saw a man that had no feet." Sometimes we become so engrossed in our own lives, and our own problems, we don't realize the troubles that someone we know may be going through. Everyone we know and meet has their own share of life's misery. They may have lost someone recently, they may have a debt that seems impossible to pay, they may know someone close who is going through a divorce, or they may have some kind of substance abuse problem be it drugs or drink or know someone close who does. They may have lost their job, they may have experienced a significant health problem, or they may have some debilitating disease or compulsion which is compromising their life. And yet most of the time no one knows because they put on a happy face and carry on with their life.

Bernice Johnson Reagan once said, "Life's challenges are not supposed to paralyze you; they're supposed to help you discover who you are." The obstacles you must confront in your journey through life are there for a reason. Meeting them head on, doing the best you can is like the fire that forges the iron ore into hardened steel. Struggling with and sometimes overcoming the difficulty reveals much about the qualities, the attributes of character you possess. Seneca had a thought which provides a great insight into the difficulties of life. He said, "It is not because things are difficult that we do not dare; it is because we do not dare that they are difficult." And I would argue that they appear to be more difficult than they really are. All too often you undervalue the fortitude and drive that must be inherent to every human, or our species would not have survived, let alone grown, demonstrating progress marked by so many modern and fantastic phenomena.

It is important to realize everyone has challenges in their life, some created by external forces, and others brought on by internal decisions and actions. These difficulties are as natural to life as breathing. It is important to remember throughout history others have experienced something similar to the load you may be carrying and sometimes they failed and sometimes they succeeded. Thomas Edison in his quest to invent things, particularly the light bulb, recognized one failure after another was leading him closer to success. He persevered, and after countless tries succeeded. Martin Luther King, Jr. encountered one set back after another in his efforts to achieve equality and the civil rights guaranteed by the Constitution for all Americans, but he never gave up. He pressed on and later wrote, "We must accept finite disappointment, but never lose infinite hope." He provided the spark of hope to multiple generations of Americans who ultimately reached the mountain top and witnessed an African-American become President of the United States. So, don't complain about not having any shoes. Look at the bright side. You can get a foot and a leg up to climb over that problem in your way.

Sincerely,

Mr. Warren

Dear Students,

Thank you for taking time to read the letters I wrote to you. I hope that you found them of interest, learned a bit about me, and discovered some things that will help you to grow succeed in school and in life.

I look forward to a positive year working together to learn about the social sciences, about our world, and about ourselves.

Reminders:

- Come to class prepared (pencil, notebook and homework)
- Be respectful when someone is talking
- Ask questions when you don't understand
- See me for help (before or after school)

- **Our task is to achieve the best that you can be**

Sincerely,
Mr. Warren

The next two days passed quickly, and my letter lesson seemed to be a hit with most of the students. By Friday, I had received several parent calls of thanks, and a few notes or comments from the kids. It sure sent me into the weekend on a high note.

In week two, the students and I kicked things into high gear as class routines became familiar and they adjusted to my style of teaching. But not all was well as Johnny Beasley was becoming a topic of discussion at team meetings. The math teacher, Jane Vogel, was having behavioral issues, while the language arts instructor, Wendy Ashman, couldn't get any work from Johnny. Fred Hammer, our science team member, indicated the student demonstrated some interest in his class. I indicated a combination of everything that had been said being exhibited in my class, too. We decided we needed to be proactive early, and called the parents for a meeting, which we set for Friday afternoon, after school.

On Thursday, Johnny and another student got into a fight in the hallway. I heard the commotion and ran into the hall and grabbed Johnny, while Fred got a hold of the other combatant. Needless to say, we had to take the boys to the office, and I found out later that both boys received Saturday Suspensions (four hours of homework from eight to noon).

That explained why Johnny was in a funk on Friday. He was listless in all our classes, and yet I could sense a simmering anger and was careful not to initiate an explosive incident. Johnny already had a lot of trouble on his plate; he sure didn't need any more.

At the end of the week, the parents met the whole team after school. We introduced ourselves and then each of us recapped our concerns regarding Johnny's classroom behavior and work habits. I was the last one to speak, and I reiterated our belief that getting parental cooperation and support early would be in Johnny's best interests. I suggested I'd be willing to help, "I get to school early, usually a little before seven. I know students don't have to be here before eight, but if you'd be willing to drop Johnny off around seven, I'd be glad to meet him and work with him to get caught up in all his classes."

Mr. Beasley opened up when I had finished making my offer, "My boy is a loser. He'll never amount to anything. He's got no drive. My wife and I have tried to give him everything he could want or need, but he's nothing but a selfish shit. He doesn't care and there's probably nothing any of you can do to turn this kid around. We've been down this road before in other schools."

I could tell we were all shocked by Mr. Beasley's admissions. Jane was looking at the floor, Wendy was shaking her head side to side, and Fred just looked stunned.

Mrs. Beasley spoke up at that point, "We do really appreciate all your efforts on Johnny's behalf, and I hope you can get some positive results, but I'm worried more now than I've ever been. I had to call the police two nights ago. My husband and son got into an argument after dinner and then it led to throwing punches. I had to call the police, I was so frightened by Johnny's violent outburst."

That omission helped to explain Johnny's behavior on Thursday and sullenness on Friday, but we were all speechless. We all looked at one another unsure of what to say. Finally, I broke the silence: "Mr. and Mrs. Beasley, let me assure you, our team will make every effort to help your son, both academically and behaviorally. We need to work together, and we need to keep in close touch. Thank you for coming in today."

As they stood up to leave, Mrs. Beasley said, "Thank you so much, and I'll have Johnny at the front of the school come seven Monday morning." She tried to smile, but it just came across as a twisted grin. I noticed tears were beginning to well up in her eyes.

As happy as I'd been last Friday, this day was a real bummer. I didn't like Mr. Beasley, who probably in many ways was responsible for the current state of affairs, but Mrs. Beasley sincerely cared about the welfare of her son. I felt sorry for her and couldn't help but wonder if there was some kind of abuse, emotional or physical, happening in the home to either Johnny or his mom.

I headed toward the parking lot, then turned around and stopped in Assistant Principal Powell's office. I asked the secretary if I could see Steve for a quick question. She went down the hall to his office, stuck her head through the open door, and then waved me back.

"What can I do for you, Skip?"

"Would you mind if I stopped by during the Saturday Suspension and met and maybe worked with Johnny for a while?" I asked.

He smiled. "No, I don't mind. It might be good for him. I'll see you tomorrow morning."

"Thanks, Steve, I'll see you then."

When I arrived in the morning, six students were sitting around the conference table busy doing school work. One student was staring at the ceiling, apparently lost in his own world of who-knowswhat thoughts. But Johnny snapped out of his zone when I walked into the office. He seemed surprised to see me. I said good morning to Steve and the students and then directed Johnny to get all his books and materials and come with me.

He readily picked up all his stuff and asked, "Where are we going?"

"My room. We can get a lot done and catch you up on some of your missing work without disturbing the other students."

We walked down the hallway together and I was surprised when he commented on my letters, "Your letters to us were nice. I never had a teacher do anything like that before. Did you really mean them?"

"Yeah, I meant every word. Your current persona may not allow you to believe this, but all your teachers, including me, want to help you succeed. We hate seeing you unhappy and in trouble, both in school and at home."

He didn't say any more. We got to work, beginning with his social studies work, and in fairly short order, we had completed two missing homework assignments, one class activity, and initiated work on a three-page essay. I told him to think of his written response as a hoagie. The top bun was his position or thesis, the salami was his main point, the ham was his second point, and the cheese was his third point. Each of these positions would be introduced in a new paragraph. The lettuce, tomatoes, onions, and oil were supporting facts for each of his three significant ideas. The bottom bun was a short closure paragraph which summarized the most important or significant elements of his thinking.

"That sounds easy enough."

"Before you get started organizing your thoughts, let me review several ways you might choose to open your essay."

I proceeded to introduce Johnny to beginning an essay with a quote (JFK and Lincoln loved to quote Shakespeare and the Bible), a bold or exclamatory statement (which is designed to provoke the reader's interest to keep reading), a question (which the essay would obviously set out to answer), or just a simple recap or restatement of the question/assignment in straightforward terms.

He spent the next hour organizing thoughts and used his text book to look up supporting facts. I checked over his work and was pleased to note he'd been pretty thorough, and I told him so in specific complementary language (much more effective than a mere "good" or "not bad").

He finally completed my essay and we moved on to his math work. This revolved around algebra, one of my favorite subjects in school. Together, we dispatched his missing assignments quickly and efficiently. Next, he wrote a poem for language arts and read a short story. Finally, he completed two science worksheets, a lab report, and did some reading. He hadn't quite finished when noon arrived, but he promised me, "I'll finish this reading tomorrow."

I told him to have a great weekend, what was left of it, and thanked him for his cooperation and hard, thorough work. That got me a smile. After he left, I stopped in to touch base with Steve. He seemed pleased by our accomplishments but indicated his worry about this troubled boy.

"I'm afraid this isn't the last Saturday our friend, Mr. Beasley, will be serving. In fact, I suspect he might end up suspended a few times. He is so obstinate and hostile to authority figures. He may even be incorrigible."

"I hope you are wrong," I exclaimed. "Have a good weekend, Steve. See you on Monday."
"You too, Skip," Steve replied.

The days passed and the first quarter was finally over. Johnny had come around for me, but not consistently for my teammates. He cooperated and participated fully in my class. I sat with him several more Saturdays and worked with him whenever mom dropped him off in the morning. With the other teachers, he was inconsistent, sometimes completing work, sometimes behaving properly and as expected, but other times not participating at all, going into a shell, or being a real pain in the ass, making instructional delivery difficult.

I felt like Johnny and I were connecting. He seemed to respect me and my efforts to assist him to become a more successful student, but he never fully bought in to what I was striving to achieve with him. He cooperated in class and most of the time did his school work. I could see potential in this young man and at times it really flourished in class activities, small group work, thoughtful essays and test results. But his behavior problems continued and escalated as the year wore on. I could only do so much.

Johnny had been suspended from school a few times the remainder of the semester, mostly for smoking on campus, but once for weed. The police had been involved by the school and his parents several times. I had heard he was creating bigger problems for himself at home and with the juvenile authorities. Brenda told me that he and Sam were missing for a while. They'd run away from home and were in the city staying with somebody named Slice. That wasn't good.

And then, he was gone. Out of my class, out of my life, permanently missing. I can honestly say I was heartbroken. I thought I'd been making enough progress with him and given enough time, maybe I could have saved him, but then again, maybe not. I was left with a very hollow feeling and lost my enthusiasm and energy for a couple of weeks after his untimely death. It was so shocking and so unexpected. I was at a loss for words and terribly confused.

The GUIDANCE COUNSELOR

"All children should be taught

to unconditionally accept,

approve, admire, appreciate,

forgive, trust, and ultimately,

love their own person."

-- Asa Don Brown

REPORTER: "Ms. Pitts, how long have you been a middle school counselor? How many students were you responsible for at Johnny Beasley's school?

I've been a counselor for fifteen years. Ten years at Johnny's school, and five at a prep school prior to that. Currently, I'm the counselor for about one hundred sixth graders, over one hundred seventh graders, and just under one hundred twenty eighth graders. I have the beginning of the alphabet from names beginning with A to last names beginning with L or M depending on where the split is fairly even. The other counselor, Bernie Greenbaum, has the other half of the school. It's a demanding position with a lot of responsibilities for both of us.

REPORTER: "I'm sure. That's a lot of students for each counselor to manage. How well do you get to know each of your assignees? In fact, how well did you really know Johnny Beasley?

I generally try to see all of my students at least once each quarter, but some are very needy, and I may see them once or twice a week. Of course, some come to me for additional counselling with an immediate problem, and at other times, teachers will ask me to speak with a student about a classroom or homework issue. The eighth graders need more of my time in the spring to get them ready for transition to the high school and to prepare a schedule of courses that will best fit their abilities and needs.

I was quite familiar with Johnny for a number of reasons. My son, Jeremy, was in Johnny's grade and they had a few classes together. They weren't friends, but I picked up on a lot of misbehaviors, as observed by Jeremy, at our dinner table. My son is very straight-laced and serious-minded, and he confessed to me that he really didn't understand students like Johnny Beasley, who smoked, did drugs, dyed their hair, wore nose rings, and defied authority, parents, teachers, or administrators. Jeremy's like a middle-aged man in a fourteen-year old's body.

For him, fitting in and being accepted by the other students is important. Likewise, being accepted by the teachers and having their approval is paramount. But growing up isn't the same experience for everyone, and I explained that to my son. When you have few or no friends, and your family is dysfunctional, and your teachers are judgmental, and sad to say, in some cases sarcastic or mean, why wouldn't you act out? Or drop out? Perhaps commit suicide, if sufficiently desperate, as too many depressed people do? They don't see any alternatives. They are beaten down by their circumstances and they don't believe their lives will ever get better.

Johnny Beasley was like most adolescents in many ways. He felt misunderstood by his parents, and he craved love and understanding, which he wasn't getting at home, and obviously, not getting enough of at school, either. I love all kids and that's why I after teaching for a few years, I chose to become a guidance counselor. I want to help kids in any way I can. I try to make my office a refuge where students can feel free to drop in and either just say hi, or unload their burdens, whatever the difficulties they face may be. But kids like Johnny, shy loners, don't usually seek me out, even if they're desperately unhappy. I have to pursue them and make sure that they know I can be trusted before they will ever seek me out on their own. I saw Johnny in seventh grade a few times more in seventh grade than I saw other students, but in his eighth-grade year, my visits with him picked up significantly.

REPORTER: "I take it Johnny didn't reach out to you, but was there anyone in the school that had any kind of rapport with him?

You are right. He didn't reach out to me, but Skip Warren, his social studies teacher, was concerned about him and he worked really hard to build a bridge between them. I met with Johnny after Skip first came to me, and Johnny was touched by the concern and effort, but he wouldn't admit to having any problems. It's awfully difficult to correct a problem; particularly, if you can't identify it or won't admit it's there. Johnny received mostly C's and D's in his classes, but he earned A's in art class and a mix of A's and B's in Mr. Warren's class. He once confided in me that Mr. Warren was the only teacher in the building who seemed "alive," the only one who had any spark. Johnny also shared that Mr. Warren had a great sense of humor, and he'd say funny things, but never at the expense of anyone in the room but himself. Johnny was impressed that Skip could be so self-deprecating. I think his personal humility and warmth helped him forge connections with all of his students, plus everyone respected his obvious intelligence. I didn't know of any kids who didn't love Mr. Warren. They used to tell him he should run for President of the United States.

REPORTER: "What about other teachers? Did they ever talk to you about Johnny?

Almost everyone who came in contact with our young Mr. Beasley came to see me at least once, if not more. Most teachers go into the profession because they care, not because the job is easy, and summers are open as the general public seems to believe. Everyone I know puts in a full day and many hours in the summer to prepare the best possible lessons to motivate and enrich their young charges. Johnny's Spanish teacher, Christine Collins, thought she smelled smoke on him when he returned from the lavatory. She wanted me to speak with him before she went to the administration. She thought maybe I could do something prior to it becoming a disciplinary issue. Ruth Wolfe, his algebra teacher, came to me for ideas on how to penetrate his thick veneer. She said it was like Johnny had erected a wall around himself that few could penetrate. She was having trouble getting assignments completed and was seeking ideas, suggestions. The other teachers came to me with similar requests. They just wanted to see him succeed. They wanted to help him have a more positive school experience and life path.

REPORTER: "Did you meet with his parents to discuss academic concerns or behavior problems?"

Discipline is handled by the administration. I might be consulted by an administrator in advance of disciplinary action to learn more about a student's history. Rumors were rampant that Johnny was in at least as much trouble outside of school as in it. I know that Mr. Powell met with Mr. and Mrs. Beasley a number of times. In fact, I heard he had their phone number memorized from so many calls. I also know a number of staff members were concerned that Johnny could become a negative influence on other students and maybe get them involved with drugs, or worse.

Teachers freely expressed those concerns to Mr. Powell.

I met with Johnny's parents on more than one occasion to discuss his work habits and grades. His father was put out the first time I called to set up a meeting. He told me the store was busy and it was hard for him to get away. Johnny told me that Mr. Beasley has to ask a neighbor to watch the store when he and his wife go somewhere because they can't afford employees. Knowing this, I told Mr. Beasley his wife could come in to school alone, but he almost bit my head off at the suggestion: "She's so befuddled, she'll get whatever you have to say all wrong!" he shouted. Then he calmed down a bit and said they'd both be coming to the meeting.

On the day of our meeting, I opened the discussion by telling the Beasleys that Johnny could be doing a lot better than he was and assured them of their son's potential based on his standardized test scores and his IQ. I shared all the teacher concerns with missing work and a lack of effort. I also threw in my express concerns about Johnny's behavior in and out of school, and that's when Mr. Beasley blew up. He shook his finger at me and scolded me in no uncertain terms to keep my nose out of any affairs that weren't school related. He added that if it wasn't a school problem, I had no business calling them for a conference, and nobody had a right to interfere with how they raised their son. Mrs. Beasley had been fidgeting in her seat, looked pale, and seemed somewhat reluctant to open her mouth, but she finally stammered, "Ralph, Mrs. Pitts is just trying to help." He snapped at her, "Don't be a dumbass, Edna. Let's go. Now!" Edna sat frozen and tears streamed from her eyes. I was taken aback by what had transpired, and before I could say anything, Mr. Beasley bellowed, "I said now, Edna, and I mean now. Get your fat ass moving." It was horrible. And then he stormed out of my office with poor Edna in his wake. The whole episode made me feel even sorrier for Johnny than I already did. His father had an awful temper and was emotionally abusive to his wife. I'm sure Johnny got his fair share, too.

REPORTER: "Did Johnny ever share any feelings about his home life?"

No, he did not, I'm afraid, but it wasn't too difficult to surmise that something was going on in the house that was negatively influencing Johnny's behavior. I realize some of the acting out was nobody's fault but his own. Teenagers are selfcentered and impulsive by nature, but there was something more sinister behind most of his actions, and after the meeting with Mr. and Mrs. Beasley, it was clear to me that the dysfunction in his family was almost entirely the source of his misconduct and low self-esteem.

Current research shows that households with regular shouting incidents are more likely to have children with lower self-esteem and much higher rates of depression. Yelling and shouting at kids produces consequences just as much as if corporal punishment were being applied. Children in these environments have higher levels of stress and depression and frequently appear anxious and demonstrate an increase in behavioral problems, both at home and in school. I believe from what I observed firsthand that there were way too many shouting and demeaning comments, like "you're stupid" or "you're a jerk" going on in his house rather than rational parenting addressing specific behaviors that needed to be improved.

I met with Johnny as much as I could, given the extensive responsibilities I have. In some of our sessions he opened up about his dream of going to art school and eventually becoming an artist. He thought he might like to have an art supply shop or maybe even teach art to young people one day.

Toward the end of the quarter we heard the news about Johnny, and I was stunned and had trouble composing myself to deal with kids who had been traumatized by Johnny's death. I suppose America's always had problems with interpersonal connections, but it seems so much worse today. It makes me very sad to see the number of young people suffering because of drugs, suffering because of loneliness, just suffering. What are we doing wrong? There are too many cases like Johnny's out there. We need to fix this.

The SCHOOL AIDE

"We rise by lifting others." -- Robert Ingersoll

REPORTER: "Mrs. Kettleman what can you tell me about the relationship between Johnny Beasley and your friend and fellow aide, Alicia Stokes?"

Alicia was great with all kids, but she really took those troubled youngsters under her wing, befriending them and gaining their confidence. She made a huge difference with many of them and was just an overall positive force with everyone throughout the school. She often said there was no job too small or too unimportant to do it thoroughly, efficiently, and, most importantly, well. You do know all the teaching staff requested her for aide time in their room.

She recognized the artist in Johnny Beasley, and he was flattered that she took such an active interest. I think she had some artistic talent that went undeveloped for far too many years. But working with Johnny helped to bring out and help refine those latent talents.

I believe Alicia was a saint for demonstrating the patience she did with kids like Johnny. I love the children, but I couldn't have succored them like she did. If a student doesn't respect me because I'm an adult and an authority figure, I'm not going out of my way to gain that respect. I figure it's their loss, but you couldn't convince Alicia of that. She got hurt some, but I figure she had more successes and bright spots than failures.

I remember the ducks. Alicia discovered a mother duck in the courtyard between the library and the art rooms. Mother duck was sitting on a nest of eggs. My loving friend put a bowl of water and another of seeds in the courtyard. Later in the spring, mom strutted around with all her little ducklings following. Johnny had seen what Alicia was up to and asked to help her. He brought the seeds in to school and got a couple of plastic owls, which he talked Mr. Powell into mounting on the roof at the corners of the court yard, to keep other birds away. I guess that's the side of Johnny Alicia saw all the time. I sure didn't.

She was dedicated to her job. She arrived an hour early and greeted all the staff as they entered the building and then when the buses started to arrive, she'd greet the students with a cheery hello. Now, that's a way to start the school day, you know, having someone say they're glad to see you.

She was so inviting and good. No, she was better than good. She was great.

Johnny really fell apart when she was killed. Heck, we all did.

REPORTER: "What happened?"

Alicia was crossing the road and was struck by a car. It was a drunk driver, and he didn't stop to help her. Finally, someone called 911 and help arrived but she died of complications at the hospital the next day. It was so sad. All the school mourned the loss, but some of those kids she was close to really took it hard and needed grief counselling. What a shame. I think that put Johnny in a free fall of bad behavior. He was always a little squirrelly, but after the accident and Alicia's death, his behavior got worse. That to me was really sad, and not what Alicia would have wanted for him.

I will say, Alicia wasn't a wealthy woman, but what she lacked in money, she made up for in empathy and serving others. With her, it wasn't the size of her bank account, it was the size of her heart. When they had the viewing at the Brown Funeral Home scheduled for seven to nine in the evening, the line started at half past six and wound all the way around the block. The family didn't stop accepting condolences until a little after ten. Almost every student in the middle school was there, and all the staff attended and paid their respects. To me, that speaks volumes about the kind of woman she was and the extent of the influence she had on people who came in contact with her.

The ADMINISTRATOR

"Out of self-image, strongly held,

essentially determines what we

become."

-- Maxwell Maltz

REPORTER: "Mr. Powell, you're aware of Johnny Beasley's recent demise. I'm trying to establish who he was and how this could happen. As an administrator and disciplinarian, what can you tell me about this troubled young man?"

Johnny Beasley, unfortunately, came to my attention early in the school year, and became a frequent flyer in my office. I can safely say he was a very troubled boy.

The first time I met him, he'd been disrespectful to one of his teachers, Jeanne Klinger, and then he was insolent and insubordinate when a fellow teacher, Ken Smithers, stepped in to help. Smithers was so red in the face as he hauled Johnny into the office, I was afraid he was going to have a stroke. Apparently, Jeanne asked Johnny to pick up some trash in the cafeteria and he told her, "No, you pick it up." Smithers overheard what had transpired and he walked up to Beasley, standing chest to chest, eye to eye, and said, "You'd better pick that up now." The kid replied, "F--- off." And Ken went ballistic, grabbing Johnny by the arm and hustling him down the hall to my office.

That was a Thursday the second week of school. After I assigned his punishment of an inschool suspension for Friday and a Saturday suspension for the following day, he grew a deep shade of scarlet, stood up grabbing the edge of my desk and tried to tip it over on me. It was way too heavy for him to lift, particularly grabbing the desk in the middle, like that. In the summer, when the custodians lift it on dollies to wash and wax the floor, it takes three of them. I wasn't worried, in fact, I even chuckled about his sad attempt, and that made him even angrier. I felt guilty about laughing, but I couldn't help myself.

As Assistant Principal of the middle school, and the chief disciplinarian, that was my introduction to Johnny Beasley. Of course, that's the first time I met Mr. and Mrs. Beasley as well. I called them and had them come in to discuss the incident and the possible consequences in the instance of any future events. Mrs. Beasley was all apologetic. "I take privileges away from, Johnny" Mrs. Beasley shared, "but it makes no difference, and he's so unhappy, I just land up giving them back to him. It breaks my heart to see Johnny so miserable. I've also tried grounding him, but again, what is the point? Johnny needs to make friends, that is part of the problem. Keeping him confined at home just makes the situation worse. I've also tried just talking to Johnny and letting him know we are here to help, but he doesn't want to talk. He just wants to be left alone. Nothing we say or do makes a difference." Mr. Beasley was something else altogether: "That no good son of mine is nothing but trouble, with a capital T. We've had to move three times due to his bad behavior, and every time he says he'll do better in the new school setting. Bullshit. He doesn't even try. He doesn't care. Mr. Powell just throw the book at him. It isn't going to change anything. I should just take him home and beat the shit out of him. That's what my father would have done to me, if I had been such a dipshit."

"Mr. Beasley, I know you're upset, but that would not be a good idea. We don't need the Division of Youth and Family Services investigating a case of child abuse. Let's try to remain calm and deal with Johnny's behavior in a rational manner," I reasoned.

Mr. Beasley's voice grew louder, and he pounded his fist on my desk: "Mr. Powell, that is easy for you to say, but I'm so frustrated and angry I don't know what else to do. I can't get through to my own kid. I know what he is doing is wrong. I have tried everything, but I can't get him to grow up. Every once in a while, I think, I brought him to this world; I sure as hell ought to be able to take him out. He is a hindrance, a menace - and I don't know how much longer I can take it. He's got another five years to go before he's an adult. How are we supposed to get through this?!"

What was I supposed to do? The guy is a maniac, incapable of reason. I wanted him out of my office before his anger escalated any further. I said, "I hear you, Mr. Beasley, and we know you and Mrs. Beasley want your son to get on track as much as we do. I'm going to set up a meeting with Johnny and his counselor, Mrs. Pitts, and I'll enlist one of his teachers to monitor him. We need to stay in close touch and work on this together. Thank you for coming in today." Then I stood up and walked toward my door, ushering them out of my office and out of the school building.

As they departed, I knew from our conversation they'd be incapable of getting Johnny back on track. Mrs. Beasley was too apathetic and inconsistent, and God knows, the one thing Johnny needed was consistency. And Mr. Beasley was a verbally abusive hothead, not what a child needed a father to be.

I followed through on my promises. Sally Pitts met with him a couple of times a week, and Skip Warren did try to take Johnny under his wing. For a short time, we seemed to be making progress, but then toward the end of the quarter, his behavior went downhill quickly.

Johnny Beasley was involved with smoking in the lavatory. He was seen going into the lavatory and when I called him into my office, sure enough he had cigarettes stuffed in the top of his sock. I gave him a Saturday. A week later, same thing, only this time he had them stuffed into the waistband of his pants with his t-shirt hanging over them. He got another Saturday. A week later he was at it again, but no smokes on his person. I went back to the lavatory and noticed the ceiling tile askew. Sure enough, when I moved the tile and opened the hole to get a better look, I found two packs of cigarettes and a lighter.

He later moved on to marijuana, and I heard from the juvenile detective he and another boy were suspected of vandalism on the west end of town. The police were well aware of Johnny Beasley and had dealt with him and his parents numerous times, as well.

One of the last incidents I had to deal with started on a Monday and ended on a Thursday. Monday morning, before school started, my secretary, Marie Royster, came to me complaining about holes in the ceiling of the women's lavatory. She took me over, and after checking it was all clear, and took me in and pointed to the ceiling over the privacy stalls. Indeed, there were round holes, about the size of a quarter, almost perfect, without flaws. I didn't know what caused them or how long they'd been there, but I assured Marie, I'd have it taken care of immediately. I went to the back of the school and located Harry in his office. I asked him to replace the tiles. He told me he'd take care of it right away.

The next day, Marie came to me again complaining that the bathroom ceiling tiles had not been fixed. I called Harry and he insisted he put in new tiles just as I asked. I thanked him and asked him to replace them again, then I walked next door to the men's lavatory and had a look around. This part of the school had been torn down and rebuilt the previous year, so the lavatories were relatively new, which made the situation all the more infuriating. I opened one of the stall doors and saw a muddy tread of a footprint on the toilet seat. I entered the stall, put my foot on the commode, and found I could reach the ceiling tile. I was expecting to see a wall to the roof of the school when I pushed the tile up and over. I was shocked to find a wall that ran no more than four inches above the ceiling. An agile young man could get a grip and pull himself into the ceiling, straddle the wall, drill holes in the tile on the women's side and spend who knows how long being a peeping Tom, getting cheap thrills from his ceiling perch.

On Wednesday, I popped into the men's room as often as I could without being too obvious about it. I was hoping I'd enter and find my culprit in the ceiling, but no such luck. Not on Thursday either. I mentioned the issue to Dave Antonelli, and he said he would look into it. Five minutes before the official school day came to end, Marie's voice announced over the P.A. for Mr. Steve Powell to report to the Principal's office immediately. When I arrived, I saw Dave was seated in my office next to Johnny.

Dave launched right into an explanation before I even got to my chair: "I walked over to the lavatory after I left finishing a few things in the office to check out your story and when I looked into the ceiling, there were a pair of eyes looking back at me. Here's your culprit. When he came down out of the ceiling, he had a quarter in his hand."

"Thank you, Mr. Antonelli. On your way out of my office, would you ask my secretary to call Mr. and Mrs. Beasley for me?" I inquired.

"Sure thing." Dave was more than happy to get away. He had done his job and there was no need to be involved beyond turning Johnny in for his delinquency.

I turned my attention to the young culprit: "What do you have to say for yourself, Johnny?"

"Nothing." Nothing? That's all he had to say? Well, so much for confessing and asking for forgiveness. He was a challenging student, no doubt about it, but so many kids these days feel so little responsibility for their actions. It's really rather incredible.

I waited until his parents arrived to speak again. By the time they were seated in front of my desk with their son, I had time to decide a course of action. After explaining what their son had been up to, I handed down the consequences for his action. I was suspending him from school Friday, and Monday and Tuesday of the following week. The suspension would remain in effect beyond Wednesday or until they obtained a letter from a psychiatrist indicating Johnny was not a threat or a danger to the school and provided such to me.

Over the weekend, the custodial crew cut wooden tiles, painted them white, and screwed them into the ceiling frame. I was determined to prevent such a thing like this from ever happening again.

Mrs. Beasley brought Johnny back to school the following Friday with the required letter. She looked as if too much makeup was covering a bruise on the side of her face and Johnny had a swollen lip. I inquired, but neither of them would say a word about their battered faces. They gave me what clearly were orchestrated excuses. It was terribly sad, but I'm sure they were afraid to come forward or just plain ashamed that this had happened. After Johnny left for class and Mrs. Beasley departed, I called the Division of Youth and Family Services. I didn't know if they'd follow through, or if they did, if they would find anything damning, but I had to be as proactive as possible. It is the law as well as a moral obligation to report suspected abuse, especially against a child.

A few days later, I walked into the cafeteria and wouldn't you know it? There was Johnny wailing away on one of his classmates, Ricky Wilson. Johnny was bent over Ricky hitting him with both fists. I quietly snuck up behind Johnny, bent slightly, slipped my hands underneath his arms and connected them behind his neck to put him in a full nelson hold. The old wrestling move came in handy at times like this. Then I carried him out of the cafeteria and didn't put him down again until we were in the hallway. He was embarrassed but calm as I walked him to my office. I told him to sit still while I tracked down Ricky, and so we could settle the matter. When I returned to the cafeteria, one table made up of mostly wrestlers from our team stood up and gave me a standing ovation. I had an inner chuckle at their display of appreciation for my move. Ricky was okay, but still shaken from his ordeal. In my office, I gave each boy the opportunity to tell me what happened and discovered when Johnny spoke that Ricky had said some nasty things about Brenda that Johnny found offensive. After some back and forth about it, Johnny started throwing punches at Ricky, and then I entered the fray. Johnny apologized to Ricky for overreacting and it seemed to me to be a genuine effort. Ricky confessed that he did say a few unkind words about Brenda, and he shouldn't have spoken that way about her, and he wouldn't do it again. I sent Ricky to class without further punishment, but I had to suspend Johnny from school for punching another student. We had a zero-tolerance policy for aggression like this. Johnny's mother picked him up from school. She looked haggard and depressed, but then, who wouldn't be in her shoes?

REPORTER: "Did the Beasleys support your efforts to guide Johnny toward better behavior, and follow through at home?"

Yes and no. We had a problem with someone scuffing the lower part of the hallway walls with a black shoe. It left an ugly mark. For several days we were unable to catch whoever was doing it. But then the custodian, Mr. Roosevelt Decker, happened to be coming down the hall toward the main office and at the bend in the hallway there was a mirror and he saw it was Johnny. Needless to say, he brought Johnny to the office. I got Mr. Beasley to come in and told him I planned to punish Johnny by having him come in on Saturday morning for four hours to wash the walls and if necessary, paint. His father argued at first, but when I suggested an at-home suspension instead, he changed his tune. I suppose he didn't want to have to deal with Johnny at home or in the store.

REPORTER: "Do parents resist the school disciplining their child?"

That's the worst thing about my job as disciplinarian. Many parents cooperate, but some fight me. Some even threaten legal action. I had a sixth grader who defecated on the lavatory floor and then smeared it on the mirrors and walls. His teacher, Mr. Bryant, caught him and was furious when he came to see me and rightly so. I was able to track down the culprit and brought his father in for a meeting. I had Roosevelt lock the bathroom and leave everything as it was. When Dad arrived, I took him to the lavatory and showed him what his son had done and admitted to doing. Billy's father asked me what consequence his son would have. I told him that I expected he would stay after school and clean the lavatory from top to bottom. Dad cut me off and said, "My son's no janitor and he's not going to clean anything." I ended up suspending Billy from school. What a waste. I always try to make the consequence appropriate and applicable to the behavior. I had a seventh-grade girl grab and swing another girl's pocketbook hitting the jungle gym. A bottle of Wite-Out exploded and ruined the purse and its contents. To me, the natural consequence was to replace the damaged items, a purse, compact, comb, and the bottle of Wite-Out. When I called the young lady's father, however, he refused to have his daughter replace the damaged items. Imagine my shock to discover he was a police officer in a neighboring town. I then had to punish her in another manner. I don't know what parents are thinking sometimes. In fact, it seems to me that sometimes they don't think at all. Don't they realize that kids need to learn there are consequences for bad behavior? Don't they want their children to learn right from wrong? I got called to the cafeteria one day by our cafeteria worker, Alicia. She was concerned after seeing a seventhgrade boy pay for his lunch with a hundred-dollar bill. She reported to me that she saw several such bills in his hand. When I inquired about it with him, he bragged to me he had ten of them. I asked him to explain. He told me his parents went to New Zealand and Australia for two weeks and left him with the money to buy lunches at school and have dinners delivered in the evening. He was home alone.

REPORTER: "What did you do?"

I found out the boy's mother had a sister in a neighboring town. I called her and indicated she needed to provide supervision until his parents returned from their vacation. I also called the Division of Youth and Family Services.

I'm sorry, I could go on all day with one story after another and that's not what this interview is about.

REPORTER: "That's okay, I can see where what you do can be frustrating at those times you meet resistance instead of cooperation from parents."

I'll just close out this interview by saying that it wasn't too long after the shoe scuffing incident that Johnny was killed. I was saddened by it, but I wasn't totally surprised. It was almost as if his life was on a collision course with a preordained destiny. It just makes you wonder if there is a grand scheme, and if so, why it unfolds the way it does for some folks. Unfortunately, I firmly believe Johnny's father expected little, or the worst, from his son. He treated him poorly and made him feel like a bad egg, and the self-fulfilling prophecy took hold. You tell a kid he's bad often enough, sure enough he'll end up bad. Sad, really.

The JUVENILE DETECTIVE

"Do not train a child to learn by force

or harshness; but

direct them to it by what amuses

their minds." --Plato

REPORTER: "Detective Hollis, I want to thank you for agreeing to this interview. I was hoping you might share your impressions of Johnny Beasley with me. What can you add to what I've learned about him to date?"

I met Johnny shortly after he had the first blow up with his father. My name is Detective Steve Hollis and I came in contact with the Beasley family through my job as Juvenile Detective with the police. He was very sullen and angry. He and his father had thrown punches at one another and Johnny's mother called the police. After interviewing all the parties, it strongly appeared I was confronting an incorrigible child. When a parent has lost a child's respect and love, behavioral manifestations can be devastating for not only the family, but the school and community as well.

Sometimes these situations end up in juvenile court and are resolved by a judge who deems there to be little choice but to admit the youngster to the justice system. This could result in the youth entering juvenile hall, a halfway house, or, in extreme cases, military-style camps for troubled teens. Despite all of these efforts, however, some young men are so oppositional in their defiance of all authority, they ultimately end up in the adult criminal system.

I wasn't sure where Johnny Beasley would end up, but after so many encounters with him over several months, I knew chances of success were minimal. He seemed to go out of his way to create situations where he ended up in trouble, and as the months passed, the trouble was bigger and more flagrant.

He came to my attention for loitering, and minor vandalizing at first. Then, the problems with pills and marijuana surfaced. He began to pal around with another middle school student who was clearly a very negative influence. In fact, they were bad for each other. Neither one had any selfcontrol, and their impulsiveness led them down one wrong path after another.

If Johnny Beasley hadn't been killed when he was, I think the judge would have finally thrown the book at him and sent him to Ranch Hope, one of those rehabilitation camps with the sole goal of stopping misbehavior and incorrigibility.

As much as I tried, I couldn't get any cooperation or consistency in handling Johnny out of Mr. and

Mrs. Beasley. He was way too hard, and she coddled the boy way too much. Johnny Beasley might have been better off with a relative or, failing that, placed in a foster home.

The last time Johnny was in juvenile detention awaiting court disposition through adjudication, he was raped by one of his cell mates. After that, I suspected this young man would be even worse than before, and I was right. My job can be depressing; particularly, when I see a young life, with some potential, end up in the court of last resort, so to speak. And without question, Johnny had reached that status. He had hit rock bottom at the tender age of 14.

The MOTHER

"If there is anything we wish

to change in the child,

we should first

examine it and see

whether it is not something

that could better be

changed in ourselves." --

Carl Jung

REPORTER: "Mrs. Beasley, I'm terribly sorry for your great loss. I know this must be difficult, but I'm trying to learn how something like this could happen, and who would better know a son, then his mother. Tell me about you and Ralph. And then, tell me a little about your boy. What kind of a young man was he? What interests did he have? Did he like school? Was he a good student? Can you explain how this tragedy could happen?"

Johnny was a challenging child from the very beginning. I loved him with all my heart but raising him was not always a joyful experience. He was a really exhausting baby, crying all the time and needing tons of attention. We had tried for years to get pregnant, but it just didn't happen, and then one winter, I had a really bad cough and took a cough syrup which I had read in a magazine made it possible for people struggling with infertility to increase their chances of getting pregnant. Anyhow, it worked. I got pregnant with Johnny. I was forty-three, and my husband was forty-five. We were old parents and I don't mind admitting, it was difficult, which surprised us considering we

339

both came from large families. Two adults and one child didn't seem like it should be so hard.

Ralph had three older sisters, and his father's parents lived with them. Occasionally a cousin lived in the home as well. Despite having so many people around, Ralph from a very early age had to look after himself. His mother didn't have time to fuss over him or even keep the house clean. One experience stuck with Ralph, and although he didn't like to talk about it, he opened up to me a couple of times. He was about four or five years old at the time, taking a nap in his room when he felt something nibbling at his leg. The sensation awakened him. He reached down his leg to scratch at the itch and saw a big rat chewing on his ankle. He was bleeding profusely and screaming at the top of his lungs. Nobody responded. His mother and grandmother were on the porch, chatting, and drinking iced tea. They didn't hear Ralph's calls for help. He was scared to death. Eventually he fell asleep, and in the morning, he decided he would keep the rat bite to himself. He thought this would prove what a "big boy" he was. A couple of days later, though, he broke out in a rash and developed a high fever, and his mother noticed the wound. Ralph admitted then that he had been bitten and his mother took him to the doctor immediately. The doctor was worried about rabies and started Ralph on shots, which were exceedingly painful. It was a very expensive treatment and Ralph's father was stressed out about the cost. He beat Ralph and hung his belt on the back of Ralph's bedroom door as a reminder of what would happen next time if he kept important information from his parents. I don't think Ralph ever forgave his father for that beating and after that, he was never really close to the old man.

There were eight kids in my family (I was the fourth child), and we slept three to a bed. Each child helped raise the children who followed. We made do with what we had, which wasn't much, and all but two of us survived into adulthood. One of my sisters died from an abnormality of her heart at the age of twelve. She was what they called a blue baby. Any exercise would cause her to turn pale, almost blue, and then she had to lie down and rest. When my parents decided to see a heart specialist who thought the problem could be repaired, thy discovered the problem was far worse than anyone suspected. Sally's heart was upside down and on the wrong side of the body. Nothing could be done. The doctor closed her up again and she died shortly afterwards. We also lost one of my brothers, Bobby, who committed suicide when he was in high school. He wasn't a popular kid and so many of his classmates either bullied him or picked on him, and he couldn't take it anymore. My mother was always busy, working to help make ends meet, and didn't have much time for anything else. I imagine it was very hard for her. My father was generally a cheerful man, but he had a serious drinking problem, and it got in the way of family concerns and responsibilities. My brothers and sisters and I learned to look after each other and fend for ourselves.

I knew Ralph from the neighborhood. We'd gone through school together and dated all through high school, so nobody was surprised when Ralph and I eloped. We didn't have a place to live at first, so we had to live with his family. It was rough with no privacy and his mother always butting in and telling me what I was doing wrong. But we did save a lot of money and neither one of us was in a rush to have children. We were well aware that raising a family was very expensive. We decided to wait and limit any children we'd have to two. I'd lie awake at night thinking about being a mother and having a baby girl. I'd name her Yvonne, which I thought at the time, was a sophisticated and beautiful name. I'd call her Evie for short. I dreamed of singing songs to her like "You Are My Sunshine" and "Mama's Little Baby Loves Shortnin Bread." Ralph was reluctant to start a family, but I finally convinced him it was time. Only it wasn't time. We tried for almost three years, and nothing. We gave up trying to get pregnant. That was hard for me. I felt so low, and ashamed of my failure to conceive that I couldn't get out of bed. It seemed as if everybody I knew was having babies, and every place I went there were babies. I became depressed and lost my appetite. My clothing hung on me as the pounds melted away and Ralph wouldn't pay for any new dresses. I had bad thoughts at times, including thoughts about killing myself. And then, funny how things work out. I'd read an article about cough medicine helping infertile women get pregnant. I thought at the time it was too good to be true. But then, I got a really bad cold and hacking cough and of course, took cough medicine. Sure enough, nine months later I delivered Johnny. It was a miracle! While I was pregnant, I painted a room for my baby and decorated it as well. Those nine months were glorious days for me. On the day I went into labor, everything happened according to the textbook. I had no complications at all. When my contractions started on a Sunday after dinner, Ralph was calm and drove me to the hospital. I wasn't worried at all. The delivery was relatively quick and easy, and Johnny was a healthy baby, twenty-two inches long and eight and a half pounds. I will admit that I was a little disappointed because I was sure I was having a girl, but Ralph was beaming and even kissed my forehead and held my hand. He promised me he'd repaint the child's room blue from the pink I had used. I thought that was sweet and it comforted me. I really enjoyed holding my baby boy and didn't want to give him back to the nurses when it was time.

We left the hospital two days later and went home. I was looking forward to the challenges of motherhood, but Ralph soon wearied of the responsibilities of fatherhood and wanted nothing to do with Johnny, so it was all up to me to deal with all an infant's needs, and Johnny was demanding. I thought I was going out of my mind. I was tired all the time. The baby couldn't be alone for a minute. It was ridiculous. He would wail as if I disappeared forever when I walked out of the room and carry on like his world was coming to an end if he soiled himself. I was up around the clock on a regular basis. And it's no surprise that this took a huge toll on our marriage. Ralph couldn't stand all the crying and stayed at the store later and later, often coming home after Johnny was in the crib for the night. Once in a while, Ralph didn't come home at all. I know he was unhappy with our sex life, which was almost non-existent, but I just plain didn't feel like it. I was too tired, and I wasn't ever in the mood for romance in those days. I had too many other things on my plate.

I managed childcare and the house without any help from Ralph or anyone else. We had no family living in the area. It would have been nice to have a mother or mother-in-law to help occasionally. Someone who could give me a brief break. Someone to understand what I was going through. Someone I could count on, unlike Ralph, who wouldn't even listen to me or give me a pat on the back for doing a good job.

Even though I wasn't especially happy, I was proud that I was a great mother. I fed my son, bathed him, dressed him, bought him toys to stimulate his brain. I did everything for him. As you might imagine, I had my hands full, but eventually, I learned to tune out Johnny's fussing, I was so used to it. I would put him in his crib and let him have at it, while I took care of other things I needed to do, like running the wash and cleaning the house. With Ralph out of the house so much, I turned my mind to projects I wanted to tackle. I made homemade Christmas cards, reorganized all the closets, painted the kitchen, and did some knitting. I never seemed able to finish my projects, though, because sometimes Johnny would throw up from all the screaming and upset, and then I was forced to change the sheets and do more laundry. On top of that, sometimes my projects were sidelined by phone calls, or I'd be distracted by a television show. There always seemed something in the way of finishing something I'd started. The house, most of the time, was a mess, and I felt fat and ugly. It made me cry. I had tearful bouts that lasted maybe an hour or more. Sometimes, I was overwhelmed by a feeling I didn't want to live any more. My heart would race as I contemplated taking my own life. My game plan varied, but I kept coming back to the same idea. I would cross into oncoming traffic as I drove. I shook these thoughts off. I couldn't really involve someone else who might be killed or seriously injured. I calmed myself down over a pint of Chunky Monkey ice cream, drink two or three or four glasses of wine, and pop a couple of sleeping pills. Then, I would get some rest, and when I awoke, it would be the same problems all over again.

Ralph was generally in a lousy mood when he was home. He never held the baby and he rarely talked to me. I tried to talk him into going to a family counselor or clergy to get some help for our marriage, but he thought that was a sign of weakness and refused. Maybe he was right. Neither of our families would ever air family troubles. They were private and nobody's business. Both our parents would have seen seeking outside help as being weak.

Eventually, the baby got past his colic, and things settled down at home for a few years. As a young child, Johnny liked watching television, playing video games, and listening to music. He always had a pair of headphones on and was plugged in to some gadget or other. He wasn't much into anything else. He was very much a loner, content to play by himself. It didn't help matters much Johnny wasn't really athletic. If he played sports, maybe that would have helped him meet other kids and become friends with them, but Johnny was an indoor kind of kid.

Johnny learned how to read in school. My husband and I aren't big readers, and we didn't read to Johnny very often, I'll admit, but Johnny didn't seem to have much difficulty learning how to read. He passed his classes with normal grades, nothing outstanding and nothing worrying, and at that time, he didn't get into much trouble. Teachers didn't call us in for conferences on a regular basis in those days. They really didn't have much to say about him at all, as far as I can recall. I only remember one time when Johnny was in fifth grade when he got into trouble. He was accused of bullying a female classmate. He called her a dummy and told her she was a fat loser. Johnny' had to apologize to the girl and he received an athome suspension for three days. We spanked him for his bad behavior, but times were tough then, and I had to put more time in at our store, because Ralph couldn't afford any help. Consequently, the suspensions landed up being like a holiday because Johnny got to stay at home and watch television all day. We couldn't stay at home and supervise our son and he would have been in the way if we took him with us to the store.

When Johnny got to the middle school, he started acting out in many different ways. I know adolescence can be a difficult time period for kids, but his behavior was over the top. It was like he was on a mission to piss off his father and punish me. I wasn't going down that road again. He'd taken enough years off my life early on, and now it was my time, time for me and me alone. If he pretended to be sick, I let him stay home from school. If he complained about dinner, I just walked away like I never even heard him. Once he threw dinner in the garbage, but Ralph came in as Johnny was in the midst of his tantrum, and my husband had such a look of despair in his eyes as he grabbed our boy by the back of the neck and forcibly stuck his head in the trash can and made him eat what he'd just thrown out. Ralph was yelling, and spitting as he did so, about being an ingrate and good-for-nothing little shit. When he finally let go, Johnny stood up and the look he gave us before he ran out of the house terrified me.

Johnny dyed his hair blue one day, and a week later it was green. Another time, he wore eyeliner and mascara. His father freaked out over that. Then he pierced his nose with that stupid gold ring. Ralph and I got into a fight over how to handle this more challenging Johnny. Our son was splitting us a part, but even though I defended my boy as any loving mother would, I had to admit to myself, his behavior was becoming worse and worse, and more indefensible. Customers would come into the store and ask us, "What's up with your son?" or "What's gotten into your son? Is he a fairy?" Ralph was mortified and I think it tipped the scales toward Ralph hating our son. I argued that Johnny just wanted to be noticed, to be different, to be himself, to be somebody. Ralph yelled at me, "Somebody, my ass! You've got to work to be somebody. It isn't being a look-alike for a circus clown or a neon pin cushion that makes somebody special or unique." We seemed to fight and argue more and more, and it always seemed to get downright nasty. After that, more and more, Johnny would sneak out of our second-floor apartment over the store at all hours of the night. I found cigarettes and a lighter in his room, and later I found marijuana. I know we were young once and did some pretty foolish things and broke the rules, but this was different. It was sick. Johnny needed help, and I didn't know where to turn or what I could do. Ralph pretty much made all the decisions and he wouldn't allow me to take Johnny to a psychiatrist. And then, it was over. Johnny passed away. It was just so sudden. I felt lost and alone. Ralph was no comfort to me. I cried for days and felt terrible. I had no motivation. Then, slowly it sank in – maybe it was for the best. I know that sounds horrible when I say it out loud, but the way Johnny was going, he might have done something really bad, hurt someone, or maybe even killed them.

The GIRLFRIEND

"A child is not born loving or

hateful. Love and hate are

learned. We have to learn to use

ourselves to teach young people

to learn to love." --

Jack Frymier

REPORTER: "Brenda, it's my understanding that you more than any other student were close to Johnny. What features or qualities about him do you remember more than any other?"

Johnny was really a sensitive and thoughtful guy, but I don't think many people saw that side of him. They didn't see his hidden talents. Of course, I got pretty close and maybe he was different around me. People often hide their real personalities. They act like somebody they aren't, so they are perceived as cool, or strong. Nobody likes to be laughed at. When Johnny got to know me really well, we shared everything. He wrote me letters and stuff and I could tell there was hurt deep inside of him. He had trouble getting along with his parents and with some of the kids at school, and it bothered him more than he let on. Johnny wrote a poem about it, which I thought was pretty good. I carry it around with me:

Living as a Process I've

seen my

needs fatly fed,

like children at a

picnic, with clothes,

toys, and

tangibles,

and they to empty

rhetoric.

I've seen my

hopes glimmer,

like tapers in

the morning, to

bloom

translucently,

then wither

without warning.

I've heard the

words crafted,

like a sculptor

sculpts his bust,

carving away the

meaning,

leaving nothing

that is just.

I've felt my

heart emptied,

like fallen logs

grown hollow,

to disengage my

parents,

and lies I could

not swallow.

I've seen my

memories

like smoke drifting

through the air, to

rendezvous en

mass,

descending to

despair.

I've seen my

happiness in tatters,   all
hope mashed

into a mess,   my

future has been

shattered,

into a lifelong loneliness.

   It's a sad poem, but Johnny was like that. He was thoughtful, sensitive and at times, oh, I don't know, deep. He could surprise you with what was going on in his head sometimes. I don't think his parents ever knew him, never really knew he was. I don't know if they cared to know. They certainly didn't try.

   We met in art class. Our teacher, Miss Day, played classical music and allowed everyone to work at their own pace on the assigned projects. The first project was a drawing of a landscape in charcoal. Everyone was busy working away and there I was staring at my blank piece of paper, wondering what to do. I'm not an outdoorsy kind of person and nothing came to mind. There was a stack of magazines in the corner of the room, so I walked over to take a look and hopefully find some scene to draw. I had to pass Johnny's seat. We were only ten minutes into class, and I noticed he had already done so much, and his landscape was really, really good. I introduced myself to him and told him I loved his drawing and he asked me how my drawing was going. I had to admit I didn't have a clue how to get started. Johnny took me to the stack of magazines and helped me find a *National*

Geographic that had some great outdoor scenes. He even pointed one out that he thought would be the easiest for me to draw. He wasn't bragging. He was just happy to help me. I liked him instantly. Anyway, that's how we met.

Mostly, Johnny and I spent time together at school, and sometimes he'd hike over to the park near my neighborhood and we'd see each other. Neither of us could drive yet, so we were pretty much dependent on our parents for transportation, and Johnny's folks could give two shits about taking turns, so they rarely drove him to my house, or anywhere else for that matter. Sometimes, I would catch a ride with mom to his apartment over the store, but I didn't like to go there if his parents were around. They were always yelling at Johnny for something, you know, demeaning him in front of me. I could tell he was boiling angry. It was tense. But if they weren't there, then his place was better than mine. He had a large bedroom and it had a couch and a long drawing table with a number of sketches and drawings. I liked to watch him work. His face got so serious, really intent as he concentrated on each line, each stroke, as if it had to be just so. He really cared about how his art turned out. He took pride in his work.

We spent a lot of time just talking. We spoke about our hopes and dreams sometimes, but mostly about music, Johnny's art, what was happening in our school. Things that were important to us. Once in a while we'd talk about places we wanted to see, also. Places we'd read about in our history class or seen on television shows. We both thought Chicago seemed like a cool city. We joked about taking a road trip there one day when we could drive, but neither of us took that too seriously. Occasionally, we talked about our families, but those conversations were mostly depressing. He didn't get along with his parents all that well, and my mom moved out. Dad didn't handle that well and seemed extra hard on me after she left. I don't know if he blamed me for her leaving or what, but times were often tense at my house, too. Johnny hated the constant screaming, yelling, and threatening going on at his house. He was lonely. I was too. We helped each other deal with it.

REPORTER: "What can you tell me about Johnny's art? Does any of his work stick out in your memory?"

He liked working with charcoal and ink, mostly. He did watercolors, too, and some of them were really beautiful. When I first met him, he was really into landscape drawings, mostly scenes around the city that he found interesting. He carried a bag with sketch pads, pencils, and charcoal, everywhere he went. So, he did a lot of his art after school.

One of my favorite sketches was of some homeless guy smoking outside of a pizza joint. Now that I think about it, I wonder if he really was a homeless guy or if it was Slice? I never met him myself, so I don't know what he looks like. Slice was a friend of Johnny's, but Slice made some people nervous. Everyone who smoked marijuana got it through Slice, but otherwise they didn't have much to do with him. But Johnny thought Slice was pretty cool and they spent a lot of time together and he kept Slice company sometimes when he did deliveries. Johnny didn't come home until late at night on those nights, but his parents didn't seem to care.

Later in the year, after we were no longer in art class together, Johnny and I didn't see as much of each other in school. It got kind of awkward and we didn't make any effort to get together after a while. During that time, I saw one of his pictures in the big art contest at school. It was a close-up of a tattooed hand, with the thumb and index finger of a left hand pointing up and the other three fingers curled under. I stared at this work for a long time. Something disturbed me about the tattoo visible on the wrist. The tattoo was super creepy looking; it was a boy's head, but it had no eyes, like they had fallen out. Tears running down the face formed a pool under the head, and the eyes were floating in that pool. It was if the boy had actually cried his eyes out. It made me want to cry along with him.

Something must have happened to make Johnny create a picture like that and hang it in public. The fingernails were black and the way the hand was shaded made it look dirty. He really made that hand come alive with the shading of the charcoal. He won the blue ribbon for most original work. I didn't say anything to Johnny about it, because we weren't really talking at that point, but I was happy for him.

REPORTER: "Why weren't you seeing Johnny? Had you broken up for good?"   Johnny was pretty frustrated with his home life and he started getting too dark and too moody for me. He got in more and more trouble in school, too. Mr. Warren, the social studies teacher, was one of the few adults he liked and respected, but everyone else, he gave a hard time. Johnny was really impressed that he cared enough to write letters to his students. Sincere letters that really conveyed his concern for us, and he did everything he could to help his students. He even went to Saturday Suspensions to help Johnny with his schoolwork. I wasn't crazy about what Johnny was doing, but I didn't want to break up with him. I still liked Johnny and hoped he'd lighten up again. The real problem was my dad heard the rumors about Johnny and he wouldn't believe me that he had nothing to worry about. He insisted that I stop seeing Johnny immediately, and he said he never wanted to hear another word about him.

A few days after dad's order, Johnny and I made secret plans to get together, but my dad found out about our plan before we met. He went ballistic. I never seen him so angry. He told me I was done with that good-for-nothing, Johnny Beasley and if he caught me like this again, I would be the sorriest girl alive. I was really upset and scared that Johnny would break up with me, but no amount of pleading made my dad change his mind. I locked myself in the bathroom with a knife and cried. I was cutting myself back then, and I cut myself deeper than I planned. I must have hit a vein or artery or something because blood started gushing out of my arm like a geyser. I started screaming and ran into the kitchen, still carrying the knife. My father was drinking coffee at the kitchen table. When he saw the blood, he jumped up and took off his belt, then wrapped it around my arm and tightened it like a tourniquet. He drove me to the emergency room at the hospital and a really nice doctor in the ER fixed me up. Afterward, she had a long talk with my dad and me, insisting that I get therapy. She gave us some names and my father told me that he was going to find someone who would see me right away. I was surprised by my dad's actions and knew he must really care about me even though he doesn't always show it. He didn't say any more about Johnny and neither did I. I didn't want to go to school and for a few days, Dad let me stay home, but then he insisted it was time to snap out of my funk. When I returned to school, I avoided Johnny as much as possible and refused to talk to him. I didn't know what to say, and I really didn't want to deal with it. But looking back now, he must have felt terrible, not knowing why I dropped him so, so, so abruptly. After that Johnny started getting in even more trouble, in school and outside of school. I didn't know things would turn out the way they did. I heard the gossip about him, and I just couldn't believe it was the same Johnny I knew.

I can't believe how this all ended for him. I feel guilty and wonder if I am responsible for what happened. And every time I look at myself in the mirror, I don't like what I see. Maybe I made him feel so bad about himself, so alone, that he stopped believing that anybody cared about him anymore or that anyone ever would. Oh my God, how could I have been so stupid? If I could go back and do it all over again, I would tell Johnny how sorry I am that I stopped talking to him. I want him to know it wasn't his fault.

THE FATHER

"Excusing personal

accountability

encourages a sense of helplessness, which leads to

an unbroken cycle of abuse, counter abuse, excuse

and violence."

- Alan M. Dershowitz

REPORTER: "Can you tell me a little bit about your son? What kind of a boy was he really, Mr. Beasley? What interests did he have? Did he like school? What kind of relationship did the two of you have?"

I'm not sure what went wrong with our family, but I guess I'd have to say, after thinking on it awhile, something the Mrs. and I did, or didn't do, played a big part in all of this mess. My old man was a "spare the rod, spoil the child" kind of guy. He said jump, and I asked how high. He was demanding and tough on the whole family and we all grew up okay.

We gave Johnny everything. Maybe he was just an ingrate, maybe he was bad in his genes. You know, some people just aren't decent people, and no matter how much discipline you give them, they won't or can't change.

I'm not sure about much anymore after this all happened, but I do think folks fall into four categories. There's a small group of what I call the "easy be's." They're your natural successes and no matter what they do, their shit don't

stink. They always come out smelling like a chocolate factory, but so much so, after a while they just plain make you nauseous. They make you want to bend over and puke. Then, you have another group I call the "going to be's." This group is a large group. They plug really hard, you know, work their asses off for what successes they achieve. And you better believe me, this group gets their full share, because they don't give up, they persevere. My old man was one of these bastards. Next, you've got an even larger group I call the "want-to be's." These poor slobs shine once in a while, but generally they ain't got the gumption, the stick-to-itiveness to really make something of themselves. They kind of float through life, not really making much of a mark on things. I don't feel any pity for this group, damn inconsistent sons-ofbitches. Finally, you've got the "never going to be's." This group is small too and they aren't worth a spit. They've got no desire, no pride, and they make little to no effort to do any goddamn thing about their woeful lot in life.

Now you know this you'll understand when I tell you, my son, Johnny Beasley, was a first class, "A" number one "never be." Oh, maybe not from the start, he wasn't, but when he hit adolescence, I couldn't get him to do shit. The older he became, the more insolent he grew, and I couldn't seem to do anything to stop it or prevent it from getting worse. He didn't listen to me, and he goddamn well didn't listen to his mother. The school people all had their hands full with him and his shenanigans. Yeah, I'd chastise him and get after him just like any parent would, but hey, kids today, what are you going to do?

Nothing we did, the Mrs. and I, nor the school, or the police and juvenile court did, made any difference. Hell, you know as well as I do, you can't shine shit! Johnny was a zero. I hate to admit it, because he sprang from my loins, but he was worthless, a fucking waste, and he single handedly tore our family apart. You give a kid, your kid, everything money can buy and more, and they take it all for granted. Why, it's enough to send parents to an early grave.

I worked hard for everything I got in life and I passed it on to him, and what the hell did I get in return? Nothing but fucking headaches. That little bastard. He gave me nothing but heartaches.

REPORTER: "Was there ever a time when Johnny wasn't difficult?"

Yeah, I got him involved in scouting and we went camping a lot during those early years. I bought a small boat and we'd drive up to the lake and set up a tent and fish for a couple of hours and while I cooked dinner, he'd go swimming by the edge of the shore. But shit, he got to be twelve or thirteen and it didn't interest him no more. I tried to get him involved in ball, you know, little league baseball or pee wee football, but it didn't fit him. My wife wanted to put him in an art camp, but that stuff's for girls and fags. I wouldn't allow it. Sometimes a man has to put his foot down. Hell, I wear the pants in my family. And shoot, I didn't think he was one of them at the time, but maybe he was heading in that direction.

My dad had a hobby whittling wood, and he taught me, although I was never as good as the old man. I thought, well if he isn't interested in camping anymore, maybe I could interest him in wood carving, and it would be something we could do together. But as always, he knew it all. He wouldn't follow my directions, then I'd get angry and before long we'd be at each other's throats. It was a terrible idea. Johnny had no patience to work with me and take directions intended to help him. What a sorry-ass kid.

All the moves we had to make once he was in middle school cost me a lot of money. I never really got what my store was worth, but we had to sell. I was at a point, I couldn't afford to hire anyone. It was just me, and occasionally the old lady would pitch in, but what a worthless good-for-nothing she was. I might as well have been doing everything by myself. She got hooked on her television shows, and booze, and then those friggin pills. Life's hard enough and then some dopes make it even harder, turn it into a living hell. Me and the old lady just began to lose it when the times got tough. I reached a point where I pretty much gave up on everything and everybody but my store.

I thought Johnny needed tough love. I was even considering having him declared incorrigible and asking the judge to send him to one of those boot camps to straighten him out, but I put off talking to Edna about it. I didn't want to listen to her sniffling about how that was too harsh. Hell, nothing we tried to that point had worked very well. I just didn't have the time nor the money to keep hiring temporary help or closing the store to go deal with my son's behavioral problems. I did sit him down and explain all that. I thought maybe if he knew the score, what it was costing the family, he'd make an effort to toe the line. That worked for all of a few days and then he was back to his antics again. And then he was gone. for good.

THE FRIEND "Of

course, new

friends are good to

have as well, but for

all their worth, they're

not the same.

We have such

small assurances of their

constancy; nor

can we feel as

sure they truly want

us in this shape, we're

in.

-- Wilson H. Ivins

REPORTER: "I'm told you were Johnny's best friend, some even say, his only friend. What can you tell me about him? What was he really like?

If he shared his innermost thoughts with you, what were they?"

I first met Johnny at the mall, but I really didn't get to know him well until he and I spent a lot of time skateboarding. At school, we were in some classes together and we hung out at lunch time and on the playground. After school, we started spending more and more time together. I didn't have many friends and Johnny was probably more important to me, than I was to him. I'm not sure he really needed me. There were times we were together, but not really. He could zone out into his own world. We spent time at the mall, sometimes the library where we could most always find Brenda, occasionally the rec center, but we got abused by a number of the jocks that hung out there. Sometimes, he'd take me to the ice cream parlor and buy me a milkshake.

I think my friend hated school almost as much as I did. It's so hard to fit in and some kids are real dipshits – they look for ways to make fun and bully other kids. I seemed to be an easy target, but Johnny stuck up for me. We tried to avoid those uptown snots as much as we could. We'd go to the park and smoke, cigarettes at first and then kush. I don't know where Johnny got it, but I know once every week or two he'd take a bus into the city and when he came back, he always had a good supply. Once in a while, he'd go in his parents' medicine cabinet and slip some pills out of his old lady's containers. He always claimed she never missed them. He said she was in a fog most of the time and didn't know her ass from page eight.

REPORTER: "I know Johnny was in trouble a lot at school. Were you too?"

Yeah, most of the time, I just followed his lead. I didn't like school and my grades were bad, but it was okay because my parents didn't give a shit. You know, the old man was always working and then hitting the bars after work. My mom worked a lot too, and she got mad at both my dad and me. He didn't take any crap from her and slapped some sense into her whenever she got too mouthy. Then, the night before school began this year, he came home late. He was drunk and the old lady made the mistake of getting out of bed and confronting him on the stairs. Boy, did he lay a hurtin' on her, and the next day she was long gone. What a stupid bitch. Hell, I know enough to lay low when the old man's been drinking. We haven't seen her since, but it gave Johnny and me the run of the house.

One afternoon, he came home early, he was sick, and caught Johnny and me smoking. He came after me, but we ran through the house and out the back door into the woods. He gave up the chase. That's when my friend and me run off. We both needed a break from our parents. I didn't know where we were going or what we'd do when we got there, but Johnny was cool. He told me he'd been slipping money out of his mom's food charge and had saved up over a hundred bucks. We figured we could eat for a week, but not in town. It'd be too easy for the Juvie Hollis to find us and pick us up. We got on a bus and rode into the city. Johnny knew a guy named Slice we could crash with. He was Johnny's dealer and they were friends. So, we went to Slice's apartment, and after slipping him sixty, he told Johnny we were good for one week, but we had to sleep on the floor.

Mostly, we stayed in Slice's apartment smoking and watching tv. A couple of days we went to the movies and roamed the streets. We sure didn't miss our parents or school. After a week, we were out of cash and Slice said hit the road. We had enough for the bus and riding home, Johnny said not to worry about it. He said he had a plan for a longer break from our shitty lives.

He talked about taking money from his old man's store, and his old lady's stash, hidden in her bureau. He said we could make our way across the country to Los Angeles. He promised we'd have the trip of our lives and we'd never have to be bothered by parents again. I believed him. Well, I wanted to believe him. I was tired of being slapped around every time my old man came home drunk or high and kicked the living shit out of me.

But that plan fell apart the night we were going to steal the money from the store. It sounded so easy to get in, get it, and get out. I'd been dreaming of sunny California at night. And then, it all went up in smoke.

You know, I can't believe the only friend I had is dead. I miss him.

The ARTIST

"Every child is an artist.

The problem is how to

remain an artist once

we grow

up.

-- Pablo Picasso

REPORTER: "Ms. Dunhill, I understand you mentored Johnny in your art shop. Tell me about your first impression of him."

I have an art supply store in one side of a duplex and an art studio in the other side, but they're both called April's. I noticed Johnny in front of my shop a number of times. He was hanging around smoking and sketching in an art pad. He was usually by himself and he appeared to be very absorbed in his work. He was around 13 or so. I don't have any kids of my own, but it worried me to see someone so young smoking and spending so much time by himself. I felt a motherly instinct as I watched from my window day in and day out. I started thinking that maybe I should just go talk to him, make some excuse so I could find out what his story was. Since he had the sketch pad and I own an art shop, I figured I'd ask him to show me his work. I didn't really expect much, but I thought this approach would seem natural. **REPORTER: "What happened?"**

Well, it was a cloudy, miserable day in late October, and I didn't have any customers in my store, so I hung up my "Be Right Back" sign on the door – it's the sign I use when I take a lunch break in the back – locked up and headed his way. I introduced myself as April Dunhill and told him that I'd often seen him sketching outside my store and I was curious if he would be interested in showing me his work. His eyes got really big, and for a moment I thought he might not allow me to take a look, but he said really quietly while looking at the ground that he was willing to show me his art but warned me not to expect much since he was not that good, yet. Well, I took the sketch book from him and was amazed. This boy could draw. He had a very keen eye and an amazing perspective. Somehow, he managed to make ordinary buildings look as if they were in conversation with one another. I couldn't help myself. I was sincerely excited about what I was viewing and exclaimed, "Wow! That's fantastic!" and "I love this one!" and a bunch of other positive responses to each turn of the page revealing another wonderful, marvelous sketch, and he could tell I meant it. He told me his name was Johnny and added he hoped one day to go to art school, but he had a lot to learn first. I invited him to come take a look at my own work as well as art pieces I sold and pointed toward the window. He told me that he had to go home but he'd come another day if that was okay with me. I responded that it was fine with me and suggested if he wanted art lessons maybe I could work something out with his parents. He lit another cigarette and off he went.

About two or three weeks later, Johnny showed up at my store. I was working with a customer, but I encouraged him to come in and take a look around at the art and all the supplies for sale, and urged him to look at the studio, which he did. When I was able to give him my attention, he asked me if there was any way he could work for me in exchange for lessons since his family would not be able to pay for them. I replied as a matter of fact, I thought we could work something out as long as he had written permission from his parents. It still made me a bit nervous that this young kid's parents didn't seem to be very involved in his life. I'm not sure if he even approached them for money for lessons, but he did return my permission form with his mother's signature. I felt confident I could make a connection with Johnny over time and help him in some way, but first I wanted to make sure he was being cared for and secondly, I wanted to protect myself. These days there are so many scandalous stories circulating in the news about adult misconduct with children, I didn't want anyone to get the wrong impression. I insisted that mom sign a permission slip for her son to volunteer in the store in exchange for free art lessons and required her to meet me in person on the first day he worked at my store. She joined him and seemed like a nice enough woman, maybe a little overwhelmed. She was wearing a housecoat and looked a mess. Her hair was disheveled, and she wore no makeup. She kind of reminded me of Edith on the old television show with Archie Bunker as the main character. What was that called again? *All in the Family*? Yeah, I think that's what it was called. Anyway, I told her I could really use some help at the store, especially when I am busy or I have to run an errand or two during the afternoon or on a Saturday, but I just didn't have the money to pay someone right now. She said that this would be fine by her and her husband as well, especially since Johnny was doing God knows what after school and on the weekends and this would be a more productive use of his time than whatever he was up to on his own. It all seemed straightforward and "normal" to me. I thanked her and reassured her she was welcome to come to the store and check on Johnny whenever he was working or taking one of his art lessons. We parted on good terms.

REPORTER: "That seems so caring of you. Were you at all nervous about what you were taking on by this offer?"

Maybe I should have been, but I am just one of those people who acts before thinking things through thoroughly, and I'm a glass half full kind of person. I look on the bright side. As far as being caring, I guess looking back, it was a caring act. I actually considered becoming a social worker before I pursued my interests in art. But being completely honest, I wasn't just doing it because I'm a caring individual. I really did need some help around the store. And, the fact of the matter, I thought Johnny was talented and I wanted to nurture his craft. I thought I had some skills and insights which would help him grow artistically.

REPORTER: "Tell me what it was like to work with Johnny. Was he responsible? Did he appreciate what you were doing for him?

I think he was very appreciative. He always thanked me when it was time for him to leave. I liked that. He was young and of course, sometimes he made mistakes when he rang up sales on the register, and he wasn't exactly gung-ho talking with customers, but he stocked the shelves and swept the store without complaining. I trusted him. When I ran errands and left him in charge, upon my return, he was busy doing what I had given him to do in my absence. None of my stock or money was ever missing, and I was never really worried that he would steal from me. He showed up on time and worked hard. And he took his art lessons seriously. I felt good about his prospects.

REPORTER: "Can you tell me about your lessons with him?"

Sure. The first thing we worked on was shading. Johnny caught on quickly and he was very devoted to practicing this skill. He filled entire notebooks practicing until he got the hang of it. I was impressed by his dedication.

After this, I showed Johnny a list of portfolio requirements for different art schools in the area and asked him if this looked like something he still wanted to study. Johnny enthusiastically said he did, so we began mapping out a long-term plan that would take him all the way through his high school years. My intention was to give Johnny goals and a structure for achieving these goals. If he still wanted to go to art school when he graduated high school, he would be prepared and competitive with kids who had far more advanced art programs in their school system. If he changed his mind, his time with me would still pay off because it would give him something to strive for in these critical years, something that gave him hope and filled him with desire to make a better future for himself.

I was devastated when...Um. This is upsetting me. I think I'm going to cry now. Are we done, or can we finish later?

REPORTER: "I have just one more question, if you think you are up to it."

Okay. I'll try.

REPORTER: "Did you ever suspect that Johnny was having trouble at home, or in the community?"

I did. It took some time for Johnny to open up to me, but about a month before his death he'd pour his heart out about his problems almost every time we were together. I cried a couple of times and the last time he cried with me. I'm ashamed to admit all this to you.

REPORTER: "Why?"

Well, for starters, I think it makes me look pretty needy, trying to be a big hero in all this by trying to save a troubled teen. And then, of course, for the obvious reason that I couldn't save him. I didn't save him. For all I did do, it wasn't enough. I'll have to live with that forever. I need to end this now. Please leave.

THE ASSOCIATED PRESS RELEASE

"Language is by all odds the

most subtle and powerful

technique we have for

controlling other people."

-- George A. Miller

REPORTER: "This story, inside the fold, piqued my curiosity and prodded me to approach my editor for permission to follow up. I wanted to interview people who knew Johnny well and, of course, Mr. and Mrs. Beasley too. I wanted to report to the readers who Johnny Beasley was and how such a tragedy could possibly occur. And to my delight, Stan said, "Go for it, Gwen.""

The following is the story compiled about Johnny

Storekeeper kills son during home/store

break-in Associated Press

Apalachicola, FL.

Shopkeeper, Ralph Beasley, hit on the head with a meat mallet by a young thief four months ago decided to fight back Thursday when an intruder broke into his store in the predawn hours. The young man he killed with his pistol, however, was his 14-year-old son, Johnny Beasley.

Beasley, 59, was not arrested charged. Police called the shooting justifiable homicide. "I guess you could say the father took the law into his own hands," said one unidentified officer who had arrested the youth before. "He finally got fed up with his kid's bad behavior. The elder Beasley would not immediately talk to reporters.

According to police sources in Apalachicola, young Beasley had been arrested seven times in the last two years for vandalism, shop-lifting, and possession of a dangerous substance. Police say Beasley surprised the intruder who appeared to be armed with a gun. He then shot the intruder to death.

"At some point during the confrontation," said Lt. Lester Browner of the County Sheriff's office, "we believe he knew it was his son." During the attempted robbery, Beasley, armed with a .38- caliber special, fired the weapon at his son. The eighth grader was shot once in the chest.

"Daddy, Daddy, why'd you shoot me?" the young man cried out, according to an unnamed source.

A teacher of Johnny Beasley, from the Jefferson Davis Middle School, Mr. Skip Warren, said that Johnny

Beasley was reasonably bright, but struggled with social and behavioral issues.

According to Warren, "He [Johnny] was a distant kid. He had few friends. It seemed as if he carried a hidden anger or resentment with him all the time, and it could surface at any time. He never really gave the other students a chance to get to know him. He wouldn't let too many people in, and few knew he was very artistic."

Another school source indicated the younger Beasley's behavior had been in a downward spiral for most of the school year. The more bizarre his appearance became, the more dangerous and extreme his behavior became too.

"Johnny planned on attending an art school after he graduated from high school," his mother said. She added, "He was a good son for a long time. He just wanted to be accepted for who he was and not for what everyone wanted him to be. He never really had a chance. Kids today are just so damned cruel."

Johnny's girlfriend, Brenda Zoppa, told this reporter her boyfriend was a sensitive, caring boy, who was mostly misunderstood. She claimed, "he was multi-talented with fantastic artistic abilities and poetry and song-writing skills."

She indicated he had just a few friends, but the ones he had were loyal.

Police said the senior Beasley had been a victim of several robbery attempts in recent months – including an incident about three or four months ago when a 13-year old boy attacked him with a meat mallet.

Young Beasley reportedly was arrested three times in one four-day period in the month before his death. "The old man was getting pretty tired of bailing his boy out," a police source told this reporter. "He was just plum worn out; Johnny exhausted his patience and his bank account," the source went on to say.

EPILOGUE

"There's no tragedy in life

like the death of a child.

things never get back to the

way they were."

-- Dwight D. Eisenhower

Beasley and his death by reporter Gwen Williamson as it appeared in *New Day* magazine.

ONE BOY'S STORY or A MODERN TRAGEDY by Gwen Williamson

Johnny Beasley's story is a modern American tragedy occurring all too often in a society moving at breakneck speed, casting aside extended families, a staple of a growing nation, and now placing too many nuclear families in jeopardy. We are witnessing a disintegration of values that regulated, that influenced, society's behavior for centuries, helping to define our country.

"Why," you ask? A combination of factors presents in everyday life, but usually not altogether in one family circle, settled into the Beasley family wreaking havoc and ultimately destroying all its members. The struggles of adolescence, the scourge of drugs, the breakdown of the family unit, the loss of long held values, the increase in technology, and poor parenting skills all tore Edna, Ralph, and Johnny Beasley asunder.

We teach our children to read and write. We teach them to drive cars. But we don't teach them parenting skills which could go a long way to combat all the negative forces pressuring the most basic unit of society. If Mr. and Mrs. Beasley had been better equipped as parents, maybe Johnny would've had a chance in life. But the inept parenting of Edna and Ralph, the abusiveness which surfaced as times became more difficult, and the loneliness of living separate lives brought this American family to the precipice of a tragedy and then over to the utter destruction. It is a story that extends beyond this one family's loss. It is the real shame of our time, a cautionary tale about the cost of our social values.

Johnny Beasley's death despite all the efforts of teachers, administrators, police and courts, friends, and parents speaks volumes about the shortcomings of our society and its institutions. Modern life is so complex and has an uncanny potential to fracture relationships into a thousandpointed splinters piercing the very fabric we've counted on for over two centuries.

How did Johnny Beasley's life end in such a grizzly manner? I spoke at length with his friend, Sam Barton, about the final moments of a life senselessly lost too soon. I spoke with his parents. I spoke with his girlfriend. And this is what I was able to piece together from all those interviews.

Sam – "On the bus ride home from the city, Johnny showed me a pistol. I asked him where he got it and he told me Slice had it hidden in a coffee can. I held it and saw that it was loaded. Johnny said we were going to get enough money so as we could stay away from home as long as we wanted.

Johnny told me his old man kept several weeks of cash in a safe in the office at the store between bank runs and he knew the combination. He said it would be a piece of cake to quietly break into the store and take the money from the safe and cash register, because his old man wouldn't have his own son arrested, not his own flesh and blood. I liked the thought of staying away from my old man for a long, long time. I told Johnny I was in.

We spent the afternoon at the movies and after, went to get something to eat. Our plan was to wait till after midnight and go in through a window in the back of the store. He bragged to me how he often would leave it unlocked so he could get out and back in late at night and his folks would be none the wiser. We smoked some dope and talked about the plan. Johnny was really hyped. I guess I was too.

We watched the store from eleven on and the lights had been out for a good hour when we went around back. The store needed a lot of work. The paint was peeling off the wall and the window sill looked like there was some rot. I could feel chills up and down my spine as Johnny put the palms of his hands on the left and right frames holding the glass. With a bend in his knees like he was doing some kind of squat thrust, he stood up. It was a great idea, but when he stood, the window didn't move with him. We both said shit and figured Mr. Beasley must have noticed it was unlocked and locked it up. Johnny began pacing and muttering that this wasn't going to stop him. I was growing even more nervous and thought I might piss myself. He moved into the shadows of the alley and came back with a small rock. I tried to talk him out of it, but he wasn't having any of it. The window had a lot of little panes and he picked the one just under the lock to smack. It was quick and while it was just a tinkling sound, to me it sounded like a cannon going off. He thrust his hand through and began turning the lock. Then, the window slid up like we thought it would when he did his knee bends. Johnny pulled himself through the open window. I looked upstairs at the windows where his folks lived and didn't see any lights. I thought that was a good sign. I could see Johnny by the safe and in less than a minute it was open, and he was emptying the contents into a bag he brought along. Next, he moved into the store area, which was out of my view. I moved along to the next set of windows, so I could see what was happening."

Edna – "I thought I heard a sound, maybe crunching broken glass, but it was muffled by the distance and floor between us, as well as the constant hum of the refrigerator units from the store below. I was sure someone was in the store, though. At this point, I woke Ralph up and told him I suspected a burglary and that he needed to call the police. He sat up in bed, listened for a short spell, and announced to me I was right. I kept urging him to call the police, but he swiveled his legs over the side of our bed and slipped on his slippers. Next, he opened the drawer of the nightstand and removed his revolver, which Ralph had purchased three or four months back, after one of the robberies. While he opened the chamber making sure it was fully loaded, I was pleading with him to call the police. He told me to shut up and call them myself. He strode to the door of our bedroom as quietly as possible, opened the door and left. I was terrified, but I managed to call, 911. The dispatcher said the police would be there in less than five minutes."

Ralph – "I hesitated at the top of the steps, my heart was beating like a drum. It seemed so loud whoever was down stairs had to hear it, I thought. Slowly and carefully, I made my descent to the store below. I even skipped the step that creaks and squeaks so loud. Then, I reached the bottom of the stairs and stopped at the door into the store. There was a light switch on the other side just to the right on the wall which would illuminate the entire area. I gathered my courage and listened to a sound coming from the area near the register. I wondered if the intruder was armed. I wasn't taking any chances and clicked off the safety. Turning the knob ever so slowly and silently, I pulled open the door with my left hand and hit the switch with my right hand, the gun hand. I was ready to blast the son-of-a-bitch into kingdom come."

Sam – "I was at one of the store windows when the lights went on. Johnny was at the register with a fistful of cash in one hand and Slice's gun in the other. It couldn't have been any more than mere seconds, Mr. Beasley, that bastard, shot Johnny right in the chest. I heard my friend call out, "Daddy, why'd you shoot me?" and the old man replied, "I brought you into this world, and I'm takin' you out!" I was stunned, and then I took off running and didn't stop until I was home. I couldn't believe what I'd seen."

This incident is a modern American tragedy. Our society is experiencing a crisis of connection. Too many families are disconnected from one another as witnessed by the divorce rate, the suicide rate, the rate of poverty, and violence within the home – spousal abuse, child abuse, and elder abuse. The tragedy of Johnny, Edna, and Ralph Beasley is a call to arms for the institutions of church and state to meet this problem head on developing solutions and putting in place safeguards and safety nets to help struggling families and individuals who are suffering through the "great" disconnect. Schools cannot carry this burden alone and be the sole solution to the problem. Unfortunately, as our society has become increasingly more complex, and parents busier and busier, we've asked our school systems to take on more and more, while simultaneously providing less funding for these increased responsibilities. Schools simply don't have the ability to fill in for the essential needs only parents can provide.

Johnny's life was a hodge-podge of idiosyncratic behaviors, some positive and good, while others were negative and bad. He, at times appeared to have a soft caring side, but at other times, he had a callousness to him, an uncaring indifference to others. In some ways he fell through the cracks. When his parents failed him, there wasn't enough there to help him get beyond that hurt. People tried, and in some cases seemed to be helping, but ultimately, Johnny made choices. Too many of them were detrimental and would lead to his death.

I remember quite well, a poem entitled "Out, Out" by Robert Frost. The poem shows an inhumane society expecting an adolescent boy to do the same lumber work an adult would normally do. He was sawing and when he became distracted at the call for lunch, the saw "leaped out at the boy's hand" and cut it up pretty badly. He begged his sister to not let the doctor amputate his hand. Under anesthesia, "the watcher at his pulse took fright." The adolescent died. The poem concludes with the line "No more to build on there. And they, since they were not the one dead, turned to their affairs." It was over and everyone moved on. If America's great institutions ignore Johnny Beasley's death, and "turn to their affairs," then society will not only have failed Johnny, but all the kids across our nation in the same situation as him – lonely, torn by drugs, lost, without sufficient guidance to grow into a contributing member of society. It's up to all of us. What can you and what will you do?

Made in the USA
Middletown, DE
12 March 2019